A MONSTROUS TRESPASS!

Retief stepped behind the shelter of the arch-way and thrust the shaft of the pike out across the opening a foot above ground level. The first Groaci through tripped over it and fell sprawl-ing. A moment later two more landed heavily on him. Another five seconds, and half a dozen Groaci were disentangling themselves from the heap. Yish advanced more cautiously, paused to look with disapproval at his disordered com-mand.

"I think you'd better schedule your boys for another thirteen weeks of basic," Retief sug-gested, "with the emphasis on obstacle-course work."

"You jape, vile Terry, but you'll rue the day you violated the Groacian Embassy."

Books by Keith Laumer

The Best of Keith Laumer
The Glory Game
A Plague of Demons
Retief and the Warlords
Retief: Diplomat at Arms
Retief: Emissary to the Stars
Retief of the CDT
Retief's War

Published by TIMESCAPE/POCKET BOOKS

RETIEF: DIPLOMAT AT ARMS

KEITH LAUMER

A TIMESCAPE BOOK
PUBLISHED BY POCKET BOOKS NEW YORK

Another *Original* publication of TIMESCAPE BOOKS

A Timescape Book published by
POCKET BOOKS, a Simon & Schuster division of
GULF & WESTERN CORPORATION
1230 Avenue of the Americas, New York, N.Y. 10020

ISBN: 0-671-44029-2

First Timescape Books printing October, 1982

10 9 8 7 6 5 4 3 2 1

Contents

". . . into the chaotic Galactic political scene of the post-Concordiat era, the CDT emerged to carry forward the ancient diplomatic tradition as a great supra-national organization dedicated to the contravention of war.* As mediators of disputes among Terrestrial-settled worlds and advocates of Terrestrial interests in contacts with alien cultures, Corps diplomats, trained in the chanceries of innumerable defunct bureaucracies, displayed an encyclopedic grasp of the nuances of Extra-Terrestrial mores as set against the labyrinthine socio-politico-economic Galactic context. Ever-zealous in its enforcement of peace, the Corps traditionally has functioned at its most scintillating level under the threat of imminent annihilation. Facing overwhelming forces at Roolit I, steely-eyed Ambassador Nitworth met the challenge unflinchingly, coolly planning his *coup*. . . ."

—extract from the *Official History of the Corps Diplomatique*, Vol. I, Reel 2, Solarian Press, New York, 479 AE (AD 2940)

Ultimatum

Ambassador Nitworth glowered across his mirror-polished, nine-foot platinum desk at his assembled staff.

"Gentlemen, are any of you familiar with a race known as the Qornt?"

There was a moment of profound silence. Nitworth nodded portentously.

* Cf. the original colorful language: "maintenance of a state of tension short of actual conflict." See CDT File 178/b/491, Col. VII, spool 12: 745 mm (code 2g).

"They were a warlike race, known in this sector back in Concordiat times—perhaps two hundred years ago. They vanished as suddenly as they had appeared. There was no record of where they went." He paused for effect.

"They have now reappeared—occupying the inner planet of this system!"

"But, sir," Second Secretary Magnan offered. "That's uninhabited Terrestrial territory . . ."

"Indeed, Mr. Magnan . . ." Nitworth smiled icily. "It appears the Qornt do not share that opinion." He plucked a heavy parchment from a folder before him, harrumphed and read aloud:

"HIS SUPREME EXCELLENCY THE QORN, REGENT OF QORNT, OVERLORD OF THE GALACTIC DESTINY, GREETS THE TERRESTRIALS AND WITH REFERENCE TO THE PRESENCE IN QORNT MANDATED TERRITORY OF TERRESTRIAL SQUATTERS, HAS THE HONOR TO ADVISE THAT HE WILL REQUIRE THE USE OF HIS OUTER WORLD ON THE THIRTIETH DAY: THEN WILL THE QORNT COME WITH STEEL AND FIRE. RECEIVE, TERRESTRIALS, RENEWED ASSURANCES OF MY AWARENESS OF YOUR EXISTENCE, AND LET THOSE WHO DARE GIRD FOR THE CONTEST."

"Frankly, I wouldn't call it conciliatory," Magnan said.

Nitworth tapped the paper with a finger.

"We have been served, gentlemen, with nothing less than an ultimatum!"

"Well, we'll soon straighten these fellows out—" the Military Attaché began.

"There happens to be more to this piece of trucolence than appears on the surface," the Ambassador cut in. He paused, waiting for interested frowns to settle into place.

"Note, gentlemen, that these invaders have appeared in force on Terrestrial-controlled soil—and without so much as a flicker from the instruments of the Navigational Monitor Service!"

The Military Attaché blinked. "That's absurd," he said flatly. Nitworth slapped the table.

"We're up against something new, gentlemen! I've considered every hypothesis from cloaks of invisibility to time travel! The fact is—the Qornt fleets are indetectable!"

The Military Attaché pulled at his lower lip. "In that case, we can't try conclusions with these fellows until we have an indetectable drive of our own. I recommend a crash project; in the meantime—"

"I'll have my boys start in to crack this thing," Chief of the Confidential Terrestrial Source Section spoke up. "I'll fit out a couple of volunteers with plastic beaks—"

"No cloak and dagger work, gentlemen! Long range policy will be worked out by Deep-Think teams back at the Department. Our role will be a holding action. Now, I want suggestions for a comprehensive, well-rounded, and decisive course for meeting this threat. Any recommendations?"

The Political Officer placed his fingertips together. "What about a stiff Note demanding an extra week's time?"

"No! No begging," the Economic Officer objected. "I'd say a calm, dignified, aggressive withdrawal—as soon as possible."

"We don't want to give them the idea we spook easily," the Military Attaché said. "Let's delay the withdrawal—say, until tomorrow."

"Early tomorrow," Magnan said. "Or maybe later today."

"Well, I see you're of a mind with me," Nitworth commented, nodding. "Our plan of action is clear, but it remains to be implemented. We have a population of over fifteen million individuals to relocate." He eyed the Political Officer. "I want five proposals for resettlement on my desk by oh-eight-hundred hours tomorrow . . ." Nitworth rapped out instructions; harried-looking staff members arose and hurried from the room. Magnan eased toward the door.

"Where are you going, Magnan?" Nitworth snapped.

"Since you're so busy, I thought I'd just slip back down to Com Inq. It was a most interesting orientation lecture, Mr. Secretary. Be sure to let us know how it works out—"

"Kindly return to your chair," Nitworth said coldly. "A number of chores remain to be assigned. I think you need a little field experience. I want you to get over to Roolit I and take a look at these Qornt personally."

Magnan's mouth opened and closed soundlessly.

"Not afraid of a few Qornt, are you, Magnan?"

"Afraid? Good lord, no, ha ha. It's just that I'm afraid I may lose my head and do something rash."

"Nonsense! A diplomat is immune to heroic impulses. Take Retief along. No dawdling now! I want you on the way in two hours. Notify the transport pool at once."

Magnan nodded unhappily and went out into the hall.

"Oh, Retief," Nitworth said. Retief turned.

"Try to restrain Mr. Magnan from any impulsive moves—in any direction."

Retief and Magnan topped a ridge and looked down across a slope of towering tree-shrubs and glossy violet-stemmed palms set among flamboyant blossoms of yellow and red, reaching down to a strip of white beach with the blue sea beyond.

"A delightful vista," Magnan said, mopping at his face. "A pity we couldn't locate the Qornt. We'll go back now and report—"

"I'm pretty sure the settlement is off to the right," Retief said. "Why don't you head back for the boat, while I ease over and see what I can observe."

"Retief, we're engaged in a serious mission. This is not a time to think of sight-seeing."

"I'd like to take a good look at what we're giving away."

"See here, Retief! One might almost receive the impression that you're questioning Corps policy."

"One might, at that. The Qornt have made their

play—but I think it might be valuable to take a look at their cards before we fold. If I'm not back at the boat in an hour, lift without me."

"You expect me to make my way back alone?"

"It's directly down-slope—" Retief broke off, listening. Magnan clutched at his arm. There was a sound of crackling foliage. Twenty feet ahead, a leafy branch swung aside. An eight-foot biped stepped into view; long, thin green-clad legs with back-bending knees moved in quick, bird-like steps. A pair of immense black-lensed goggles covered staring eyes set among bushy green hair above a great bone-white beak. The crest bobbed as the creature cocked its head, listening.

Magnan gulped audibly. The Qornt froze, head tilted, beak aimed directly at the spot where the Terrestrials stood in the deep shade of a giant trunk.

"I'll go for help," Magnan squeaked. He whirled and took three leaps into the brush; a second great green-clad figure rose up to block his way. He spun, darted to the left. The first Qornt pounced, grappled Magnan to its narrow chest. Magnan yelled, threshing and kicking, broke free, turned—and collided with the nine-foot alien, coming in fast from the right. All three went down in a tangle of limbs.

Retief jumped forward, hauled Magnan free, thrust him aside, and stopped, right fist cocked. The two Qornt lay groaning, moving feebly.

"Nice piece of work, Mr. Magnan," Retief said. "You nailed both of them."

"Those, undoubtedly, are the most blood-thirsty, aggressive, merciless countenances it has ever been my misfortune to encounter," Magnan said. "It hardly seems fair: eight feet tall AND faces like that . . ."

The smaller of the two captive Qornt ran long, slender fingers over a bony shin from which he had turned back the tight-fitting green trousers.

"It's not broken," he whistled nasally in passable Terrestrial, eyeing Magnan through the heavy goggles, now badly cracked. "Small thanks to you."

Magnan smiled loftily. "I daresay you'll think twice before interfering with peaceable diplomats in future."

"Diplomats? Surely you jest."

"Never mind us," Retief said. "It's you fellows we'd like to talk about. How many of you are there?"

"Only Zubb and myself—"

"I mean altogether. How many Qornt?"

The alien whistled shrilly.

"Here, no signaling!" Magnan snapped, looking around.

"That was merely an expression of amusement—"

"You find the situation amusing? I assure you, sir, you are in perilous straits at the moment. I MAY fly into another rage, you know."

"Please, restrain yourself. I was merely somewhat astonished—" a small whistle escaped—"at being taken for a Qornt."

"Aren't you a Qornt?"

"I? Great snail trails, no!" More stifled whistles of amusement escaped the beaked face. "Both Zubb and I are Verpp. Naturalists, as it happens."

"You certainly LOOK like Qornt."

"Oh, not at all—except perhaps to a Terrestrial. The Qornt are sturdily-built rascals, all over ten feet in height. And, of course, they do nothing but quarrel. A drone caste, actually."

"A caste? You mean they're biologically the same as you—"

"Not at all! A Verpp wouldn't think of fertilizing a Qornt."

"I mean to say, you're of the same basic stock—descended from a common ancestor, perhaps."

"We are all Pud's creatures."

"What are the differences between you and them?"

"Why, the Qornt are argumentative, boastful, lacking in appreciation for the finer things of life. One dreads to contemplate descending to their level."

"Do you know anything about a Note passed to the Terrestrial Ambassador at Smørbrød?"

The beak twitched. "Smørbrød? I know of no place called Smørbrød."

"The outer planet of this system."

"Oh, yes; we call it Guzzum. I had heard that some sort of creatures had established a settlement there, but I confess I pay little note to such matters."

"We're wasting time, Retief," Magnan said. "We must truss these chaps up, hurry back to the boat, and make our escape. You heard what they said—"

"Are there any Qornt down there at the harbor, where the boats are?" Retief asked.

"At Tarroon, you mean? Oh, yes. A large number; the Qornt are making ready for one of their adventures."

"That would be the invasion of Smørbrød," Magnan said. "And unless we hurry, Retief, we're likely to be caught there with the last of the evacuees—"

"How many Qornt would you say there are at Tarroon?"

"Oh, a very large number. Perhaps fifteen or twenty."

"Fifteen or twenty what?" Magnan looked perplexed.

"Fifteen or twenty Qornt."

"You mean that there are only fifteen or twenty individual Qornt in all?"

Another whistle. "Not at all. I was referring to the local Qornt only. There are more at the other Centers, of course."

"And the Qornt are responsible for the Ultimatum—unilaterally?"

"I suppose so; it sounds like them. A truculent group, you know. And interplanetary relations are rather a hobby of theirs."

Zubb moaned and stirred. He sat up slowly, rubbing his head. He spoke to his companion in a shrill alien clatter of consonants.

"What did he say?"

"Poor Zubb. He blames me for his bruises, since it was my idea to gather you as specimens."

"You should have known better than to tackle that

fierce-looking creature," Zubb said, pointing his beak at Magnan.

"How does it happen that you speak Terrestrial?" Retief asked.

"Oh, one picks up all sorts of dialects."

"It's quite charming, really," Magnan said. "Such a quaint, archaic accent."

"Suppose we went down to Tarroon," Retief asked. "What kind of reception would we get?"

"That depends. I wouldn't recommend interfering with the Gwil or the Rheuk; it's their nest-mending time, you know. The Boog will be busy mating—such a tedious business—and of course the Qornt are tied up with their ceremonial feasting. I'm afraid no one will take any notice of you."

"Do you mean to say," Magnan demanded, "that these ferocious Qornt, who have issued an ultimatum to the Corps Diplomatique Terrestrienne—who openly avow their intention to invade a Terrestrial-occupied world—would ignore Terrestrials in their midst?"

"If at all possible."

Retief got to his feet.

"I think our course is clear, Mr. Magnan. It's up to us to go down and attract a little attention."

"I'm not at all sure we're going about this in the right way," Magnan puffed, trotting at Retief's side. "These fellows Zubb and Slun—Oh, they seem affable enough—but how can we be sure we're not being led into a trap?"

"We can't."

Magnan stopped short. "Let's go back."

"All right," Retief said. "Of course, there may be an ambush—"

Magnan moved off. "Let's keep going."

The party emerged from the undergrowth at the edge of a great brush-grown mound. Slun took the lead, rounded the flank of the mound, halted at a rectangular opening cut into the slope.

"You can find your way easily enough from here," he said. "You'll excuse us, I hope—"

"Nonsense, Slun!" Zubb pushed forward. "I'll escort our guests to Qornt Hall." He twittered briefly to his fellow Verpp. Slun twittered back.

"I don't like it, Retief," Magnan whispered. "Those fellows are plotting mischief."

"Threaten them with violence, Mr. Magnan. They're scared of you."

"That's true—but the drubbing they received was well-deserved. I'm a patient man, but there are occasions—"

"Come along, please," Zubb called. "Another ten minutes' walk—"

"See here, we have no interest in investigating this barrow," Magnan announced. "We wish you to take us direct to Tarroon to interview your military leaders regarding the Ultimatum!"

"Yes, yes, of course. Qornt Hall lies here inside the village."

"This is Tarroon?"

"A modest civic center, sir, but there are those who love it."

"No wonder we didn't observe their works from the air," Magnan muttered. "Camouflaged." He moved hesitantly through the opening.

The party moved along a wide, deserted tunnel which sloped down steeply, then leveled off and branched. Zubb took the center branch, ducking slightly under the nine-foot ceiling lit at intervals with what appeared to be primitive incandescent panels.

"Few signs of an advanced technology here," Magnan whispered. "These creatures must devote all their talents to warlike enterprise."

Ahead, Zubb slowed. A distant susurration was audible, a sustained high-pitched screeching. "Softly, now. We approach Qornt Hall. They can be an irascible lot when disturbed at their feasting."

"When will the feast be over?" Magnan called hoarsely.

"In another few weeks, I should imagine, if, as you say, they've scheduled an invasion for next month."

"Look here, Zubb." Magnan shook a finger at the tall alien. "How is it that these Qornt are allowed to embark on piratical ventures of this sort without reference to the wishes of the majority—"

"Oh, the majority of the Qornt favor the move, I imagine."

"A handful of hotheads are permitted to embroil the planet in war?"

"Oh, they don't embroil the planet in war. It's merely a Qornt enterprise. We Verpp ignore such goings-on."

"Retief, this is fantastic! I've heard of iron-fisted military cliques before, but this is madness!"

"Come softly, now . . ." Zubb beckoned, moving toward a bend in the yellow-lit corridor. Retief and Magnan moved forward. The corridor debouched through a high double door into a vast oval chamber, high-domed, gloomy, panelled in dark wood and hung with tattered banners, scarred halberds, pikes, rusted long-swords, crossed spears, patinaed hauberks, pitted radiation armor, corroded power rifles, the immense mummified heads of horned and fanged animals. Great guttering torches in wall brackets and in stands along the length of the long table shed a smoky light that reflected from the mirror polish of the red granite floor, gleamed on polished silver bowls and paper-thin glass, shone jewel-red and gold through dark bottles—and cast long flickering shadows behind the fifteen trolls who loomed in their places at the board. Lesser trolls—beaked, bush-haired, great-eyed—trotted briskly, bird-kneed, bearing steaming platters, stood in groups of three strumming slender bottle-shaped lutes, or pranced in intricately-patterned dance, unnoticed in the shrill uproar as each of the magnificently draped, belted, feathered, and bejeweled Qornt carried on a shouted conversation with an equally noisy fellow.

"A most interesting display of barbaric splendor," Magnan breathed. "Now we'd better be getting back—"

"Ah, a moment," Zubb said. "Observe the Qorn—

the tallest of the feasters—he with the headdress of crimson, purple, silver and pink—"

"Twelve feet if he's an inch," Magnan estimated. "And now we really must hurry along—"

"That one is chief among these rowdies. I'm sure you'll want a word with him. He controls not only the Tarroonian vessels but those from the other Centers as well."

"What kind of vessels? Warships?"

"Certainly. What other kind would the Qornt bother with?"

"I don't suppose," Magnan said casually, "that you'd know the type, tonnage, armament, and manning of these vessels? And how many units comprise the fleet? And where they're based at present?"

"They're fully automated twenty-thousand ton all-purpose dreadnoughts. They mount a variety of weapons—the Qornt are fond of that sort of thing—and each of the Qornt has his own, of course. They're virtually identical, except for the personal touches each individual has given his ship."

"Great Heavens, Retief!" Magnan exclaimed in a whisper. "It sounds as though these brutes employ a battle armada as simpler souls might a set of toy sailboats!"

Retief stepped past Magnan and Zubb to study the feasting hall. "I can see that their votes would carry all the necessary weight."

"And, now, an interview with the Qorn himself," Zubb shrilled. "If you'll kindly step along, gentlemen . . ."

"That won't be necessary," Magnan said hastily. "I've decided to refer the entire matter to a committee—"

"After having come so far," Zubb said, "it would be a pity to miss having a cosy chat . . ."

There was a pause.

"Ah . . . Retief," Magnan said. "Zubb has just presented a most compelling argument . . ."

Retief turned. Zubb stood, gripping an ornately

decorated power pistol in one bony hand, a slim needler in the other. Both were pointed at Magnan's chest.

"I suspected you had hidden qualities, Zubb," Retief commented.

"See here, Zubb; we're diplomats—" Magnan started.

"Careful, Mr. Magnan; you may goad him to a frenzy."

"By no means," Zubb whistled. "I much prefer to observe the frenzy of the Qornt when presented with the news that two peaceful Verpp have been assaulted and kidnaped by bullying interlopers. If there's anything that annoys the Qornt, it's Qornt-like behavior in others. Now, step along, please."

"Rest assured, this will be reported—"

"I doubt it."

"You'll face the wrath of Enlightened Galactic Opinion—"

"Oh? How big a navy does Enlightened Galactic Opinion have?"

"Stop scaring him, Mr. Magnan. He may get nervous and shoot." Retief stepped into the banquet hall, headed for the resplendent figure at the head of the table. A trio of flute-players broke off in mid-bleat, staring. An inverted pyramid of tumblers blinked as Retief swung past, followed by Magnan and the tall Verpp. The shrill chatter at the table faded.

Qorn turned as Retief came up, blinking three-inch eyes. Zubb stepped forward, gibbered, waving his arms excitedly. Qorn pushed back his chair—a low, heavily padded stool—and stared unwinking at Retief, moving his head to bring first one great round eye, then the other, to bear. There were small blue veins in the immense fleshy beak. The bushy hair, springing out in a giant halo around the greyish, porous-skinned face, was wiry, stiff, moss-green, with tufts of chartreuse fuzz surrounding what appeared to be tympanic membranes. The tall headdress of scarlet silk and purple feathers was slightly askew, and a loop of pink pearls had slipped down above one eye.

Zubb finished his speech, fell silent, breathing hard. Qorn looked Retief over in silence, then belched.

"Not bad," Retief said admiringly. "Maybe we could get up a match between you and Ambassador Sternwheeler. You've got the volume on him, but he could spot you points on timbre."

"So," Qorn hooted in a resonant tenor. "You come from Guzzum, eh? Or Smørbrød, as I think you call it. What is it you're after? More time? A compromise? Negotiations? Peace?" He slammed a bony hand against the table. "The answer is NO!"

Zubb twittered. Qorn cocked an eye, motioned to a servant. "Chain him, then . . ." he indicated Magnan. His eyes went to Retief. "This one's bigger; you'd best chain him, too."

"Why, Your Excellency—" Magnan started, stepping forward.

"Stay back!" Qorn hooted. "Stand over there where I can keep an eye on you."

"Your Excellency, I'm empowered—"

"Not here, you're not!" Qorn trumpeted. "Want peace, do you? Well, I don't want peace! I've had a surfeit of peace these last two centuries! I want action! Loot! Adventure! Glory!" He turned to look down the table. "How about it, fellows? It's war to the knife, eh?"

There was a momentary silence.

"I guess so," grunted a giant Qornt in iridescent blue with flame-colored plumes.

Qorn's eyes bulged. He half rose. "We've been all over this!" he bassooned. He clamped bony fingers on the hilt of a light rapier. "I thought I'd made my point . . ."

"Oh, sure, Qorn,"

"You bet."

"I'm convinced."

Qorn rumbled and resumed his seat. "All for one and one for all, that's us."

"And you're the one, eh Qorn?" Retief commented.

Magnan cleared his throat. "I sense that some of you

gentlemen are not convinced of the wisdom of this move," he piped, looking along the table at the silks, jewels, beaks, feather-decked crests, and staring eyes.

"Silence!" Qorn hooted. "No use your talking to my loyal lieutenants anyway," he added. "They do whatever I convince them they ought to do."

"But I'm sure that on more mature consideration—"

"I can lick any Qornt in the house," Qorn said. "That's why I'm Qorn." He belched again.

A servant came up staggering under a weight of chain, dropped it with a crash at Magnan's feet. Zubb aimed the guns while the servant wrapped three loops around Magnan's wrists, snapped a lock in place.

"You, next!" The guns pointed at Retief's chest. He held out his arms. Four loops of silvery-grey chain in half-inch links dropped around them. The servant cinched them up tight, squeezed a lock through the ends and closed it.

"Now," Qorn said, lolling back in his chair, glass in hand. "There's a bit of sport to be had here, lads. What shall we do with them?"

"Let them go," the blue-and-flame Qornt said glumly.

"You can do better than that," Qorn hooted. "Now, here's a suggestion: we carve them up a little—lop off the external labiae and pinnae, say—and ship them back—"

"Good lord! Retief, he's talking about cutting off our ears and sending us home mutilated! What a barbaric proposal!"

"It wouldn't be the first time a Terrestrial diplomat got a trimming," Retief commented.

"It should have the effect of stimulating the Terries to put up a reasonable scrap," Qorn said judiciously. "I have a feeling that they're thinking of giving up without a struggle."

"Oh, I doubt that," the blue-and-flame Qornt said. "Why should they?"

Qorn rolled an eye at Retief and another at Magnan. "Take these two," he hooted. "I'll wager they came here to negotiate a surrender!"

"Well," Magnan started.

"Hold it, Mr. Magnan," Retief said, "I'll tell him."

"What's your proposal?" Qorn whistled, taking a gulp from his goblet. "A fifty-fifty split? Monetary reparations? Alternate territory? I can assure you, it's useless. We Qornt LIKE to fight—"

"I'm afraid you've gotten the wrong impression, Your Excellency," Retief said blandly. "We didn't come to negotiate. We came to deliver an ultimatum . . ."

"What?" Qorn trumpeted. Behind Retief, Magnan spluttered.

"We plan to use this planet for target practice," Retief said. "A new type hell bomb we've worked out. Have all your people off of it in seventy-two hours, or suffer the consequences."

"You have the gall," Qorn stormed, "to stand here in the center of Qornt Hall—uninvited, at that—and in chains—"

"Oh, these," Retief said. He tensed his arms; the soft aluminum links stretched, broke. He shook the light metal free. "We diplomats like to go along with colorful local customs, but I wouldn't want to mislead you. Now, as to the evacuation of Roolit I—"

Zubb screeched, waved the guns. The Qornt at the table craned, jabbering.

"I told you they were brutes," Zubb shrilled.

Qorn slammed his fist down on the table. "I don't care what they are!" he honked. "Evacuate, hell! I can field eighty-five combat-ready ships—"

"And we can englobe every one of them with a thousand Peace Enforcers, with a hundred megatons/second fire-power each."

"Retief—" Magnan tugged at his sleeve. "Don't forget their superdrive—"

"That's all right; they don't have one."

"But—"

"We'll take you on!" Qorn French-horned. "We're

the Qorn! We glory in battle! We live in fame or go down in—"

"Hogwash," the flame-and-blue Qorn cut in. "If it wasn't for you, Qorn, we could sit around and feast and brag and enjoy life without having to prove anything."

"Qorn, you seem to be the firebrand here," Retief said. "I think the rest of the boys would listen to reason—"

"Over my dead body!"

"My idea exactly," Retief said. "You claim you can lick any man in the house. Unwind yourself from your ribbons and step out here on the floor, and we'll see how good you are at backing up your conversation."

Magnan hovered at Retief's side. "Twelve feet tall," he moaned. "And did you notice the size of those hands?"

Retief watched as Qorn's aides helped him out of his formal trappings. "I wouldn't worry too much, Mr. Magnan. This is a light-Gee world. I doubt if old Qorn would weigh up at more than two-fifty standard pounds here."

"But that phenomenal reach—"

"I'll peck away at him at knee level; when he bends over to swat me, I'll get a crack at him."

Across the cleared floor, Qorn shook off his helpers with a snort.

"Enough! Let me at the upstart!"

Retief moved out to meet him, watching the upraised backward-jointed arms. Qorn stalked forward, long lean legs bent, long horny feet clacking against the polished floor. The other aliens—both servitors and bejeweled Qornt—formed a wide circle, all eyes unwaveringly on the combatants.

Qorn struck suddenly, a long arm flashing down in a vicious cut at Retief, who leaned aside, caught a lean shank below the knee. Qorn bent to haul Retief from his leg—and staggered back as a haymaker took him just below the beak. A screech went up from the crowd as Retief leaped clear.

Qorn hissed and charged. Retief whirled aside, then struck the alien's off-leg in a flying tackle. Qorn leaned, arms windmilling, crashed to the floor. Retief whirled, dived for the left arm, whipped it behind the narrow back, seized Qorn's neck in a stranglehold, and threw his weight backward. Qorn fell on his back, his legs squatted out at an awkward angle. He squawked, beat his free arm on the floor, reaching in vain for Retief.

Zubb stepped forward, pistols ready. Magnan stepped before him.

"Need I remind you, sir," he said icily, "that this is an official diplomatic function? I can brook no interference from disinterested parties."

Zubb hesitated. Magnan held out a hand. "I must ask you to hand me your weapons, Zubb."

"Look here," Zubb began.

"I MAY lose my temper," Magnan hinted. Zubb lowered the guns, passed them to Magnan. He thrust them into his belt with a sour smile, turned back to watch the encounter.

Retief had thrown a turn of violet silk around Qorn's left wrist, bound it to the alien's neck. Another wisp of stuff floated from Qorn's shoulder. Retief, still holding Qorn in an awkward sprawl, wrapped it around one outflung leg, trussed ankle and thigh together. Qorn flopped, hooting. At each movement, the constricting loop around his neck jerked his head back, the green crest tossing wildly.

"If I were you, I'd relax," Retief said, rising and releasing his grip. Qorn got a leg under him. Retief kicked it. Qorn's chin hit the floor with a hollow clack. He wilted, an ungainly tangle of over-long limbs and gay silks.

Retief turned to the watching crowd. "Next?" he called.

The blue-and-flame Qornt stepped forward. "Maybe this would be a good time to elect a new leader," he said. "Now, my qualifications—"

"Sit down," Retief said loudly. He stepped to the head of the table, seated himself in Qorn's vacated chair. "A couple of you finish trussing Qorn up; then stack him in the corner—"

"But we must select a leader!"

"That won't be necessary, boys. I'm your new leader."

"As I see it," Retief said, dribbling cigar ashes into an empty wine glass, "you Qornt like to be warriors, but you don't particularly like to fight."

"We don't mind a little fighting—within reason. And, of course, as Qornt, we're expected to die in battle. But what I say is—why rush things?"

"I have a suggestion," Magnan said. "Why not turn the reins of government over to the Verpp? They seem a level-headed group—"

"What good would that do? Qornt are Qornt; and it seems there's always one among us who's a slave to instinct—and, naturally, we have to follow him."

"Why?"

"Because that's the way it's done."

"Why not do it another way?" Magnan offered. "Now, I'd like to suggest Community singing—"

"If we gave up fighting, we might live too long; then what would happen?"

"Live too long . . ." Magnan looked puzzled.

"When estivating time comes, there'd be no burrows for us; and anyway, with the new Qornt stepping in next Awakening—"

"I've lost the thread," Magnan said. "Who are the new Qornt?"

"After estivating, the Verpp moult, and then they're Qornt, of course. The Gwil become Boog, the Boog become Rheuk, the Rheuk metamorphosize into Verpp—"

"You mean Slun and Zubb—the mild-natured naturalists—will become warmongers like Qorn?"

"Very likely; 'the milder the Verpp, the wilder the Qornt,' as the old saying goes."

"What do Qornt turn into?" Retief asked.

"Hmmmm. That's a good question. So far, none have survived Qornthood."

"Have you thought of forsaking your warlike ways?" Magnan asked. "What about taking up sheepherding and regular church attendance—"

"Don't mistake me. We Qornt like a military life. It's great sport to sit around roaring fires and drink and tell lies and then go dashing off to enjoy a brisk affray and some leisurely looting afterward. But we prefer a nice numerical advantage. Now, this business of tackling you Terrestrials over on Guzzum—that was a mad notion. We had no idea what your strength was—"

"But now that's all off, of course," Magnan chirped. "Now that we've had diplomatic relations and all—"

"Oh, by no means. The fleet lifts in thirty days; after all, we're Qornt; we have to satisfy our drive to action."

"But Mr. Retief is your leader, now. He won't let you . . ."

"Only a dead Qornt stays home when Attack Day comes. And even if he orders us all to cut our own throats, there are still the other Centers—all with their own leaders. No, gentlemen, the invasion is definitely on."

"Why don't you go invade somebody else?" Magnan suggested. "Now, I could name some very attractive prospects—outside my sector, of course."

"Hold everything," Retief said. "I think we've got the basis of a deal here . . ."

At the head of a double column of gaudily caparisoned Qornt, Retief and Magnan strolled across the ramp toward the bright tower of the CDT Sector HQ. Ahead, gates opened, and a black Corps limousine emerged, flying an Ambassadorial flag below a plain white banner.

"Curious," Magnan commented. "I wonder what the significance of the white ensign might be?"

Retief raised a hand. The column halted with a clash of accoutrements, a rasp of Qornt boots. Retief looked back along the line. The high white sun flashed on bright silks, polished buckles, deep-dyed plumes, cere-

monial swords, the polished butts of pistols, the soft
gleam of leather.

"A brave show indeed," Magnan commented approvingly. "I confess the idea has merit—"

The limousine pulled up with a squeal of brakes,
stood on two fat-tired wheels, gyros humming softly.
The hatch popped up. A portly diplomat stepped out.

"Why, Ambassador Nitworth," Magnan glowed.
"This is very kind of you—"

"Keep cool, Magnan," Nitworth said in a strained
voice. "We'll attempt to get you out of this . . ." He
stepped past Magnan's outstretched hand and looked
hesitantly at the ramrod-straight line of Qornt, eighty-
five strong—and beyond at the eighty-five tall Qornt
dreadnoughts.

"Good afternoon, sir . . . ah, Your Excellency," Nitworth said, blinking up at the leading Qornt. "You are
Commander of the Strike Force, I assume?"

"Nope," the Qornt said shortly.

"I . . . ah . . . wish to request seventy-two hours in
which to evacuate the Headquarters," Nitworth plowed
on.

"Mr. Ambassador," Retief said. "This—"

"Don't panic, Retief. I'll attempt to secure your release," Nitworth hissed over his shoulder. "Now—"

"You will address our leader with more respect!"
the tall Qornt hooted, eyeing Nitworth ominously from
eleven feet up.

"Oh, yes indeed, sir . . . Your Excellency . . . Commander. Now, about the invasion—"

"Mr. Ambassador." Magnan tugged at Nitworth's
sleeve.

"In heaven's name, permit me to negotiate in peace!"
Nitworth snapped. He rearranged his features. "Now,
Your Excellency, we've arranged to evacuate Smør-
brød, of course, just as you requested—"

"Requested?" the Qornt honked.

"Ah . . . demanded, that is. Quite rightly of course.
Ordered. Instructed. And, of course, we'll be only too

pleased to follow any other instructions you might have—"

"You don't quite get the big picture, Mr. Ambassador," Retief said. "This isn't—"

"Silence, confound you!" Nitworth barked. The leading Qornt looked at Retief. He nodded. Two bony hands shot out, seized Nitworth, and stuffed a length of bright pink silk into his mouth, then spun him around and held him facing Retief.

"If you don't mind my taking this opportunity to brief you, Mr. Ambassador," Retief said blandly, "I think I should mention that this isn't an invasion fleet. These are the new recruits for the Peace Enforcement Corps."

Magnan stepped forward, glanced at the gag in Ambassador Nitworth's mouth, hesitated, then cleared his throat. "We felt," he said, "that the establishment of a Foreign Brigade within the P E Corps structure would provide the element of novelty the Department has requested in our recruiting, and at the same time would remove the stigma of Terrestrial chauvinism from future punitive operations."

Nitworth stared, eyes bulging. He grunted, reaching for the gag, caught the Qornt's eye on him, dropped his hands to his sides.

"I suggest we get the troops in out of the hot sun," Retief said. Magnan edged close. "What about the gag?" he whispered.

"Let's leave it where it is for a while," Retief murmured. "It may save us a few concessions."

An hour later, Nitworth, breathing freely again, glowered across his desk at Retief and Magnan.

"This entire affair," he rumbled, "has made me appear to be a fool!"

"But we who are privileged to serve on your staff already know just how clever you are," Magnan burbled.

Nitworth purpled. "You're skirting insolence, Magnan," he roared. "Why was I not informed of the

arrangements? What was I to assume at the sight of
eighty-five war vessels over my headquarters, unannounced?"

"We tried to get through, but our wave-lengths—"

"Bah! Sterner souls than I would have quailed at the
spectacle of those armed horrors advancing."

"Oh, you were perfectly justified in panicking—"

"I did NOT panic!" Nitworth bellowed. "I merely
adjusted to the apparent circumstances. Now, I'm of
two minds as to the advisability of this foreign legion
idea of yours. Still, it may have merit. I believe the
wisest course would be to dispatch them on a long
training cruise in an uninhabited sector of space—"

The office windows rattled. "What the devil—!" Nitworth turned, stared out at the ramp where a Qornt
ship rose slowly on a column of pale blue light. The
vibration increased as a second ship lifted, then a
third—

Nitworth whirled on Magnan. "What's this! Who
ordered these recruits to embark without my permission?"

"I took the liberty of giving them an errand to run,
Mr. Secretary," Retief said. "There was that little matter of the Groaci infiltrating the Sirenian System. I sent
the boys off to handle it."

"Call them back! Call them back at once!"

"I'm afraid that won't be possible. They're under
orders to maintain total communications silence until
completion of the mission."

Nitworth drummed his fingers on the desk top. Slowly, a thoughtful expression dawned. He nodded. "This
may work out," he said. "I should call them back, but
since the fleet is out of contact, I'm unable to do so,
correct? Thus, I can hardly be held responsible for
any over-enthusiasm in chastising the Groaci." He
closed one eye in a broad wink at Magnan.

"Very well, gentlemen, I'll overlook the irregularity
this time. Magnan, see to it the Smørbrødian public are
notified they can remain where they are. And by the

way, did you by any chance discover the technique of the indetectable drive the Qornt use?"

"No, sir. That is, yes, sir."

"Well? Well?"

"There isn't any. The Qornt were there all the while. Underground."

"Underground? Doing what?"

"Hibernating—for two hundred years at a stretch."

Outside in the corridor, Magnan came up to Retief, who stood talking to a tall man in a pilot's coverall.

"I'll be tied up, sending through full details on my— our—your recruiting scheme, Retief," Magnan said. "Suppose you run into the city to assist the new Verpp Consul in settling in."

"I'll do that, Mr. Magnan. Anything else?"

Magnan raised his eyebrows. "You're remarkably compliant today, Retief. I'll arrange transportation—"

"Don't bother, Mr. Magnan. Cy here will run me over. He was the pilot who ferried us over to Roolit I, you recall."

Magnan nodded curtly.

"I'll be with you as soon as I pack a few phone numbers, Retief," the pilot said. He moved off. Magnan followed him with a disapproving eye. "An uncouth sort, I fancied. I trust you're not consorting with his kind socially . . ."

"I wouldn't say that, exactly," Retief said. "We just want to go over a few figures together."

"For all their professional detachment from emotional involvement in petty local issues, tough-minded CDT envoys have ever opened their hearts to long-suffering peoples striving to cast off the yoke of economic oppression. At Glave, Ambassador Sternwheeler's dedicated group selflessly offered their services, assisting the newly unshackled populace in savoring the first fruits of freedom . . ."

—Vol. IV, Reel 71, 492 AE (AD 2953)

Native Intelligence

Retief turned back the gold-encrusted scarlet cuff of the mess jacket of a First Secretary and Consul, gathered in the three eight-sided black dice, shook them by his right ear, and sent them rattling across the floor to rebound from the bulkhead.

"Thirteen's the point," the Power Section Chief called. "Ten he makes it!"

"Oh . . . Mr. Retief." A tall thin youth in the black-trimmed grey of a Third Secretary flapped a sheet of paper from the edge of the circle surrounding the game. "The Ambassador's compliments, sir, and will you join him and the staff in the conference room at once . . ."

Retief rose and dusted his knees. "That's all for now, boys," he said. "I'll take the rest of your money later." He followed the junior diplomat from the ward room, along the bare corridors of the crew level, past the glare panel reading NOTICE—FIRST CLASS ONLY BEYOND THIS POINT, through the chandeliered and draped ballroom and along a stretch of soundless carpet to a heavy door bearing a placard with the legend CONFERENCE IN SESSION.

"Ambassador Sternwheeler seemed quite upset, Mr. Retief," the messenger said.

"He usually is, Pete." Retief took a cigar from his breast pocket. "Got a light?"

The Third Secretary produced a permatch. "I don't know why you smoke those things instead of dope sticks, Mr. Retief," he said. "The Ambassador hates the smell."

Retief nodded. "I only smoke this kind at conferences; it makes for shorter sessions." He stepped into the room. Ambassador Sternwheeler eyed him down the length of the conference table.

"Ah, Mr. Retief honors us with his presence. Do be seated, Retief." He fingered a yellow Departmental despatch. Retief took a chair, puffed out a dense cloud of smoke.

"As I have been explaining to the remainder of my staff for the past quarter hour," Sternwheeler rumbled, "I've been the recipient of important intelligence." He blinked at Retief expectantly. Retief raised his eyebrows in polite inquiry.

"It seems," Sternwheeler went on, "that there has been a change in regime on Glave. A week ago, the government which invited the dispatch of this mission— and to which we're accredited—was overthrown. The former ruling class has fled into exile, and a popular workers' and peasants' junta has taken over."

"Mr. Ambassador," Counselor Magnan broke in, rising; "I'd like to be the first—" he glanced around the table—"or one of the first, anyway—to welcome the new government of Glave into the family of planetary ruling bodies—"

"Sit down, Magnan!" Sternwheeler snapped. "Of course the Corps always recognizes *de facto* sovereignty. The problem is merely one of acquainting ourselves with the policies of this new group—a sort of blue-collar coalition, it seems. In what position that leaves this Embassy I don't yet know."

"I suppose this means we'll spend the next month in a parking orbit," Counselor Magnan sighed.

"Unfortunately," Sternwheeler went on, "the entire affair has apparently been carried off without recourse to violence, leaving the Corps no excuse to step in— that is, it appears our assistance in restoring order will not be required."

"Glave was one of the old Contract Worlds," Retief said. "What's become of the Planetary Manager General and the technical staff?—And how do the peasants and workers plan to operate the atmospheric purification system, and weather control station, and the tide-regulation complexes?"

"I'm more concerned at present with the status of the Mission. Will we be welcomed by these peasants and workers, or peppered with buckshot?"

"You say that this is a popular junta, and that the former leaders have fled into exile," someone asked. "May I ask the source of this information, Mr. Ambassador?"

"The despatch cites a 'reliable Glavian source.' "

"That's officialese for something cribbed from a broadcast news tape," Retief commented. "Presumably the Glavian news services are in the hands of the revolution. In that case—"

"Yes, yes, there is the possibility that the issue is yet in doubt; of course, we'll have to exercise caution in making our approach; it wouldn't do to make overtures to the wrong side."

"Oh, I think we need have no fear on that score," the Chief of the Political Section spoke up. "I know these entrenched cliques; once challenged by an aroused populace, they scuttle for safety—with large balances safely tucked away in neutral banks."

"I'd like to go on record," Magnan piped, "as registering my deep gratification at this fulfillment of popular aspirations—"

"The most popular aspiration I know of is to live high off someone else's effort," Retief said. "I don't know of anyone outside the Corps who's managed it."

"I'd like to propose that immediate arrangements be made for a technical mission," Magnan said. "It's my experience that one of the most pressing needs of newly established democracies is—"

"Is someone to tell them how to run what they've stolen after they've kicked out the legitimate owners," Retief suggested.

The Political Officer blinked at Retief. "Are you implying approval of technocratic totalitarianism?"

"I won't know," Retief said, "until I look that up in a dictionary."

"Gentlemen!" Sternwheeler bellowed. "I'm awaiting your constructive suggestions—not an exchange of political views. We'll arrive off Glave in less than six hours. I should like before that time to have developed some notion regarding to whom I shall expect to offer my credentials!"

There was a discreet tap at the door; it opened and the young Third Secretary poked his head in.

"Mr. Ambassador, I have a reply to your message— just received from Glave. It's signed by the Steward of the GFE, and I thought you'd want to see it at once . . ."

"Yes, of course; let me have it."

"What's the GFE?" someone asked.

"It's the revolutionary group," the messenger said, passing the message over.

"GFE? GFE? What do the letters signify?"

"Glorious Fun Eternally," Retief suggested. "Or possibly Goodies For Everybody."

"I believe that's 'Glavian Free Electorate'," the Third Secretary said.

Sternwheeler stared at the paper, lips pursed. His face grew pink. He slammed the paper on the table.

"Well, gentlemen! It appears our worst fears have been realized! This is nothing less than a warning! A threat! We're advised to divert course and by-pass Glave entirely. It seems the GFE wants no interference from meddling foreign exploiters, as they put it!"

Magnan rose. "If you'll excuse me, Mr. Ambassador,

I want to get off a message to Sector HQ to hold my old job for me—"

"Sit down, you idiot!" Sternwheeler roared. "If you think I'm consenting to have my career blighted—my first Ambassadorial post whisked out from under me—the Corps made a fool of—"

"I'd like to take a look at that message," Retief said. It was passed along to him. He read it.

"I don't believe this applies to us, Mr. Ambassador."

"What are you talking about? It's addressed to me—by name!"

"It merely states that 'meddling foreign exploiters' are unwelcome. Meddling foreigners we are, but we don't qualify as exploiters unless we show a profit—and this appears to be shaping up as a particularly profitless venture."

"What are you proposing, Mr. Retief?"

"That we proceed to make planetfall as scheduled, greet our welcoming committee with wide diplomatic smiles, hint at largesse in the offing, and settle down to observe the lie of the land."

"Just what I was about to suggest," Magnan said.

"That might be dangerous," Sternwheeler said.

"That's why I didn't suggest it," Magnan said.

"Still it's essential that we learn more of the situation than can be gleaned from official broadcasts," Sternwheeler mused. "Now, while I can't justify risking the entire Mission, it might be advisable to dispatch a delegation to sound out the new regime—"

"I'd like to volunteer," Magnan said, rising.

"Of course, the delegates may be murdered—"

"—but unfortunately, I'm under treatment at the moment." Magnan sat down.

"—which will place us in an excellent position, propaganda-wise."

"What a pity I can't go," the Military Attaché said. "But my place is with my troops."

"The only troops you've got are the Assistant Attaché and your secretary," Magnan pointed out.

"Say, I'd like to be down there in the thick of things,"

the Political Officer said. He assumed a grave expression. "But, of course, I'll be needed here, to interpret results."

"I appreciate your attitude, gentlemen," Sternwheeler said, studying the ceiling. "But I'm afraid I must limit the privilege of volunteering for this hazardous duty to those officers of more robust physique, under forty years of age—"

"Tsk. I'm forty-one," Magnan said.

"—and with a reputation for adaptability." His glance moved along the table.

"Do you mind if I run along now, Mr. Ambassador?" Retief said. "It's time for my insulin shot."

Sternwheeler's mouth dropped open.

"Just kidding," Retief said. "I'll go. But I have one request, Mr. Ambassador: no further communication with the ground until I give the all-clear."

Retief grounded the lighter in the center of Glave spaceport, cycled the lock, and stepped out. The hot yellow Glavian sun beat down on a broad expanse of concrete, an abandoned service cart, and a row of tall ships casting black shadows toward the silent control tower. A wisp of smoke curled up from the shed area at the rim of the field. There was no other sign of life.

Retief walked over to the cart, tossed his valise aboard, climbed into the driver's seat, and headed for the operations building. Beyond the port, hills rose, white buildings gleaming against the deep green slopes. Near the ridge, a vehicle moved ant-like along a winding road, a dust trail rising behind it. Faintly, the tiny rap! of a distant shot sounded.

Papers littered the ground before the Operations Building. Retief pushed open the tall glass door, stood listening. Slanting sunlight reflected from a wide, polished floor, at the far side of which illuminated lettering over empty counters read IMMIGRATION, HEALTH, and CUSTOMS. He crossed to the desk, put the valise down, then leaned across the counter. A worried face under an over-sized white cap looked up at him.

"You can come out now," Retief said. "They've gone."

The man rose, dusting himself off. He looked over Retief's shoulder. "Who's gone?"

"Whoever it was that scared you."

"Whatta ya mean? I was looking for my pencil."

"Here it is." Retief plucked a worn stub from the pocket of the soiled shirt sagging under the weight of braided shoulder-boards. "You can sign me in as a Diplomatic Representative; a break for you—no formalities necessary. Where can I catch a cab for the city?"

The man eyed Retief's bag. "What's in that?"

"Personal belongings under duty-free entry."

"Guns?"

"No, thanks, just a cab, if you don't mind."

"You got no gun?" the man raised his voice.

"That's right, fellows," Retief called out. "No gun; no knife, not even a small fission bomb; just a few pairs of socks and some reading matter."

A brown-uniformed man rose from behind the Customs counter, holding a long-barreled blast-rifle centered on the Corps insignia stitched to the pocket of Retief's powder-blue blazer.

"Don't try nothing," he said. "You're under arrest."

"It can't be overtime parking; I've only been here five minutes."

"Hah!" The gun-handler moved out from the counter, came up to Retief. "Empty out your pockets!" he barked. "Hands over head!"

"I'm just a diplomat, not a contortionist," Retief said, not moving. "Do you mind pointing that thing in some other direction?"

"Looky here, Mister, I'll give the orders. We don't need anybody telling us how to run our business—"

"I'm telling you to shift that blaster before I take it away from you and wrap it around your neck," Retief said conversationally. The cop stepped back uncertainly, lowering the gun.

"Jake! Horny! Pud! Come on out!"

Three more brown uniforms emerged from concealment.

"Who are you fellows hiding from? The top sergeant?" Retief glanced over the ill-fitting uniforms, the
unshaved faces, the scuffed boots. "Tell you what;
when he shows up, I'll engage him in conversation,
and you beat it back to the barracks and grab a quick
bath—"

"That's enough smart talk," the biggest of the three
newcomers moved up to Retief. "You stuck your nose
in at the wrong time. We just had a change of manage-
ment around here."

"I heard about it," Retief said. "Who do I complain
to?"

"Complain? What about?"

"The port's a mess," Retief barked. "Nobody on
duty to receive official visitors! No passenger service
facilities! Why, do you know I had to carry my own
bag—"

"All right, all right, that's outside my department.
You better see the boss."

"The boss? I thought you got rid of the bosses."

"We did, but now we got new ones."

"They any better than the old ones?"

"This guy asks too many questions," the man with
the gun said. "Let's let Sozier answer 'em."

"Who's he?"

"He's the Military Governor of the City."

"Now we're getting somewhere," Retief said. "Lead
the way, Jake—and don't forget my bag."

Sozier was a small man with thin hair oiled across a
shiny scalp, prominent ears, and eyes like coal chips
set in rolls of fat. He glowered at Retief from behind a
polished desk occupying the center of a spacious office.

"I warned you off," he snapped. "You came anyway." He leaned forward and slammed a fist down on
the desk. "You're used to throwing your weight around,
but you won't throw it around here! There'll be no
spies pussy-footing around Glave!"

"Looking for what, Mr. Sozier?"

"Call me General!"

"Mind if I sit down?" Retief pulled out a chair, seated himself, and took out a cigar. "Curiously enough," he said, lighting up, "the Corps has no intention of making any embarrassing investigations. We deal with the existing government, no questions asked—" His eyes held the other's. "Unless, of course, there are evidences of atrocities or other illegal measures."

The coal-chip eyes narrowed. "I don't have to make explanations to you or anybody else—"

"Except, presumably, the Glavian Free Electorate," Retief said blandly. "But tell me, General—who's actually running the show?"

A speaker on the desk buzzed. "Hey, Corporal Sozier! Wes's got them two hellions cornered. They're holed up in the Birthday Cake—"

"*General* Sozier, damn you! And plaster your big mouth shut!" He gestured to one of the uniformed men standing by.

"You! Get Trundy and Little Moe up here—pronto!" He swiveled back to Retief. "You're in luck; I'm too busy right now to bother with you. You get back over to the port and leave the same way you came—and tell your blood-sucking friends the easy pickings are over as far as Glave's concerned. You won't lounge around here living high and throwing big parties and cooking up deals to get fat on at the expense of the working man."

Retief dribbled ash on Sozier's desk and glanced at the green uniform front bulging between silver buttons.

"Who paid for *your* pot-belly, Sozier?" he inquired carelessly.

Sozier's eyes narrowed to slits. "I could have you shot—"

"Stop playing games with me, Sozier," Retief rapped. "There's a squadron of Peace Enforcers standing by just in case any apprentice statesmen forget the niceties of diplomatic usage. I suggest you start showing a little intelligence about now, or even Horny and Pud are likely to notice."

Sozier's fingers squeaked on the arms of his chair. He swallowed.

"You might start by assigning me an escort for a conducted tour of the capital," Retief went on. "I want to be in a position to confirm that order has been re-established, and that normal services have been restored—otherwise, it may be necessary to send a Monitor Unit to straighten things out."

"You can't meddle with the internal affairs of a sovereign world—"

Retief sighed. "The trouble with taking over your boss's job is discovering its drawbacks. It's disillusioning, I know, Sozier—but—"

"All right! Take your tour! You'll find everything running as smooth as silk! Utilities, police, transport, environmental control—"

"What about Space Control? Glave Tower seems to be off the air."

"I shut it down. We don't need anything from outside."

"Where's the new Premier keeping himself? Does he share your passion for privacy?"

The general got to his feet. "I'm letting you take your look, Mr. Big Nose. I'm giving you four hours. Then out! And the next meddling bureaucrat that tries to cut atmosphere on Glave without a clearance gets burned!"

"I'll need a car."

"Jake! You stick to this bird. Take him to the main power plant, the water works, and the despatch center, ride him around town and show him we're doing OK without a bunch of leeches bossing us; then dump him at the port—and see that he leaves."

"I'll plan my own itinerary, thanks. I can't promise I'll be finished in four hours—but I'll keep you advised."

"I warned you—"

"I heard you. Five times. And I only warned you

once. You're getting ahead of me." Retief rose, motioned to the hulking guard. "Come on, Jake; we've got a lot of ground to cover before dinner."

At the curb, Retief held out his hand. "Give me the power cylinder out of your rifle, Jake."

"Huh?"

"Come on, Jake. You've got a nervous habit of playing with the firing stud. We don't want any accidents."

"How do you get it out? They only give me this thing yesterday."

Retief pocketed the cylinder. "You sit in back. I'll drive." He wheeled the car off along a broad avenue crowded with vehicles and lined with flowering palms behind which stately white buildings reared up into the pale sky.

"Nice looking city, Jake," Retief said conversationally. "What's the population?"

"I dunno. I only been here a year."

"What about Horny and Pud? Are they natives?"

"Whatta ya mean, natives? They're just as civilized as me."

"My boner, Jake. Known Sozier long?"

"Sure; he useta come around to the club."

"I take it he was in the army under the old regime?"

"Yeah—but he didn't like the way they run it. Nothing but band playing and fancy marching. There wasn't nobody to fight."

"Just between us, Jake—where did the former Planetary Manager General go?" Retief watched Jake's heavy face in the mirror. Jake jumped, clamped his mouth shut.

"I don't know nothing."

Half an hour later, after a tour of the commercial center, Retief headed toward the city's outskirts. The avenue curved, leading up along the flank of a low hill.

"I must admit I'm surprised, Jake," Retief said. "Everything seems orderly; no signs of riots or panic. Power, water, communications normal—just as the general said. Remarkable, isn't it, considering that the entire managerial class has packed up and left . . ."

"You wanta see the Power Plant?" Retief could see perspiration beaded on the man's forehead under the uniform cap.

"Sure. Which way?" With Jake directing, Retief ascended to the ridge top, cruised past the blank white facade of the station.

"Quiet, isn't it?" Retief pulled the car in to the curb. "Let's go inside."

"Huh? Corporal Sozier didn't say nothing—"

"You're right, Jake. That leaves it to our discretion."

"He won't like it."

"The corporal's a busy man, Jake. We won't worry him by telling him about it."

Jake followed Retief up the walk. The broad double doors were locked.

"Let's try the back."

The narrow door set in the high blank wall opened as Retief approached. A gun barrel poked out, followed by a small man with bushy red hair. He looked Retief over.

"Who's this party, Jake?" he barked.

"Sozier said show him the plant," Jake said.

"What we need is more guys to pull duty, not tourists. Anyway, I'm chief Engineer here. Nobody comes in here 'less I like their looks."

Retief moved forward, stood looking down at the red-head. The little man hesitated, then waved him past. "Lucky for you, I like your looks."

Inside, Retief surveyed the long room, the giant converter units, the massive bussbars. Armed men—some in uniform, some in work clothes, others in loud sport shirts—stood here and there. Other men read meters, adjusted controls, or inspected dials.

"You've got more guards than workers," Retief said. "Expecting trouble?"

The red-head bit the corner from a plug of spearmint. He glanced around the plant. "Things is quiet now; but you never know . . ."

"Rather old-fashioned equipment, isn't it? When was it installed?"

"Huh? I dunno. What's wrong with it?"

"What's your basic power source, a core sink? Lithospheric friction? Sub-crustal hydraulics?"

"Beats me, Mister. I'm the boss here, not a dern mechanic."

A grey-haired man carrying a clip-board walked past, studied a panel, made notes, glanced up to catch Retief's eye, moved on.

"Everything seems to be running normally," Retief remarked.

"Sure; why not?"

"Records being kept up properly?"

"Sure; some of these guys, all they do is walk around looking at dials and writing stuff on paper. If it was me, I'd put 'em to work."

Retief strolled over to the grey-haired man, now scribbling before a bank of meters. He glanced at the clip-board.

Power off at sunset. Tell Corasol was scrawled in block letters across the record sheet. Retief nodded, rejoined his guard.

"All right, Jake. Let's have a look at the communications center."

Back in the car, headed west, Retief studied the blank windows of office buildings, the milling throngs in beer bars, shooting galleries, tattoo parlors, billiards halls, pin-ball arcades, bordellos, and half-credit casinos.

"Everybody seems to be having fun," he remarked.

Jake stared out the window. "Yeah."

"Too bad you're on duty, Jake. You could be out there joining in."

"Soon as the corporal gets things organized, I'm opening me up a place to show dirty tri-di's. I'll get my share."

"Meanwhile, let the rest of 'em have their fun, eh, Jake?"

"Look, Mister, I been thinking: Maybe you better gimme back that kick-stick you taken outa my gun . . ."

"Sorry, Jake; no can do. Tell me, what was the real cause of the revolution? Not enough to eat? Too much regimentation?"

"Naw, we always got plenty to eat. There wasn't none of that regimentation—up till I joined up in the corporal's army."

"Rigid class structure, maybe? Educational discrimination?"

Jake nodded. "Yeah, it was them schools done it. All the time trying to make a feller go to some kind of class. Big shots. Know it all. Gonna make us sit around and view tapes. Figgered they was better than us."

"And Sozier's idea was you'd take over, and you wouldn't have to be bothered."

"Aw, it wasn't Sozier's idea. He ain't the big leader."

"Where does the big leader keep himself?"

"I dunno. I guess he's pretty busy right now." Jake snickered. "Some of them guys call themselves colonels turned out not to know nothing about how to shoot off the guns."

"Shooting, eh? I thought it was a sort of peaceful revolution; the managerial class were booted out, and that was that."

"I don't know nothing," Jake snapped. "How come you keep trying to get me to say stuff I ain't supposed to talk about? You want to get me in trouble?"

"Oh, you're already in trouble, Jake. But if you stick with me, I'll try to get you out of it. Where exactly did the refugees head for? How did they leave? Must have been a lot of them; I'd say in a city of this size they'd run into the thousands."

"I don't know."

"Of course, it depends on your definition of a big shot. Who's included in that category, Jake?"

"You know, the slick-talking ones; the fancy dressers; the guys that walk around and tell other guys what to do. We do all the work and they get all the big pay."

"I suppose that would cover scientists, professional men, executives, technicians of all sorts, engineers, teachers—all that crowd of no-goods."

"Yeah, them are the ones."

"And once you got them out of the way, the regular fellows would have a chance; chaps that don't spend all their time taking baths and reading books and using big words; good Joes that don't mind picking their noses in public."

"We got as much right as anybody—"

"Jake, who's Corasol?"

"He's—I don't know."

"I thought I overheard his name somewhere."

"Uh, here's the communication center," Jake cut in.

Retief swung into a parking lot under a high blank facade. He set the brake and stepped out.

"Lead the way, Jake."

"Look, Mister, the corporal only wanted me to show you the outside—"

"Anything to hide, Jake?"

Jake shook his head angrily and stamped past Retief. "When I joined up with Sozier, I didn't figger I'd be getting in this kind of mess . . ."

"I know, Jake; it's tough. Sometimes it seems like a fellow works harder after he's thrown out the parasites than he did before."

A cautious guard let Retief and Jake inside, followed them along bright lit aisles among consoles, cables, batteries of instruments. Armed men in careless uniforms lounged, watching. Here and there a silent technician worked quietly.

Retief paused by one, an elderly man in a neat white coverall, with a purple spot under one eye.

"Quite a bruise you've got there," Retief commented heartily. "Power failure at sunset," he added softly. The technician hesitated, nodded, and moved on.

Back in the car, Retief gave Jake directions. At the end of three hours, he had seen twelve smooth-running, heavily guarded installations.

"So far, so good, Jake," he said. "Next stop, Substation Number Nine." In the mirror, Jake's face stiffened. "Hey, you can't go down there—"

"Something going on there, Jake?"

"That's where—I mean, no; I don't know."

"I don't want to miss anything, Jake. Which way?"

"I ain't going down there," Jake said sullenly.

Retief braked. "In that case, I'm afraid our association is at an end, Jake."

"You mean . . . you're getting out here?"

"No, you are."

"Huh? Now wait a minute, Mister; the corporal said I was to stay with you."

Retief accelerated. "That's settled, then. Which way?"

Retief pulled the car to a halt two hundred yards from the periphery of a loose crowd of brown-uniformed men who stood in groups scattered across a broad plaza, overflowing into a stretch of manicured lawn before the bare, functional facade of Sub-station Number Nine. In the midst of the besieging mob, Sozier's red face and bald head bobbed as he harangued a cluster of green-uniformed men from his place in the rear of a long open car.

"What's it all about, Jake?" Retief inquired. "Since the parasites have all left peacefully, I'm having a hard time figuring out who'd be holed up in the pumping station—and why. Maybe they haven't gotten the word that it's all going to be fun and games from now on."

"If the corporal sees you over here—"

"Ah, the good corporal. Glad you mentioned him, Jake. He's the man to see." Retief stepped out of the car and started through the crowd. A heavy lorry loaded with an immense tank with the letter H blazoned on its side trundled into the square from a side street, moved up to a position before the building. A smaller car pulled alongside Sozier's limousine. The driver stepped down, handed something to Sozier. A moment later, Sozier's amplified voice boomed across the crowd.

"You in there, Corasol. This is General Sozier, and

I'm warning you to come out now or you and your smart friends are in for a big surprise. You think I won't blast you out because I don't want to wreck the plant. You see the tank aboard the lorry that just pulled up? It's full of gas—and I got plenty of hoses out here to pump it inside with. I'll put men on the roof and squirt it in the ventilators . . ."

Sozier's voice echoed and died. The militiamen eyed the station. Nothing happened.

"I know you can hear me, damn you!" Sozier squalled. "You'd better get the doors open and get out here fast—"

Retief stepped to Sozier's side. "Say, Corporal, I didn't know you went in for practical jokes—"

Sozier jerked around to gape at Retief.

"What are you doing here!" he burst out. "I told Jake—where is that—"

"Jake didn't like the questions I was asking," Retief said, "so he marched me up here to report to you."

"Jake, you damn fool!" Sozier roared. "I gotta good mind—"

"I disagree, Sozier," Retief cut in. "I think you're a complete imbecile. Sitting out here in the open yelling at the top of your lungs, for example: Corasol and his party might get annoyed and spray that fancy car you've swiped with something a lot more painful than words."

"Eh?" Sozier's head whipped around to stare at the building.

"Isn't that a gun I see sticking out?"

Sozier dropped. "Where?"

"My mistake; just a foreign particle on my contact lenses." Retief leaned on the car. "On the other hand, Sozier, most murderers are sneaky about it; I think making a public announcement is a nice gesture on your part. The Monitors won't have any trouble deciding who to hang when they come in to straighten out this mess."

Sozier scrambled back onto his seat. "Monitors?" he snarled. "I don't think so. I don't think you'll be around to do any blabbering to anybody." He raised his voice. "Jake! March this spy over to the sidelines. If he tries anything, shoot him!" He gave Retief a baleful grin. "I'll lay the body out nice and ship it back to your cronies. Accidents will happen, you know. It'll be a week or two before they get around to following up— and by then I'll have this little problem under control."

Jake looked at Retief uncertainly, fingering his empty rifle.

Retief put his hands up. "I guess you got me, Jake," he said. "Careful of that gun, now."

Jake glanced at Sozier, gulped, aimed the rifle at Retief, and nodded toward the car. As Retief moved off, a murmur swept across the crowd. Retief glanced back; a turret on the station roof was rotating slowly. A shout rose; men surged away from the building, scuffling for way; Sozier yelled. His car started up, moved forward, horns blaring. As Retief watched, a white stream arced up from the turret, catching the sun as it spanned the lawn, down to strike the massed men in a splatter of spray. It searched across the mob, came to rest on Sozier's car. Uniformed men scrambled for safety as the terrified driver gunned the heavy vehicle. The hose followed the car, dropping a solid stream of water on Sozier, kicking and flailing in the back seat. As the car passed from view down a side street, water was overflowing the sides.

"The corporal will feel all the better for an invigorating swim in his mobile pool," Retief commented. "By the way, Jake, I have to be going now. It wouldn't be fair to send you back to your boss without something to back up your story that you were outnumbered, so—"

Retief's left fist shot out to connect solidly with Jake's jaw. Jake dropped the gun and sat down hard. Retief turned and headed for the pumping station. The hose had shut down now. A few men were standing, eyeing the building anxiously. Others watched his progress across the square. As Retief passed, he caught scattered comments:

"—seen that bird before."

"—where he's headed."

"—feller Sozier was talkin to . . ."

"Hey, you!" Retief was on the grass now. Ahead, the blank wall loomed up. He walked on, briskly.

"Stop that jasper!" a shout rang out. There was a sharp whine and a black spot appeared on the wall ahead. Near it, a small personnel door abruptly swung inward. Retief sprinted, plunged through the opening as a second shot seared the paint on the doorframe. The door clanged behind him. Retief glanced over the half-dozen men confronting him.

"I'm Retief, CDT, Acting Chargé," he said. "Which of you gentlemen is Manager-General Corasol?"

Corasol was a tall, wide-shouldered man of fifty, with shrewd eyes, a ready smile, capable-looking hands, and an urbane manner. He and Retief sat at a table at one side of the large room, under a maze of piping, tanks and valves; Corasol poured amber fluid into square glass tumblers.

"We spotted you by the blazer," he said. "Baby blue and gold braid stand out in a crowd."

Retief nodded. "The uniform has its uses," he agreed. He tried the drink. "Say, what is this? It's not bad."

"Sugar-weed rum; made from a marine plant. We have plenty of ocean here on Glave; there's only the one continent, you know, and it's useless for agriculture."

"Weather?"

"That's part of it; Glave is moving into what would be a major glaciation if it weren't for a rather elaborate climatic control installation. Then there are the tides; half the continent would be inundated twice a year when our satellite is at aphelion; there's a system of baffles, locks and deep-water pumps that maintain the shore-line more or less constant; we still keep our cities well inland. Then there are the oxygen generators, the atmosphere filtration complex, vermin control, and so on. Glave in its natural state is a rather hostile world."

"I'm surprised that your mines can support it all."

"Oh, they don't." Corasol shook his head. "Two hundred years ago, when the Company first opened up Glave, it was economical enough. Quintite was a precious mineral in those days. Synthetics have long since taken over. Even fully automated, the mines barely support the public services and welfare system."

"I seem to recall a reference in the Post Report to the effect that a Company petition to vacate its charter had been denied . . ."

Corasol nodded, smiling wryly. "The CDT seemed to feel that as long as any of the world's residents desired to remain, the Company was constrained to oblige them. The great majority departed long ago, of course—relocated to other operational areas. Only the untrainables, living off welfare funds—and a skeleton staff of single men to operate the technical installations—have stayed on."

"What do you mean—untrainable?"

"There's always a certain percentage of any population with the conviction that society is a conspiracy to deny them their rights. The right to be totally ignorant of any useful knowledge seems to be the basic one. Most societies can carry the burden of these drones—along with the criminal and idiot classes—as mere minority problems. Here on Glave, they've constituted the population—with the planet operated to maintain them. Some of them have opened small businesses—of the kind that require only a native shrewdness and a stomach for the popular tastes. Of course, they still regard any material advantages possessed by the productive as flagrant evidence of discrimination."

"That explains the mechanics of the recent uprising," Retief said.

The bottle clinked against glasses for a second round. "What about the good corporal?" Retief asked. "Assuming he's a strong swimmer, you should be hearing from him soon."

Corasol glanced at his finger watch. "I imagine he'll be launching his gas attack any minute."

"The prospect doesn't seem to bother you."

"Sozier is a clever enough chap in his own way," Corasol said. "But he has a bad habit of leaping to conclusions. He's gotten hold of a tank of what someone has told him is gas—as indeed it is. Hydrogen, for industrial use. It seems the poor fellow is under the impression that anything masquerading as gas will have a lethal effect."

"He may be right—if he pumps it in fast enough."

"Oh, he won't be pumping it—not after approximately five minutes from now."

"Hmmm. I think I'm beginning to see the light. 'Power off at sunset . . .' "

Corasol nodded. "I don't think he realizes somehow that all his vehicles are operating off broadcast power."

"Still, he has a good-sized crowd of hopefuls with him. How do you plan to get through them?"

"We don't; we go under. There's an extensive system of service ways underlying the city; another detail which I believe has escaped the corporal's notice."

"You'll be heading for the port?"

"Yes—eventually. First, we have a few small chores to see to. Sozier has quite a number of our technical men working at gun point to keep various services going."

Retief nodded. "It won't be easy breaking them out; I made a fast tour of the city this afternoon; locked doors, armed guards—"

"Oh, the locks are power-operated, too. Our fellows will know what to do when the power fails. I think the sudden darkness will eliminate any problem from the guards."

The lights flickered and died. The whine of the turbines was suddenly noticeable, descending. Faint cries sounded from outside.

Corasol switched on a small portable lantern. "All ready, gentlemen?" he called, rising. "Let's move out. We want to complete this operation before dawn."

Four hours later, Retief stood with Corasol in a low-ceilinged tunnel, white-tiled, brilliantly lit by a central glare strip, watching as the last of the column of men released from forced labor in the city's utilities installations filed past. A solidly-built man with pale blond hair came up, breathing hard.

"How did it go, Taine?" Corasol asked.

"They're beginning to catch on, Mr. Corasol. We had a brisk time of it at Station Four. Everybody's clear now. No one killed, but we had a few injuries."

Corasol nodded. "The last few crews in have reported trouble. Ah—what about—"

Taine shook his head. "Sorry, Sir. No trace. No one's seen them. But they're probably at the port ahead of us, hiding out. They'd know we'd arrive eventually."

"I suppose so. You sent word to them well in advance . . ."

"Suppose I stand by here with a few men; we'll patrol the tunnels in case they show up. We have several hours before daylight."

"Yes. I'll go along and see to the preparations at Exit Ten. We'll make our sortie at oh-five-hundred. If you haven't seen anything of them by then . . ."

"I'm sure they're all right."

"They'd better be," Corasol said grimly. "Let's be off, Retief."

"If it's all the same to you, Mr. Manager-General, I'll stay here with Taine; I'll join you later."

"As you wish. I don't imagine there'll be any trouble—but if there is, having a CDT observer along will lend a certain air to the operation." He smiled, shook Retief's hand and moved off along the tunnel. The echo of feet and voices grew faint, faded to silence. Taine turned to the three men detailed to him, conversed briefly, sent them off along branching corridors. He glanced at Retief.

"Mr. Retief, you're a diplomat. This errand is not a diplomatic one."

"I've been on a few like that, too, Mr. Taine."

Taine studied Retief's face. "I can believe that," he said. "However, I think you'd better rejoin the main party."

"I might be of some use here, if your missing men arrive under fire."

"Missing men?" Taine's mouth twisted in a sour smile. "You fail to grasp the picture, Mr. Retief. There'll be no missing men arriving."

"Oh? I understood you were waiting here to meet them."

"Not men, Mr. Retief. It happens that Corasol has twin daughters, aged nineteen. They haven't been seen since the trouble began."

Half an hour passed. Retief leaned against the tunnel wall, arms folded, smoking a cigar in silence. Taine paced, ten yards up the corridor, ten yards back . . .

"You seem nervous, Mr. Taine," Retief said.

Taine stopped pacing, eyed Retief coldly. "You'd better go along now," he said decisively. "Just follow the main tunnel; it's about a mile—"

"Plenty of time yet, Mr. Taine." Retief smiled and drew on his cigar. "Your three men are still out—"

"They won't be back here; we'll rendezvous at Exit Ten."

"Am I keeping you from something, Taine?"

"I can't be responsible for your safety if you stay here."

"Oh? You think I might fall victim to an accident?"

Taine narrowed his eyes. "It could happen," he said harshly.

"Where were the girls last seen?" Retief asked suddenly.

"How would I know?"

"Weren't you the one who got word to them?"

"Maybe you'd better keep out of this."

"You sent your men off; now you're eager to see me retire to a safe position. Why the desire for solitude, Taine? You wouldn't by any chance have plans . . . ?"

"That's enough," Taine snapped. "On your way. That's an order!"

"There are some aspects of this situation that puzzle me, Mr. Taine. Mr. Corasol has explained to me how he and his Division Chiefs—including you—were surprised in the Executive Suite at Planetary Central, by a crowd of Sozier's bully-boys. They came in past the entire security system without an alarm. Corasol and the others put up a surprisingly good fight and made it to the service elevators—and from there to the Substation. There was even time to order an emergency alert to the entire staff—but somehow, they were all caught at their stations and kept on the job at gun point. Now, I should think that you, as Chief of Security as well as Communications, should have some ideas as to how all this came about."

"Are you implying—"

"Let me guess, Taine. You have a deal with Sozier. He takes over, ousts the legal owners, and sets himself up to live off the fat of the land, with you as his technical chief. Then, I imagine, you'd find it easy enough to dispose of Sozier—and you'd be in charge."

Without warning, Taine put his head down and charged. Retief dropped his cigar, side-stepped, and planted a solid right on Taine's jaw. He staggered, went to his hands and knees.

"I suppose you'd like to get word to Sozier that his work force is arriving at the port at oh-five-hundred," Retief said. "Of course, he'll want to have a good-sized reception committee on hand as they come out—"

Taine plunged to his feet, threw a vicious left that went past Retief's ear, then abruptly dropped, clamped a lock on Retief's leg, twisted—

The two men rolled, came to rest with Taine on top, Retief face-down, his arm bent back and doubled. Taine, red-faced and puffing, grunted as he applied pressure.

"You know a lot about me," he granted, "but you overlooked the fact that I've been Glavian Judo champion for the past nine years."

"You're a clever man, Taine," Retief said between clenched teeth. "Too clever to think it will work."

"It will work. Glave's never had a CDT mission here before; we're too small. Corasol invited your Embassy in because he had an idea there was something in the wind. That forced my hand. I've had to move hastily. But by the time I invite observers in to see for themselves, everything will be running smoothly. I can even afford to let Corasol and the others go—I'll have hostages for his good behavior."

"You've been wanting to boast about it to someone who could appreciate your cleverness, I see. Sozier must be an unappreciative audience."

"Sozier's a filthy pig—but he had his uses."

"What do you plan to do now?"

"I've been wondering that myself—but I think the best solution is to simply break your arm for now. You should be easy to control then. It's quite simple; I merely apply pressure, thus . . ."

"Judo is a very useful technique," Retief said. "But in order to make it work, you have to be a pretty good man . . ." He moved suddenly, shifting his position. Taine grabbed, holding Retief's arm by the wrist and elbow, his own arm levering Retief's back, back . . . Retief twisted onto his side, then his back. Taine grunted, following the movement, straining. Slowly, Retief sat up against Taine's weight. Then, with a surge, he straightened his arm. Taine's grip broke. Retief came to his feet. Taine scrambled up in time to meet a clean uppercut.

"Ah, there you are," Retief said as Taine's eyes fluttered and opened. "You've had a nice nap—almost fifteen minutes. Feeling better?"

Taine snarled, straining against the bonds on his wrists.

"Gold braid has its uses," Retief commented. "Now that you're back, perhaps you can answer a question for me. What's the Birthday Cake?"

Taine spat. Retief went to stand over him.

"Time is growing short, Mr. Taine. It will be dawn in another two hours. I can't afford the luxury of coaxing you. You'd better answer my question."

"You won't get away with this."

Retief looked at the glowing end of his cigar. "This won't be subtle, I agree—but it will work . . ."

"You're bluffing."

Retief leaned closer. "In my place—would you hesitate?" he asked softly.

Taine cursed, struggled to break free, eyes on the cigar.

"What kind of diplomat are you?" he snarled.

"The modern variety; throat-cutting, thumb-screws, poison and stiletto work were popular in Machiavelli's time; nowadays we go in more for the administrative approach—but the cigar-end still has its role."

"Look—we can come to an agreement—"

"What's the Birthday Cake?" Retief snapped.

"I'm in a position to do a lot for you—"

"Last chance—"

"It's the official Residence of the Manager-General!" Taine screeched, writhing away from the cigar.

"Where is it? Talk fast!"

"You'll never get close! There's a seven-foot wall and by this time the grounds are swarming with Sozier's men—"

"Nevertheless, I want to know where it is—and the information had better be good. If I don't come back, you'll have a long wait."

Taine groaned. "All right. Put that damned cigar away. I'll tell you what I can . . ."

Retief stood in the shadow of a vine-grown wall, watching the five-man guard detail at the main gate to the Residence grounds. The bluish light of the Glavian satellite reflected from the rain-pocked street, glinted from the leaves of a massive tree ten yards from the gate. The chill in the air cut through Retief's wet clothes; the men at the gate huddled, hands in pockets, coat collars turned up, backs to the wind—and to Retief. He moved silently forward, caught a low branch of the tree, pulled himself up. The men at the gate exchanged muttered remarks. One lit a cigarette. Retief waited, then moved higher. The guards talked in low

voices, edged closer to the shelter of the gate-house.
Retief lowered himself onto the wall, dropped down
onto the sodden lawn, crouched, waiting. There was
no alarm.

Through the trees the dark shape of the house
loomed up, its top story defiantly ablaze with lights.
Retief moved off silently, from the shadow of one
tree to the next, swinging in an arc that would bring
him to the rear of the great round structure. He froze
as the heavy footfalls of one of Sozier's pickets slogged
past five yards from him, then moved on. The glow
of a camp-fire flickered near the front of the house. Retief
could make out the shapes of men around it—a dozen
or two, at least. Probably as many more warmed themselves at each of the other fires visible on the grounds—
and most of the rest had doubtless found dryer shelter
in the lee of the house itself.

Retief reached the conservatory at the rear of the
house, studied the dark path leading to the broad terrace, picked out the squat shape of the utilities manifold behind a screen of shrubbery. So far, Taine's
information had been accurate. The next step was to—

There was a faint sound from high above, followed
by a whoosh!—Then, with a sharp crack, a flare appeared overhead, rocking gracefully, floating down
gently under a small parachute. Below it, inky shadows
rocked in unison. In the raw white light, Retief counted
eighteen men clinging to handholds on the side of the
house, immobile in the pitiless glare. Above them, a
face appeared, then a second, peering over the edge of
the fourth-story gallery. Both figures rose, unlimbering
four-foot bows, fitting arrows to strings—

Whok! Whok! Two men lost their holds and fell,
yelling, to slam into the heavy shrubbery. A second
flight of arrows found marks. Retief watched from the
shadows as man after man dropped to flounder in the
wet foliage. Several jumped before the deadly bows
were turned on them. As the flare faded, the last of
the men plunged down to crash among their fellows.
Retief stepped out, ran swiftly to the manifold, forcing

his way among the close-growing screen, scrambled
to its top. His hand fell on a spent arrow. He picked
it up. It was a stout wooden shaft twenty inches long,
terminating in a rubber suction cup. Retief snorted,
dropped the arrow and started up.

Twenty feet above ground level, the wide windows
of the third floor sun terrace presented a precarious
handhold as Retief swung back a foot, kicked in a
panel. Inside, he dimly made out the shape of a broad
carpeted room, curving out of sight in both directions.
There were wide-leaved tropical plants in boxes, groups
of padded chairs, low tables with bowls of fruit. Retief
made his way past them, found an inner door, went into
a dark hall. At the far end, voices exchanged shouted
questions. Feet pounded. A flicker of light from a hand
lantern splashed across the wall, disappeared. Retief
found a stair, went up it noiselessly. According to
Taine, the elevator to the top floor apartment should be
to the left—
Retief flattened himself to the wall. Footsteps
sounded near at hand. He moved quickly to a doorway. There was a murmur of voices, the wavering light
of lanterns. A party of uniformed men tiptoed past a
cross corridor, struggling under the weight of a massive
log, two feet in diameter and twelve feet long.

". . . on signal, hit all together. Then . . ." someone
was saying.

Retief waited, listening. There was the creak of a
door, the fumbling of awkwardly-laden feet on a
stair, hoarse breathing, a muffled curse.

". . . got my fingers, ya slob . . ." a voice snarled.

"Shaddup!" another voice hissed.

There was a long moment of silence, then a muffled
command—followed an instant later by a thunderous
crash, a shout—cut off abruptly by a ponderous blam!
followed instantly by a roar like a burst dam, mingled
with yells, thumps, crashes. A foamy wash of water
surged along the cross corridor, followed a moment

later by a man sliding on his back, then another, two
more, the log, fragments of a door, more men.

In the uproar, Retief moved along to the elevator,
felt over the control panel, located a small knurled
button. He turned it; the panel came away. He fumbled
cautiously, found a toggle switch, flipped it. A light
sprang up in the car; instantly, Retief flipped the light
switch; the glow faded. He waited. No alarm. Men
were picking themselves up, shouting.

". . . them broads dropped a hundred gallon bag of
water . . ." someone complained.

". . . up there fast, men. We got the door OK!"

Feet thumped. Yells sounded.

"No good, Wes! They got a safe or something in the
way!"

Retief silently closed the lift door, pressed the button. With a sigh, the car slid upward, came to a gentle
stop. He eased the door open, looked out into a dim-
lit entrance hall. Footsteps sounded beyond a door. He
waited, heard the clack of high heels crossing a floor.
Retief stepped out of the car, went to the door, glanced
into a spacious lounge with rich furniture, deep rugs,
paintings, a sweep of glass, and in an alcove at the far
side, a bar. Retief crossed the room, poured a stiff
drink into a paper-thin glass, and drained it.

The high-heeled steps were coming back now. A
door opened. Two leggy young women in shorts, with
red-gold hair bound back by ribbons—one green, one
blue—stepped into the room. One held a coil of in-
sulated wire; the other carried a heavy-looking grey-
enameled box eight inches on a side.

"Now, see if you can tinker that thing to put out
about a thousand amps at two volts, Lyn," the girl
with the wire said. "I'll start stringing . . ." her voice
died as she caught sight of Retief. He raised his glass.
"My compliments, ladies. I see you're keeping yourselves amused."

"Who . . . who are you?" Lyn faltered.

"My name's Retief; your father sent me along to
carry your bags. It's lucky I arrived when I did, before

any of those defenseless chaps outside were seriously injured."

"You're not . . . one of them?"

"Of course he's not, Lyn," the second girl said. "He's much too good-looking."

"That's good," Lyn said crisply. "I didn't want to have to use this thing." She tossed a bright-plated 2mm needler onto a chair and sat down. "Dad's all right, isn't he?"

"He's fine, and we've got to be going. Tight schedule, you know. And you'd better get some clothes on. It's cold outside."

Lyn nodded. "Environmental Control went off the air six hours ago; you can already feel snow coming."

"Don't you suppose we have time to just rig up one little old circuit?" the other twin wheedled. "Nothing serious; just enough to tickle."

"We planned to wire all the window frames, the trunk we used to block the stair, the lift shaft—"

"And then we thought we'd try to drop a loop down and pick up the gallery guard rail, and maybe some of that wrought-iron work around the front of the house—"

"Sorry, girls; no time."

Five minutes later, the twins were ready, wrapped in fur robes. Retief had exchanged his soaked blazer for a down-lined weatherproof.

"The lift will take us all the way down, won't it?" he asked.

Lyn nodded. "We can go out through the wine cellar."

Retief picked up the needler and handed it to Lyn. "Hang on to this," he said. "You may need it yet."

A cold wind whipped the ramp as dawn lightened the sky.

"It's hard to believe," Corasol said. "What made him do it?"

"He saw a chance to own it all."

"He can have it." Corasol's communicator beeped.

He put it to his ear. "Everything's ship-shape and ready to lift," a tiny voice said.

Corasol turned to Retief. "Let's go aboard—"

"Hold it," Retief said. "There's someone coming . . ."

Corasol spoke into the communicator. "Keep him covered, but don't fire unless he does."

The man slogging across the concrete was short, wrapped in heavy garments. Over his head a white cloth fluttered from a stick.

"From the set of those bat-ears, I'd say it was the good corporal."

"I wonder what he wants."

Sozier stopped twenty feet from Retief and Corasol.

"I want to . . . ah . . . talk to you, Corasol," he said.

"Certainly, General. Go right ahead."

"Look here, Corasol. You can't do this. My men will freeze. We'll starve. I've been thinking it over, and I've decided we can reach an understanding."

Corasol waited.

"I mean, we can get together on this thing. Compromise. Maybe I acted a little hasty." Sozier looked from Corasol to Retief. "You're from the CDT. You tell him. I'll guarantee his people full rights . . ."

Retief puffed at his cigar in silence; Sozier started again.

"Look, I'll give you a full voice in running things. A fifty-fifty split. Whatta you say?"

"I'm afraid the proposal doesn't interest me, General," Corasol said.

"Never mind the General stuff," Sozier said desperately. "Listen, you can run it. Just give me and my boys a little say-so."

"Sorry," Corasol shook his head. "Not interested, General."

"OK, OK! You win! Just come on back and get things straightened out! I got a belly full of running things!"

"I'm afraid I have other plans, General. For some time I've wanted to transfer operations to a world called Las Palmas on which we hold a charter. It has a naturally delightful climate, and I'm told the fishing is good. I leave Glave to the Free Electorate with my blessing. Goodbye, General." He turned to the ship.

"You got to stay here!" Sozier howled. "We'll complain to the CDT! And don't call me General. I'm a Corporal—"

"You're a General now—whether you like it or not." Corasol said bluntly. He shivered. There was a hint of ice in the air. "If you or any of your men ever decide to go to work, General, I daresay we can train you for employment on Las Palmas. In the meantime— Long Live the Revolution!"

"You can't do this! I'll sue!"

"Calm down, Sozier," Retief said. "Go back to town and see if you can get your radio working. Put in a call for Mr. Magnan aboard the CDT vessel. Tell him your troubles. It will make his day. And a word of advice: Mr. Magnan hates a piker—so ask for plenty."

"My boy, I'm delighted," Ambassador Sternwheeler boomed. "A highly professional piece of work. A stirring testimonial to the value of the skilled negotiator! An inspiration to us all!"

"You're too kind, Mr. Ambassador," Retief said, glancing at his watch.

"And Magnan tells me that not only will the mission be welcomed, and my job secure for another year—that is, I shall have an opportunity to serve—but a technical mission has been requested as well. I shall look forward to meeting General Sozier. He sounds a most reasonable chap."

"Oh, you'll like him, Mr. Ambassador. A true democrat, willing to share all you have."

Counselor of Embassy Magnan tapped and entered the office.

"Forgive the intrusion, Mr. Ambassador," he said breathlessly, "but—"

"Well, what is it, man! The deal hasn't gone sour . . . ?"

"Oh, far from it! I've been exploring General Sozier's economic situation with him via scope—and it seems he'll require a loan . . ."

"Yes, yes? How much?"

Magnan inhaled proudly. "Twenty. Million. Credits."

"No!"

"Yes!"

"Magnificent! Good lord, Magnan, you're a genius! This will mean promotions all around. Why, the administrative load alone—"

"I can't wait to make planetfall, Mr. Ambassador. I'm all abubble with plans. I hope they manage to get the docking facilities back in operation soon."

"Help is on the way, my dear Magnan. I'm assured the Environmental Control installations will be coming back in operation again within a month or two."

"My, didn't those ice-caps form quickly—and in the open sea."

"Mere scum-ice. As my Counselor for Technical Affairs, you'll be in charge of the ice-breaking operation once we're settled in. I imagine you'll want to spend considerable time in the field. I'll be expecting a record of how every credit is spent."

"I'm more the executive type," Magnan said. "Possibly Retief—"

A desk speaker hummed. "Mr. Corasol's lighter has arrived to ferry Mr. Retief across to the Company ship . . ."

"Sorry you won't be with us, Retief," Sternwheeler, said heartily. He turned to Magnan. "Manager-General Corasol has extended Retief an exequatur as Consul General to Las Palmas."

Retief nodded. "Much as I'd like to be out in that open boat with you, breaking ice, I'm afraid duty calls elsewhere."

"Your own post? I'm not sure he's experienced enough, Mr. Ambassador. Now, I—"

"He was requested by name, Magnan. It seems the Manager-General's children took a fancy to him."

"Eh? How curious. I never thought you were particularly interested in infant care, Retief."

"Perhaps I haven't been, Mr. Magnan." Retief draped his short blue cape over his left arm and turned to the door. "But remember the diplomat's motto: be adaptable . . ."

"The ancient defender of the principle of self-determination of peoples threw the elite of its diplomatic shock troops into the fight when local tradition was threatened at Elora. Holding himself aloof from internal bickering, Ambassador Hidebinder dealt shrewdly with diverse elements of the power picture, to forge a bright new page in Corps history . . ."

—Vol. VIII, Reel 7, 490 AE (AD 2951)

The Prince and the Pirate

Retief reined in the tall-shouldered urze-beast with a jangle of the hunting-bells attached to the long-legged mount's harness. The trail of the dirosaur led straight ahead, into a dense thicket of iron-rod trees fifty feet distant, now bent and twisted by the passing of the wounded monster. Far away, the hunting horns of the main party sounded; Retief smiled. Prince Tavilan would employ a choice selection of royal oaths when he learned that a mere diplomat had beaten him to the quarry's turn-at-bay . . .

A windy screech sounded from the depths of the thicket; Retief raised his saddle-horn, blew an answering blast. There was a clanging of branches, a scraping of armored hide on metallic bark. Retief dropped the horn to swing at the pommel; with a pull of a lever, he cocked his cross-bow, sat his mount, waiting. A tiny head, mostly jaws, armed with a foot-long spike below the mouth, snaked out from the grove, hissing a ferocious warning. Retief's urze-beast stirred, tossed its head at the scent of the dirosaur. Trees shuddered aside as the great carnivore forced its bulk between them, its golden-yellow eyes fixed on the man. A clawed foreleg as big as a man's body set with rusty scales raked the ground, dragging the predator's multi-ton bulk into the clear. With a final clangorous flick of its log-like tail, the dirosaur broke free, reared its head into striking position, and charged. Retief raised the cross-bow, took aim—

The cross-bow bucked; Retief spurred aside; he had a momentary glimpse of a two-foot shaft of polished steel protruding from the eye socket of the monster as it blundered past, the long neck falling, to collapse in a cloud of dust, lie twitching, then still.

It was five minutes before the hunt galloped into view, Prince Tavilan's black crested urze-beast in the lead. He slowed to a canter, rode up beside the fallen dirosaur, sat looking down at the open-jawed head, the yellow eyes, glazing in death.

"That's another barrel of royal vintage I owe you, Retief," he said. "If I ever see the palace cellars again." He was a tall, wide, sandy-haired man with a turned-up sun-burned nose. His leather forest garb was well worn; there were cockleburrs in the snow-tiger facings of his royal Eloran blue cape. The cross-bow across his back was his only weapon.

"We're wasting time hunting game," a rider at the prince's side said. "There's a plentiful supply of cross-bow bolts at the lodge; I propose we ride down to Elora City and distribute them among the good Prime Minister's Greenbacks—point first."

"The King still has hopes the CDT will revise its policy," Tavilan glanced at Retief. "If the triple-damned embargo were lifted, Minister Prouch and his talk of a regency would evaporate faster than the royal treasury has under his control."

"Oh, it's not an Embargo, Your Highness," Retief said. "I believe Ambassador Hidebinder refers to it as a unilateral shift in emphasis balance-of-trade-wise to a more group-oriented—"

"What it adds up to is the Royal Eloran Navy grounded, while traitors plot in the palace and Dangredi's pirates raid shipping at the edge of Eloran atmosphere!" Tavilan smacked a fist into his palm. "I've got the finest corps of naval-combat commanders in the Eastern Arm, forty-five battle-ready ships of the line— and, thanks to CDT policy, no fuel! So much for my co-operation with your Ambassador, Retief!"

"Didn't he explain that, Your Highness? If you had the Big Picture, it would all make sense. Of course, I'm a Small Picture man myself, so I'm afraid I can't be of much help."

"It's not your doing, Retief. But ten million Elorans are about to have a dictatorship clamped on them because I lack a few megaton/seconds of firepower . . ."

"Your great-grandfather's mistake was in being a romantic. If he'd named his planet Drab Conformity, set up a committee of bureaucrats to run it and used the forest to supply paper mills instead of hunting in them, you'd be the apple of the collective CDT eye today."

"The old man led a hard life; when he found Elora it was a wilderness. He made his fortune—and then arranged matters here to suit himself—and we Elorans still like parties!"

Retief glanced at the sun. "Speaking of which, I'd better be starting back; the Grande Balle d'Elore is tonight and Mr. Magnan will be upset if I'm not there to help him hover nervously for at least an hour before the Ambassador comes down."

"Retief, you're not riding back to the city . . . ?" Count Arrol looked up from cutting out the dirosaur's chin-horn. He stood. "I told you what my man reported. Your sympathies are too well-known to suit Prouch. Tonight, at the ball—"

"I don't think the worthy Prime Minister will go that far. He's dependent on the good will of the CDT— and diplomat-killing is bad publicity."

"The Palace Guard is still loyal," Tavilian said. "And remember the lad, Aric; you can trust him with any mission within his strength. He's working in the palace as a mess-servant." He laughed bitterly. "Think of us as you dance with the fair ladies of the court, Retief. If you see my father, tell him that my Invincibles and I will continue to skulk here in the Deep Forest as he commands—but we long for action."

"I'll get word to you, Tavilan," Retief said. "My conspiratorial instinct tells me that there'll be action enough for everybody before sunrise tomorrow."

In the Grand Ballroom at the Palace of Elora, Retief cast an eye over the chattering elite of the court, the gorgeously gowned and uniformed couples, the glum representatives of the People's Party, the gaudily uniformed diplomats from Yill, Fust, Flamme, and half a hundred other worlds. A cluster of spider-lean Groaci whispered together near a potted man-eating plant, one leaf of which quivered tentatively, seemed to sniff the aliens, withdrew hastily. Retief plucked a glass from a wide silver tray offered by a bright-eyed mess-boy in a brocaded bolero jacket and a cloth-of-gold turban, who glanced quickly around the crowded ballroom, then stepped close to whisper:

"Mr. Retief—the rascals are forcing the lock on your room!"

Retief passed the glass under his nose, sipped.

"Exactly which rascals do you mean, Aric?" he murmured. "We've got about four sets to choose from."

Aric grinned. "A couple of the Groaci Ambassador's boys," he whispered. "The ones he usually uses for high-class back-alley work."

Retief nodded. "That would be Yilith and Sith, formerly of the Groaci Secret Police. Things must be coming to a head. It's not like old Lhiss to take such direct action." He finished the drink in his hand, put the empty glass on a black marble table.

"Come on, Aric. Ditch that tray and let's take a walk."

In the broad mirror-hung corridor, Retief turned to the right.

"But, Mr. Retief," Aric said. "Your apartment's in the other direction . . ."

"They won't find anything there, Aric—and it would be embarrassing for all concerned if I caught them red-handed. So while they're occupied, I'll just take this opportunity to search their rooms."

At the top of the wide spiral staircase that led from the public areas of the palace to the living quarters assigned to foreign diplomatic missions, Retief paused.

"You wait here, Aric." He went along the corridor to the third door, a simple white-painted panel edged with a tiny carved floral design. He tried the large gold doorknob, then took a slender instrument from an inner pocket of his silver-epauletted tangerine mess jacket and delicately probed the lock. The bolt snicked back. He eased the door open, glanced around, then stepped back out and beckoned Aric to him.

"How'd you get it open, Mr. Retief?"

"Locks are a hobby of mine. Patrol the corridor, and if you see anybody, cough. If it's one of my Groaci colleagues, have a regular paroxysm. I won't be long."

Inside the room, Retief made a fast check of the desk, the dresser drawers, the undersides of furniture. He slapped sofa cushions, prodded mattresses for tell-tale cracklings, then opened the closet door. Through the wall, faint voices were audible, scratchy with the quality of narrow-range amplification. He stooped, plucked a tiny earphone from a miniature wall bracket. Ambassador Lhiss, it appeared, was not immune from eavesdropping by his own staff . . .

Retief put the 'phone to his ear.

". . . agreed, then," Ambassador Hidebinder's voice was saying. "Seventy-two hours from now, and not a moment before."

"Just see that you keep your end of the bargain," a thin Groaci voice lisped. "This would be a poor time for treachery . . ."

"I want it clearly understood that our man will be treated in a reasonably civilized fashion, and quietly released to us when the affair is completed."

"I suggest you avoid over-complicating the arrangements with last minute conditions," the Groaci voice said.

"You've done very well in this affair," Hidebinder came back. "Your profits on the armaments alone—"

"As I recall, it was you who proposed the scheme; it is you who wish to place homeless Soetti rabble on Elora, not we . . ."

Retief listened for another five minutes before he snapped the phone back in its bracket, stepped quickly to the door; in the hall, Aric came to meet him.

"Find anything, Mr. Retief?"

"Too much . . ." Retief took a pen from his pocket, jotted a note.

"See that this gets to Prince Tavilan at the lodge; tell him to get the Invincibles ready, but to do nothing until I get word to him—no matter what."

"Sure, Mr. Retief, but—"

"Let's go, Aric. And remember: you're more help to me outside than inside . . ."

"I don't follow you, Mr. Retief . . ." Aric trotted at his side. "Outside what . . . ?"

"We'll know in a few minutes; but wherever I wind up, watch for a signal . . ."

From the head of the Grand Staircase, Retief saw the glint of light on steel. Two men in the dull black and green of the People's Volunteers stood in the corridor.

"Hey, Mr. Retief," Aric whispered. "What are Greenbacks doing in the palace . . . ?"

"Simple, Aric. They're standing guard over my door."

"Maybe somebody caught those Groaci trying to break in . . ."

"Drop back behind me, Aric—and remember what I said . . ."

Retief walked up to his door, took out an old-fashioned mechanical key, inserted it in the lock. One of the two armed soldiers stepped up, made a threatening motion with his rifle butt.

"Nobody goes in there, you," he growled. He was a broad-faced blonde, a descendant of the transported felons who had served as contract labor on Elora a century earlier.

Retief turned casually, moved to one side far enough that the man before him was between him and his companion, then moved suddenly, caught the stock of the rifle in his left hand and with his right yanked the barrel forward; the butt described a short arc, smashed against the soldier's chin. He gave a choked yell, stumbled back. Retief jerked the door open, slipped inside, slammed it behind him. He shot the bolt, then started a fast check of his room. The door rattled; heavy poundings sounded. Retief pulled open the desk; a loose heap of unfamiliar papers lay there. A glance at one showed the letterhead of the Office of the Commercial Attaché, Terrestrial Embassy. It appeared to be a delivery order for one hundred thousand rounds of fractional-ton ammunition made out to a Bogan armaments exporter. Another was an unsigned letter referring to drop-points and large sums of money. A heavy parchment caught Retief's eye. It was stamped in red: UTTER TOP SECRET. Below the seal of the Eloran Imperial Department of War was a detailed break-out of the disposition of units of the Imperial Fleet and the Volunteer Reserve.

The telephone buzzed. Retief picked it up. There was a sound of breathing at the other end.

"Yilith . . . ?" a faint voice inquired.

"No, you damned fool!" Retief snapped. "They finished up ten minutes ago. When do the Greenbacks arrive?"

"Why, they should be there now. The pigeon has left the ballroom—" There was a pause. "Who is this?"

Retief slammed down the phone, whirled to the wide fireplace, flipped the switch that started a cheery blaze licking over the pseudo-logs. He grabbed up a handful of papers from the desk, tossed them into the fire, started back for another—

With a rending of tough plastic panels, the door bulged, then slammed open. Half a dozen Greenbacks charged into the room, short bayonets fixed and leveled. Retief's hand went behind him, felt over the small table at his back, plucked open the drawer, fished out a tiny slug gun, dropped it into a back pocket.

A tall man with a small head, a body like a bag of water, and tiny feet bellied his way through the armed men. He wore a drab cutaway of greyish-green adorned with the star of the Order of Farm Production. Behind him, the small, spindle-armed figure of the Groaci Military Attaché was visible, decked out in formal jewel-studded eyeshields and a pink and green hip-cloak.

"Don't touch anything!" the water-bag man called in a high, excited voice. "I want everything undisturbed!"

"What about the fire, Mr. Minister?" the Groaci lisped. "The miscreant seems to have been burning something . . ."

"Yes, yes. Rake those papers out of there!" The large man wobbled his chin agitatedly. He fixed Retief with eyes like peeled eggs. "I'm warning you, don't make any violent moves—"

"Let me have a crack at him," a Greenback said. "He fixed Horney so he won't be able to eat nothing but mush for six months—"

"None of that!" the big-bellied man folded his arms. A striped vest bulged under his voluminous frock coat like a feather mattress. "We'll just hold him for the criminal authorities."

"Any particular reason why you and your friends came to play in my room?" Retief inquired mildly. "Or were you under the impression it was my birthday?"

"Look here," a man called from across the room. "Under the mattress . . ." He held up a paper. "A letter from the pirate, Dangredi, addressed to Retief, thanking him for the latest consignment of arms and supplies!"

"If you'll wait just a minute," Retief said, "I'll get my scrapbook; it's full of all kinds of incriminating evidence I've been saving for just this occasion."

"Ah, then you confess! Where is it?" the Groaci whispered hoarsely, pushing to the fore.

"Oh, I forgot; when I heard you coming, I ate it."

There was a stir at the rear of the group. The ranks parted and a short, round Terrestrial with a stiff white moustache and a mouth like a change-purse pushed through. He yanked at the overlapping lapels of a grape-juice colored mess-jacket caked with decorations.

"Here, what's this, Mr. Retief! Contraband? Pilfered documents? Evidence of traffic with piratical elements?"

"No, Mr. Ambassador," Retief said, "I'm only charging them with breaking and entering, assault with a deadly weapon, abuse of diplomatic privilege, and loitering. If you'll—"

"Here, don't let him confuse the issue, Ambassador Hidebinder!" The egg-like eyes rolled toward the stout diplomat. "He stands self-convicted—"

"Don't say too much, Mr. Minister," Retief cut in. "After all, you haven't had time yet to read those scraps the boys are fishing out of the fire, so it wouldn't do for you to know what they are."

"Enough of this pointless chatter!" Prime Minister Prouch piped. "Obviously, there's treason afoot here!" He jabbed a finger at the Terrestrial Ambassador. "In view of the seriousness of the offense—in a time of grave crisis in inter-world affairs—I demand that you suspend this criminal's diplomatic immunity!"

The Groaci spoke up: "As a neutral party, I propose that he be turned over to my mission for restraint until the time of trial."

"Well . . ." Ambassador Hidebinder blinked. "I'm not at all sure . . ."

"We'll tolerate no stalling tactics!" the Minister squeaked. "The security of Elora is at stake!" He motioned. The troops closed in around Retief.

"I propose to take this man into custody at once," he bulged his eyes at Hidebinder. "I trust there will be no protest . . . !"

Hidebinder looked around at the room, the scattered papers, the smoldering fire, then past Retief's ear.

"Your penchant for mischief is well-known, Mr. Retief," he said solemnly. "I'm sure this fits the pattern nicely."

"Not as nicely as you seem to imagine," Retief said. "Maybe you'd better think it over—without any help from Ambassador Lhiss."

Hidebinder purpled; he sputtered. "The man's insane! You have my permission to place him under protective restraint!" He stamped from the room.

General Hish stepped forward. "Soldiers, you heard the order of the Minister," he hissed. "Take the criminal away . . ."

The cell was ten feet square, with a twelve by eighteen inch opening just under the ten-foot high ceiling. The furnishings included a plastic cot with one blanket, the minimum in plumbing facilities, one small, unshielded neon lamp, numerous large roaches, and a bristly rat over a foot long, which sat by the open floor drain from which it had emerged, regarding Retief with beady eyes.

Retief's hand went slowly to the small, hard pillow on the cot beside him. He picked it up, pegged it suddenly; with a squeal of rage, the rat dove for cover, scrabbled for a moment in a frantic attempt to squirm past the cushion, now wedged in the drain; then it darted for the darkest corner of the cell.

Retief picked up the blanket and a length of yarn worked from it earlier, moved toward the rat. It crouched, making a sound like a rusty bed-spring. Suddenly it leaped—straight at Retief's face—and met the enveloping blanket in mid-air. Cautiously, Retief folded back the blanket to expose the chinless, snouted face, armed with back-slanting yellow fangs half an inch long. He looped the string over the vicious head, drew it snug and knotted it.

He went to the drain, kicked the obstruction from it, then released the tethered rat. It dived down the dark opening and was gone. The carefully coiled string paid out rapidly, loop after loop. It slowed, then fed down the drain more slowly as the rat traveled through the piping. The guard's footsteps approached. Retief jumped for the cot; he was stretched out at ease when the sentry looked in. When he had passed, Retief looped the end of the string over his finger, pulled in the slack. In the gloomy light of the neon lamp, the thread was invisible against the dark floor. He sat on the bunk and waited.

An hour passed. The barred rectangle of moonlight slanting through the window crept across the floor. Regularly, at nine-minute intervals, feet sounded in the passage outside the metal slab door. Suddenly the string in Retief's hand twitched, once, twice, three times. He gave three answering tugs. For a moment there was no response; then there was a single firm tug. Aric was on the job . . .

Retief pulled at the string; it dragged heavily. He hauled it in slowly, hand over hand. Twice it caught on some obstruction far away in the drain line; he tugged gently until it came free. He thrust the accumulating pile of thread under the mattress. Each time the guard looked in, he was sitting quietly, staring at the wall. Suddenly, the end of a half-inch rope appeared, securely tied to the end of the string. Retief let it slip back a few inches, waited until the sentry passed, then quickly began hauling in the rope.

Five minutes later, a hundred feet of polyon cable was tucked out of sight under the mattress. Retief slipped the bundle of hacksaw blades which had been tied to the end of the rope into the pocket of the gold-braided white trousers which he had been allowed to retain along with his short boots. He stood under the window, gauged the distance, then jumped; he pulled himself up, got a firm grip on the bars, then took out a saw and started in.

An hour later, both bars were cut through, ready to be removed by a single firm twist. Retief waited for the guard to pass, then dropped the blades down the drain, looped the cable over his shoulder and leaped up to the window again. Far below, he could see the moonlight sparkling on a fountain in the palace garden; the shadows of trees and hedges were dark against the grass. On the graveled walks, armed sentries passed.

Retief wrenched the bars free, tied the rope to one, tossed the coil of rope through the window, then pulled himself up, and carefully fitted the short bar across the corner of the window opening on the inside. Keeping pressure on the rope, he eased out, then slid quickly down.

Twenty feet below, Retief dropped onto a narrow balcony before a rank of darkened glass doors. With a flick, he freed the upper end of the rope; the bar clattered against the stone wall as it fell; he pulled the rope in, dropped it in a heap, then tried door handles, found one that turned. He stepped in through heavy drapes, felt his way across to a door, opened it and looked out into a wide corridor. At the far end, two ornately uniformed guards stood stiffly at attention. There was no one else in sight. Retief slipped the slug gun into the palm of his hand, stepped out, walked boldly toward the guards. They stood unmoving. As he passed, one spoke quietly from the corner of his mouth:

"Greenbacks patrolling one flight up . . ."

"They're on the look-out for any suspicious activity," the other sentry added.

"If you see any, let us know," the first said.

"I'll do that," Retief said softly. "If you hear any loud noises, pay no attention. General Hish will be entertaining a guest . . ."

Retief followed the corridor, took a turn to the left, then a right, found the passage housing the Groaci

Embassy, now brightly lit. The apartment of the Military Attaché was on the left, four doors along . . .

A black-booted Greenback officer stepped into view from the far end of the passage, paused at sight of Retief striding unconcernedly toward him. The Greenback narrowed his eyes uncertainly, started along the corridor toward Retief. At fifteen feet, sure now of the identity of the intruder, he snapped back the flap covering his side-arm, tugged at the heavy power pistol. Retief brought the slug gun up, fired at point-blank range. At the muffled whoomp! the officer slammed back, hit the floor and lay sprawled; his gun bounced against the wall. Retief scooped it up, turned to the door of the Groaci General's quarters, needle-beamed the lock at low power. The hardware dissolved in a wash of blue flame, an acrid stink of burned plastic and metal. He kicked the door wide, caught the fallen Greenback by the ankles, dragged him inside. A swift examination of the room revealed that it was deserted. He picked up the phone, dialed.

"Post number twenty-nine," a crisp voice answered promptly.

"This is the General's guest," Retief said. "The light in the hall might hurt the General's eyes; corridor 9-C. Think you could douse it?"

"We've had some trouble with fuses in that wing lately; I've got a feeling one might go out any minute now—and it will take maybe an hour to fix." The phone clicked off.

Retief flipped off the lights in the room, went into the small, lavishly equipped kitchen, rummaged through the supplies of Groaci delicacies, found a one-pound jar of caviar and a package of grain wafers. He ate hurriedly, keeping an eye on the door, drank a small bottle of Green Yill wine, then returned to the living room. He stripped the Greenback, donned the drab uniform.

The phone buzzed. Retief went to it, lifted the receiver.

"Two-minute alert," a low voice said. "He's alone . . ."

Retief went to the door, opened it half an inch, stood in the shadows beside it. He heard the soft approach of mincing Groaci footsteps, then a soft exclamation—

He swung the door open, reached out, caught the Groaci by the throat and dragged him inside. He grunted as a booted foot caught him in the ribs; then he jammed the pistol hard against the Groaci's horny thorax.

"No loud noises, please, General; it's my hour for meditation . . ."

Retief pushed the door shut with a foot, leaned against the light button; a soft glow sprang up. Retief released the Groaci, holding the gun aimed at a three-inch broad *Grand Cordon* of the Legion d'Cosme crossing the bulging abdomen.

"I'm going out; you're coming with me. Better hope we make it."

He holstered the pistol, showed the small, smooth-stone-shaped slug gun. "This will be a foot from your back, so be a good little soldier and give all the right answers."

The Groaci's throat sacs dilated, vibrating. He cast a sidelong glance at the stripped body of the Greenback.

"The swift inevitability of your death," he hissed in Groaci. "To anticipate with joy your end in frightful torment . . ."

"To button your mandible and march," Retief interrupted. He pulled the door open. "After you, General . . ."

The blaze of stars scattered from horizon to horizon above the palace roof gleamed on the polished fittings of a low-slung heli parked on the royal pad. As Retief and his prisoner emerged from the service stair into the cold night air, there was a crunch of boots on gravel, the snick! of a power gun's action. A dark shadow moved before Retief. Abruptly a searchlight's beam glared in his eyes.

"Stand aside, idiot!" the Groaci hissed. The light flashed across to him; five beady, stemmed eyes glinted angrily at the guard.

"General Hish, sir . . ." The guard snapped off the light, presented arms hurriedly. Other boots sounded, coming across the rooftop helipad.

"What's going on here? Tell these—" the voice broke off. In the gloom, barely relieved by starlight, Retief saw the newcomer start, then put a hand to his pistol butt.

"We require the use of the royal gig," Hish whispered. "Stand aside!"

"But the orders—" the first guard started.

"General, drop!" the second bawled, hauling his gun out. Retief shot him, took a short step and drove a hard punch to the jaw of the first Greenback, then caught the Groaci's arm, jumped for the heli. Yells sounded across the room. A yard-wide light-cannon, gymbal-mounted atop the guard shack, winked on, throwing a grey-blue tunnel of light into the sky; it pivoted, depressed, swept a burning disc across to Retief—

He drew the power pistol, thumbed it to narrow beam, blasted the light; it exploded in a shower of tinkling glass, a billow of orange smoke that faded, winked out.

Retief shoved the slender Groaci ahead of him, yanked wide the heli's entry hatch, tumbled his prisoner in, jumped after him. He flipped switches, rammed the control lever to EMERGENCY FULL CLIMB. With a whine of power, the finely-engineered craft leaped from the room, surged upward in a buffet of suddenly stirred air. From below, the blue and yellow flashes of blasters winked briefly against the discs of the screaming rotors; then they dwindled away and were gone.

*   *   *

Half an hour later, Retief dropped the heli in low over the black tree-tops of the Deep Forest. A gleam of light reflected across rippling water. He edged the machine forward, swung out over the lake; below, the water churned in the down-draft from the rotors as the heli settled gently into two feet of water. Retief cut the engine and popped the hatch. Cold mountain air swirled in; somewhere, water lizards shrilled.

"What place of infamy is this?" the captive general hissed. He stared out into the darkness. "Do you bring me here to slay me unseen, vile disrespecter of diplomatic privilege?"

"The idea has merit," Retief said, "but I have other plans for you, General." He climbed down, motioned the Groaci out. Hish grumbled, scrambling down into the icy water of the lake, slogging to shore. From the darkness, a night-fowl called. Retief whistled a reply. There was the sound of a footstep in the brush, the click! of a cross-bow's cocking mechanism.

"It's Retief," he called. "I have a guest: General Hish, of the Groaci Embassy."

"Ah, welcome, Retief," a soft voice drawled. "We're honored, General. Good of you to call. His Highness was hoping you'd be along soon . . ."

Inside the high-beamed lodge, Prince Tavilan came across the room; behind him, Aric grinned.

"I caught the rat all right, Mr. Retief—"

"Retief!" Tavilan clapped him on the shoulder. "Aric reached me with your message an hour ago. I heard the news of your arrest on Tri-D; they broke into a concert to announce that a plot involving the CDT and reactionary Royalist elements had been uncovered."

"Hidebinder will be very unhappy with that version of events," Retief said. "The agreement was that it was all to be blamed on a rotten apple in the Corps barrel, namely me—"

"We were saddling up to storm the palace and free you, when your message reached me—"

"How many reliable men do you have available on short notice, Your Highness?" Retief cut in.

"I have thirty-eight of the Invincibles with me here; at least three others are under arrest on various pretexts. Four more managed to report in that they're pinned down by 'protective escorts' but we can still strike—"

Retief shook his head. "That was the idea of arresting me, Your Highness—as a personal challenge to you, since my sympathies are well-known. Prouch wanted to bring you out into the open. An armed attack was just what he needed—and he was ready for you. He has at least two hundred Greenbacks in the palace—armed to the nines. Your raid would have been the signal for his take-over—to preserve the domestic tranquillity, of course—and your death in the fighting would have left him a clear field."

"What about the Palace Guard? They haven't gone over . . . ?"

"Of course not . . ." Retief accepted a cigar, took a seat by the fire. "They're standing fast, playing it by ear. The Grand Ball tonight gave them an excuse for full dress, including weapons, of course. The Greenbacks aren't quite ready to start anything with them—yet."

Tavilan stamped across the fire-beast-hide rug. "Blast it, Retief, we can't sit here and watch Prouch and his mob move in unopposed! If we hit them now—before they've had time to consolidate—"

"—you'll get every Royalist supporter in Elora City killed," Retief finished for him. "Now, let's consider the situation. Item: the Royal Fleet is grounded, courtesy of CDT policy. Item two: Prouch's People's Volunteer Naval Reserve Detachment of late-model Bogan destroyers is sitting in its launch-cradles at Grey Valley, fifteen miles from here—"

"They're no threat to us; they can't operate without fuel either."

"They won't have to," Retief said, puffing out smoke. "Corps policy is nothing if not elastic. It seems that the

Big Picture called for the supplying of the Volunteer Reserve with full magazines—"

"What!"

"—and the topping off of all tanks."

Tavilan's face was pale. "I see," he said quietly, nodding. "The CDT talked disarmament to me while it was arming Prouch's revolutionaries. It never intended to see the monarchy survive."

"Well, Your Highness, the CDT is a very cleanminded organization, and it heard somewhere that 'monarchy' was a dirty word—"

"All right!" Prince Tavilan turned to Count Arrol. "We have mounts for every man—and plenty of crossbow bolts. There'll be Greenback blood on the palace floors before the night is out—"

"If I might make a suggestion . . . ?"

"You're not involved in this, Retief. Take the copter and get clear—"

"Clear to where? I've been disowned by my colleagues and slapped in jail by the Prime Minister. To get back to the Little Picture: I see no point in our riding into Elora City and being shot down at long range by Greenbacks—"

"We'll ride in at the Marivale Gate, move up through the fire-lanes—"

"If you'll pardon my saying so," Retief said, "I've got a better idea. It's only fifteen miles to the Grey Valley . . ."

"So?"

"So I suggest we take a ride over and look at the Volunteer Navy."

"You've just told me Prouch's renegades are armed to the teeth . . ."

Retief nodded. "Since we need guns, Your Highness, I can't think of a closer place to get 'em . . ."

At the head of the troop of thirty-eight riders, including General Hish, lashed to a mount, Retief and Tavilan reined in at the crest of the slope that faced the barracks of the People's Volunteer Naval Reserve, a blaze of light all across the narrow valley. On the ramp a quarter of a mile beyond the administrative and shop areas, fifty slim destroyers loomed, bathed in the glare of polyarcs. Prince Tavilan whistled.

"Prouch and the CDT seem to have struck it off even better than I thought. That's all brand-new equipment."

"Just defensive, of course," Retief said. "I believe Minister Prouch has given assurances that the elimination of Dangredi's freebooters will be carried out with dispatch—just as soon as the CDT recognizes his regime."

Tavilan laughed shortly. "I could have swept Dangredi off the space lanes six months ago—if the CDT hadn't blockaded me."

"Such are the vagaries of Galactic policy—"

"I know: the Big Picture again." Tavilan turned to Arrol. "We'll split into two parties, work around both ends of the valley, and pick our target at close range. Retief, you ride with me. Let's move out."

It was a forty-minute ride along the forested slopes walling the valley to the rendezvous point Prince Tavilan had designated, a sheltered ravine less than a hundred yards from the nearest of the parked war vessels. The access ladder was down, and light spilled from the open entry port. A Reservist in baggy grey and green lounged in the opening. Two more stood below, power rifles slung across their backs.

"You could pick those three off from here," Retief remarked. "Cross-bows are a nice quiet weapon—"

Tavilan shook his head. "We'll ride down in formal battle-order. No war's been declared. They won't fire on the Prince Royal."

"There may be forty more inside—to say nothing of the crews of the next ships in line, sentries, stand-by riot squads, and those two pill-boxes commanding the ends of the valley."

"Still—I must give those men their chance to declare themselves."

"As the Prince wishes—but I'll keep my blaster loose in its holster—just in case . . ."

The Prince rode in the lead with his guidon at his left, followed by thirty-five men, formed up in a precise triangle of seven ranks, with two honor guards out on the flanks. The rear guard followed, holding the reins of the mount to which General Hish, still hissing bitter complaints, was lashed.

The Invincibles moved down the slope and out onto the broad tarmac, hooves clattering against the paved surface. The two men on the ramp turned, stood gaping. The one above at the ship's entry port whirled, disappeared inside.

The troop rode on; they were halfway to the ship now. One of the waiting Greenbacks unlimbered his power gun, cranked the action, the other followed suit. Both stepped forward half a dozen paces, brought their weapons up uncertainly.

"Halt! Who the Hell's there!" one bawled.

Tavilan flipped the corner of his hunting cape forward over his shoulder to show the royal Eloran device, came on in silence.

The taller of the two Greenbacks raised his rifle, hesitated, half-lowered it. Riding half a pace behind Tavilan, Retief eased his pistol from its holster, watching the doorway above. On his right, Count Arrol held his cross-bow across his knee, a bolt cocked in the carriage, his finger on the trigger.

Ten feet from the two Greenback sentries, Prince Tavilan reined in.

"Aren't you men accustomed to render a proper salute when your Commander makes a surprise inspection?" he said calmly.

The Greenbacks looked at each other, fingering their guns.

"It looks as though the word had gone out," Arrol whispered to Retief.

"You cover the Prince; I'll handle the entry port," Retief murmured.

At that moment a figure eased into view at the port; light glinted from the front sight of a power gun as it came up, steadied—

Retief sighted, fired; in the instantaneous blue glare, the man at the port whirled and fell outward. The Greenback nearest Tavilan made a sudden move to swing his gun on the Prince—then stumbled back, a steel quarrel from Arrol's cross-bow standing in his chest. The second Greenback dropped his weapon, stood with raised hands, his mouth open and eyes wide, then turned and ran.

Tavilan leaped down from his steed, dashed for the access ladder, his cross-bow ready. As though on command, four men followed him, while others scattered to form a rough semi-circle at the base of the ladder. Sheltered behind a generator unit, Retief and Arrol covered the port. Tavilan disappeared inside, the men at his heels. There was a long half-minute of dead silence. Then a shout sounded from the next vessel in line, a hundred yards distant. Tavilan reappeared, gestured.

"Everybody in," Arrol called. The men went for the ladder, sprang up in good order; those waiting on the ramp faced outward, covering all points.

A light flashed briefly from the adjacent vessel; a sharp report echoed. A man fell from the ladder; others caught him, lifted him up. Far away, a harsh voice bellowed orders.

"They aren't using any heavy stuff," Arrol said. "They wouldn't want to nick the paint on their new battle wagon . . ."

A squad of men appeared, running from the shadows at the base of the ship from which the firing had come. Most of the troop were up the ladder now; two men hustled the struggling Groaci up. Beside Retief, Arrol launched three bolts in rapid-fire order. Two of the oncoming men fell. The blue flashes of power guns winked; here and there, the surface of the tarmac boiled as wild shots struck.

"Come on . . ." The two men ran for the ladder; Arrol sprang for it, swarmed up. Retief followed; molten metal spattered as a power-gun bolt vaporized the handrail. Then hands were hauling him inside.

"Hit the deck," Arrol yelled. "We're lifting . . . ?"

"We took one burst from an infinite repeater," an officer reported, "but no serious damage was done. They held their fire just a little too long."

"We were lucky," Prince Tavilan said. "One man killed, one wounded. It's fortunate we didn't select the next ship in line; we'd have had a hornet's nest on our hands."

"Too bad we broke up the battalion crap game," Retief commented. "But by now they'll be lifting off after us—a few of them, anyway."

"All right—we'll give them a warm welcome before they nail us—"

"If I may venture to suggest—"

Tavilan waved a hand, grinning. "Every time you get so damned polite, you've got some diabolical scheme up your sleeve. What is it this time, Retief?"

"We won't wait around to be nailed. We'll drive for Deep Space at flank speed—"

"And run into Dangredi's blockade? I'd rather use my firepower on Prouch's scavengers."

"That's where our friend the General comes in." Retief nodded toward the trussed Groaci. "He and Dangredi are old business associates. We'll put him on the screen and see if he can't negotiate a brief truce. With the approval of Your Highness, I think we can make an offer that will interest him . . ."

The flagship of the pirate fleet was a four-hundred-year-old, five-hundred-thousand-ton dreadnought, a relic of pre-Concordiat times. In the red-lit gloom of its cavernous Command Control deck, Retief and Prince Tavilan relaxed in deep couches designed for the massive frames of the Hondu corsairs. Opposite them, Dangredi, the Hondu chieftain, lounged at ease, his shaggy, leather-strapped, jewel-spangled 350-pound bulk almost overflowing his throne-like chair. At Retief's side, General Hish perched nervously. Half a dozen of Tavilian's Invincibles stood around the room, chatting with an equal number of Dangredi's hulking officers, whose greenish fur looked black in the light from the crimson lamps.

"What I failing to grasp," Dangredi rumbled, "is reason for why suddenly now changing of plan previously okayed."

"I hardly think that matters," Tavilan said smoothly. "I've offered to add one hundred thousand Galactic Credits to the sum already agreed on."

"But the whole idea was compensate me, Grand Hereditary War Chief of Hondu people, for not fight; now is offering more pay for stand and give battle . . ."

"I thought you Hondu loved war," an Eloran officer said.

Dangredi nodded his heavy green-furred head, featureless but for two wide green-pupiled eyes. "Crazy mad for warring, and also plenty fond of cash. But is smelling rodent somewhere in woodpile . . ."

"It's very simple, Commodore," Retief said. "General Hish here had arranged with you to flee when the People's Volunteer forces attacked; now changing conditions on Elora make it necessary that you fight—and in place of the loot you would otherwise so rightly expect, you'll collect a handsome honorarium—"

Suddenly the Groaci leaped to his feet, pointed at Retief. "Commodore Dangredi," he hissed. "This renegade diplomat beside me holds a gun pointed at my vitals; only thus did he coerce me to request this parley. Had I guessed his intention, I would have dared him to do his worst. Seize the traitor, Excellency!"

Dangredi stared at the Groaci.

"He—and these strutting popinjays—plot against the security of the People's State of Elora!" Hish whispered urgently. "The plan remains unchanged! You are to flee engagement with the forces of Minister Prouch!"

The great green head bobbed suddenly; hooting laughter sounded. A vast hand slapped a thigh like a shaggy beer keg.

"Aha! At last is getting grasp of situation," Dangredi bellowed. "Now is little honest treachery, kind of dealing Hondu understanding!" He waved a hand at a servitor standing by. "Bringing wassail bowl, plenty meat!" He brought his hands together with a dull boom, rubbed them briskly. "Double-cross, plenty fighting, more gold at end of trail! Is kind of operation I, Dangredi, Hereditary War Chief, dreaming of in long nights of tooth-shedding time!"

"But these—these criminal kidnapers have no authority to deal—"

"Groaci-napping is harmless pastime—like stealing wine-melons when cub. Unless, maybe . . ." he cocked a large emerald eye at Hish. ". . . you maybe raising ante?"

"I . . . I will match the offer of the saboteurs of interplanetary amity! One hundred thousand in Groaci gold!"

Dangredi considered briefly. "No good. What about fighting? You give Hondu gunners targets in sights? Or maybe chance for rough-and-tumble, hand-to-hand, cold steel against enemy blades?"

General Hish shuddered. "In the name of civilization, I appeal—"

"Shove civilization in ventral orifice! Hondu taking good, crooked, blood-thirsty barbarians every time. Now disappearing quietly, Groaci, while I and new buddies planning strategy. Maybe later I sending for you and bending arms and legs until you tell all about enemy battle plan . . ."

"The Groaci is our hostage," Tavilan said as the general was led away. "He's not to be bent without my prior approval."

"Sure; just having little joke." Dangredi leaned back,

accepted a vast drumstick and a tank of wine, waited
while his guests accepted proffered delicacies.

"Now, Retief, you say attack coming when . . . ?"

"I must confess," Counselor Magnan said, "I don't
quite understand how it happened that after trouncing
the Eloran Volunteers, the pirate Dangredi voluntarily
gave himself up and offered the services of his entire
fleet as a reserve force to replace the very units he
destroyed."

"Never mind that, Magnan," Ambassador Hidebinder said. "As seasoned campaigners must, we shall
accept the *fait accompli*. Our resettlement plans are set
back a year, at least. It's doubly unfortunate that Prime
Minister Prouch suffered a fall just at this time. Magnan, you'll attend the funeral."

"With pleasure, Mr. Ambassador," Magnan said.
"That is, I'll be honored—"

"Retief . . ." Hidebinder glared across the table.
"I'm not going to press civil charges, since the Eloran
government, at the behest of Prince Tavilan, has
dropped the case. However, I may as well tell you at
once—your future with the Corps is non-existent. A
trifling embezzlement of official funds, I could wink at.
Embellished reports, slack performance of duty, cow-
ardice in the face of the enemy—these I could shrug off
as youthful peccadillos. But foot-dragging in the carrying out of Corps policy—" his fist thumped the desk.
"Intolerable!"

A messenger entered the conference room, handed a
note to Magnan, who passed it to Hidebinder; he
opened it impatiently, glanced at it. His jaw dropped.
He read it through again. His mouth closed; his jowls
paled, quivering.

"Mr. Ambassador—what is it?" Magnan gasped.

Hidebinder rose and tottered from the room. Magnan snatched up the paper, read it through, then stared
at Retief.

"He's been—declared *persona non grata*—The Im-

perial government gives him twelve hours to leave
Elora . . . !"

Retief glanced at the wall clock. "If he hurries, he
can catch the mail boat."

"And you, Retief . . . !"

Retief raised his eyebrows. Magnan glanced around
the table. "If you gentlemen will excuse us for a few
moments . . . ?" Half a dozen frowning diplomats filed
from the room. Magnan cleared his throat. "This is
most irregular, Retief! The Imperial government re-
quests that you present credentials as Minister Plenipotentiary and Ambassador Extraordinary at once . . .
they will accept no other appointee . . ."

Retief tsked. "I told Prince Tavilan I wouldn't have
time for a ceremonial job. I have a suggestion, Mr.
Magnan: suppose I nominate you for the post?"

"Over the heads of a hundred senior officers?" Magnan gasped. "Retief, dear boy . . ."

"That is, if your distaste for monarchies isn't overwhelming . . . ?"

"Eh? Oh, well, as to that," Magnan sat erect, tugged
his lapels into place. "I've always had a sneaking ad-
miration for absolute royalty."

"Fine. Dangredi will be along in a few minutes to
arrange for supplies; it seems there are a few shiploads
of CDT-sponsored undesirables already landing on the
northern continent who'll have to be warned off. It's
probably just a slip. I'm sure our former Ambassador
wouldn't have jumped the gun in violation of solemn
treaties."

"Ah," Magnan said.

"And, of course, the Royal Navy will require pro-
visioning—just to be sure the new Reservists don't get
any large ideas . . ."

"Uh . . ."

"And, of course, a new treaty plainly guaranteeing
the territorial integrity of Elora will have to be worked
up at once . . ."

"Oh . . ."

Retief rose. "All of which I'm sure you'll handle

brilliantly, Mr. Ambassador. And by the way—I think I could best serve the mission in some other capacity than as Admin Officer . . ."

Magnan pulled at his collar, waiting . . .

"I think I'd better work closely with Prince Tavilan, the heir apparent," Retief said blandly. "He does a lot of hunting, so perhaps you'd better designate me as Field and Stream Attaché . . ." He picked up his crossbow from the corner.

"I leave the details to you, Mr. Ambassador. I'm going hunting."

"Ever mindful of its lofty mission as guardian of the territorial integrity of Terrestrial-settled worlds against forays by non-social-minded alien groups, the Corps, in time of need, dispatched inobtrusive representatives to threatened areas, thus dynamically reaffirming hallowed Corps principles of Terrestrial solidarity. The unflinching support tendered by Deputy Ass't Under-Secretary Magnan to Jorgensen's Worlds in their hour of crisis added a proud page to Corps history . . ."

—Vol. X, Reel 9, 493 AE (AD 2954)

Courier

"It *is* rather unusual, Retief," Deputy Assistant Under-Secretary Magnan said, "to assign an officer of your rank to courier duty; but this is an unusual mission."

Retief drew on his cigar and said nothing. Just before the silence grew awkward, Magnan went on.

"There are four planets in the group," he said. "Two double planets, all rather close to an unimportant star listed as DRI-G 814369. They're called Jorgensen's Worlds, and in themselves are of no importance whatever. However, they lie deep in the sector into which the Soetti have been penetrating.

"Now," Magnan leaned forward and lowered his voice, "we have learned that the Soetti plan a bold step forward. They've been quietly occupying non-settled worlds. Since they've met no opposition so far in their infiltration of Terrestrial space, they intend to seize Jorgensen's Worlds by force."

Magnan leaned back, waiting for Retief's reaction. Retief drew carefully on his cigar and looked at Magnan. Magnan frowned.

"This is open aggression, Retief, in case I haven't made myself clear. Aggression on Terrestrial-occupied territory by an alien species. Obviously, we can't allow it." He drew a large folder from his desk.

"A show of resistance at this point is necessary. Unfortunately, Jorgensen's Worlds are backward, technologically undeveloped areas. They're farmers, traders; their industry is limited to a minor role in their economy—enough to support the merchant fleet, no more. The war potential, by conventional standards, is nil."

Magnan tapped the folder before him.

"I have here," he said solemnly, "information which will change that picture completely." He leaned back, blinked at Retief.

"All right, Mr. Secretary," Retief said. "I'll play along; what's in the folder?"

Magnan spread his fingers, folded one digit down.

"First," he said, "the Soetti War Plan—in detail. We were fortunate enough to make contact with a defector from a party of renegade Terrestrials who've been advising the Soetti." He folded another finger. "Next, a battle plan for the Jorgensen's people, worked out by the Theory Group." He wrestled a third finger down. "Lastly, an Utter Top Secret schematic for conversion of a standard anti-acceleration field into a potent weapon—a development our Systems people have been holding in reserve for just such a situation."

"Is that all? You've still got two fingers sticking up."

Magnan looked at the fingers and put them away. "This is no occasion for flippancy, Retief. In the wrong hands, this information could be catastrophic. You'll memorize it before you leave this building—"

"I'll carry it, sealed," Retief said. "That way nobody can sweat it out of me."

"As you wish. Now, let me caution you against personal emotional involvement here. Overall policy calls for a defense of these back-water worlds; otherwise, the

Corps would prefer simply to allow History to follow its natural course, as always."

"When does this attack happen?"

"In less than four weeks."

"That doesn't leave me much time."

"I have your itinerary here. Your accommodations are clear as far as Aldo Cerise. You'll have to rely on your ingenuity to get you the rest of the way."

"And what do I rely on to get me back?"

Magnan looked casually at his fingernails. "Of course, you *could* refuse the assignment . . ."

Retief smiled, directed a smoke ring past Magnan's ear.

"This antiac conversion; how long does it take?"

"A skilled electronics crew can do the job in a matter of minutes. The Jorgensens can handle it very nicely; every second man is a mechanic of some sort."

Retief opened the envelope Magnan handed him and looked at the tickets inside.

"Less than four hours to departure time," he said. "I'd better not start any long books."

"You'd better waste no time getting over to Indoctrination," Magnan said.

Retief stood up. "If I hurry, maybe I can catch the cartoon."

"The allusion escapes me," Magnan said coldly. "And one last word: the Soetti are patrolling the trade lanes into Jorgensen's Worlds. Don't get yourself interned."

"I'll tell you what," Retief said soberly, "in a pinch, I'll mention your name."

"You'll be traveling with Class X credentials," Magnan snapped. "There must be nothing to connect you with the Corps."

"I'll pose as a gentleman. They'll never guess."

"You'd better be getting started." Magnan shuffled papers.

"You're right. If I work at it, I might manage a snootful by take-off." He went to the door, looked back.

"No objection to my checking out a needler, is there?"

Magnan looked up. "I suppose not. What do you want with it?"

"Just a feeling I've got."

"Please yourself."

"Some day," Retief said, "I may take you up on that."

Retief put down the heavy, travel-battered suitcase and leaned on the counter, studying the schedules chalked on the board under the legend ALDO CERISE INTERPLANETARY. A thin clerk in a faded sequined blouse and a plastic snakeskin cummerbund groomed his fingernails and watched Retief from the corner of his eye; he nipped off a ragged corner with rabbit-like front teeth, spat it on the floor. "Was there something?" he said.

"Two-twenty-eight, due out today for the Jorgensen group. Is it on schedule?"

The clerk nibbled the inside of his right cheek, eyed Retief.

"Filled up. Try again in a couple of weeks."

"What time does it leave?"

The clerk smiled pityingly. "It's my lunch hour. I'll be open in an hour." He held up a thumb nail, frowned at it.

"If I have to come around this counter," Retief said, "I'll feed that thumb to you the hard way."

The clerk looked up, opened his mouth, caught Retief's eye. He closed his mouth and swallowed.

"Just as it says there," he said, jerking the thumb at the board. "Lifts in an hour. But you won't be on it," he added.

Retief looked at him.

"Some . . . ah . . . VIPs required accommodation," the clerk said. He hooked a finger inside the sequined collar. "All tourist reservations were canceled," he went on. "You'll have to try to get space on the Four-Planet Line ship next—"

"Which gate?" Retief said.

"For . . . ah . . . ?"

"Two-twenty-eight for Jorgensen's Worlds."

"Well!" said the clerk. "Gate 19," he added quickly. "But—"

Retief picked up his suitcase and walked away toward the glare sign reading "To gates 16–30."

"Smart-alec," the clerk said behind him.

Retief followed the signs, threaded his way through crowds, found a covered ramp with the number 228 posted over it. A heavy-shouldered man with a scarred jawline and small eyes, wearing a rumpled grey uniform, put out a hand as Retief started past him.

"Lessee your boarding pass," he growled.

Retief pulled a paper from an inside pocket, handed it over.

The guard blinked at it. "Whassat?"

"A 'gram confirming my space. Your boy on the counter says he's out to lunch."

The guard crumpled the 'gram, dropped it on the floor, lounged back against the handrail.

"On your way, bum," he said.

Retief put his suitcase down carefully, took a step and drove a right into the guard's midriff, stepped aside as the man doubled and went to his knees.

"You were wide open, ugly. I couldn't resist." Retief picked up his bag. "Tell your boss I sneaked past while you were resting your eyes." He stepped over the man and went up the gangway into the ship. A pimply youth in stained whites came along the corridor.

"Which way to cabin fifty-seven?" Retief asked.

"Up there." The boy jerked his head, hurried on. Retief made his way along the narrow hall, found signs, followed them to cabin fifty-seven. The door was open. Inside, unfamiliar baggage was piled in the center of the floor. Retief put his bag down. He turned at a sound behind him. A tall florid man with an expensive coat belted over a massive paunch stood in the open door. He looked at Retief. Retief looked back. The florid man clamped his jaws together, turned to speak over his shoulder.

"Somebody in the cabin. Get 'em out." He rolled a cold eye at Retief, backed out of the room. A short thick-necked man appeared.

"What are you doing in Mr. Tony's room?" he barked. "Never mind; clear out of here, fellow. You're keeping Mr. Tony waiting."

"Too bad," Retief said. "Finders keepers."

"You nuts or something?" The thick-necked man stared at Retief. "I said it's Mr. Tony's room."

"I don't know Mr. Tony. He'll have to bull his way into other quarters."

"We'll see about you, mister." The man turned and went out. Retief sat on the bunk and lit a cigar. There was a sound of voices in the corridor. Two burly baggage-smashers appeared, straining at an oversized trunk. They maneuvered it through the door, lowered it with a crash, glanced at Retief, and went out. The thick-necked man appeared again.

"All right, you; out," he growled. "Or have I got to have you thrown out?"

Retief rose, clamped the cigar between his teeth. He gripped a handle of the brass-bound trunk in each hand, bent his knees and heaved the trunk up to chest level, then raised it overhead. He turned to the door.

"Catch," he said between clenched teeth. The trunk slammed against the far wall of the corridor and burst. Retief turned to the baggage on the floor, tossed it into the hall. The face of the thick-necked man appeared cautiously around the door jamb.

"Mister, you must be—"

"If you'll excuse me," Retief said. "It's time for my nap." He flipped the door shut, pulled off his shoes, and stretched out on the bed.

Five minutes passed before the door rattled and burst open. Retief looked up. A gaunt leathery-skinned man wearing white ducks, a blue turtleneck sweater, and a peaked cap tilted raffishly over one eye stared at Retief.

"Is this the joker?" he grated.

The thick-necked man edged past him, looked at Retief, snorted. "That's him, sure."

"I'm Captain of this vessel," the gaunt man said. "You've got two minutes to haul your freight out of here. Get moving, Buster."

"When you can spare the time," Retief said, "take a look at Section Three, Paragraph One, of the Uniform Code. That spells out the law on confirmed space on vessels engaged in interplanetary commerce."

"A space lawyer." The captain turned. "Throw him out, boys," he called.

Two big men edged into the cabin, stood looking at Retief. "Go on, pitch him out," the captain snapped.

Retief put his cigar in an ashtray, swung his feet off the bunk. One of the two wiped his nose on a sleeve, spat on his right palm, and stepped forward, then hesitated.

"Hey," he said. "This the guy tossed the trunk off the wall?"

"That's him," the thick-necked man called. "Spilled Mr. Tony's possessions right on the deck."

"Deal me out," the bouncer said. "He can stay put as long as he wants to. I signed on to move cargo. Let's go, Moe."

"You'd better be getting back to the bridge, Captain," Retief said. "We're due to lift in twenty minutes."

The thick-necked man and the captain both shouted at once. The captain's voice prevailed. "—twenty minutes . . . Uniform Code . . . gonna do?"

"Close the door as you leave," Retief said.

The thick-necked man paused at the door. "We'll see you when you come out."

Four waiters passed Retief's table without stopping. A fifth leaned against the wall nearby, a menu under his arm. At a table across the room, the captain, now wearing a dress uniform and with his thin red hair neatly parted, sat with a table of male passengers. He talked loudly and laughed frequently, casting occasional glances Retief's way.

A panel opened in the wall behind Retief's chair. Bright blue eyes peered out from under a white chef's cap.

"Givin' you the cold shoulder, heh, mister?"

"Looks like it, old-timer. Maybe I'd better go join the skipper; his party seems to be having all the fun."

"Fella has to be mighty careless who he eats with to set over there."

"I see your point."

"You set right where you're at, mister. I'll rustle you up a plate."

Five minutes later, Retief cut into a thirty-two-ounce Delmonico nicely garnished with mushrooms and garlic butter.

"I'm Chip," the chef said. "I don't like the cap'n. You can tell him I said so. Don't like his friends, either. Don't like them dern Sweaties; look at a man like he was a worm."

"You know how to fry a steak, Chip," Retief said. He poured red wine into a glass. "Here's to you."

"Dern right," Chip said. "Dunno who ever thought up broiling 'em. I got a Baked Alaska comin' up in here for dessert. You like brandy in yer coffee?"

"Chip, you're a genius."

"Like to see a fella eat. I gotta go now; if you need anything, holler."

Retief ate slowly. Time always dragged on ship-board. Four days to Jorgensen's Worlds. Then, if Magnan's information was correct, there would be four days to prepare for the Soetti attack. It was a temptation to scan the tapes built into the handle of his suitcase; it would be good to know what Jorgensen's Worlds would be up against.

Retief finished the steak, and the chef handed out the Baked Alaska and coffee. Most of the other passengers had left the dining room. Mr. Tony and his retainers still sat at the captain's table.

As Retief watched, four men arose from the table, sauntered across the room. The first in line, a stony-faced thug with a broken ear, took a cigar from his mouth as he reached the table, dipped the lighted end in Retief's coffee, looked at it, dropped it on the tablecloth.

The others came up, Mr. Tony trailing.

"You must want to get to Jorgensen's pretty bad," the thug said in a grating voice. "What's your game, hick?"

Retief looked at the coffee cup, picked it up.

"I don't think I want my coffee," he said. He looked at the thug. "You drink it."

The thug squinted at Retief. "A wise hick," he began.

With a flick of the wrist, Retief tossed the coffee into the thug's face, then stood and slammed a straight right to the chin. The thug went down.

Retief looked at Mr. Tony, who stood open-mouthed.

"You can take your playmates away now, Tony," he said. "And don't bother to come around yourself. You're not funny enough."

Mr. Tony found his voice. "Take him, Marbles," he growled.

The thick-necked man slipped a hand inside his tunic, brought out a long-bladed knife. He licked his lips and moved in.

Retief heard the panel open beside him. "Here you go, mister," Chip said. Retief darted a glance; a well-honed French knife lay on the sill.

"Thanks, Chip. I won't need it for these punks."

Thick-neck lunged and Retief hit him square in the face, knocking him under the table. The other man stepped back, fumbled a power pistol from his shoulder holster.

"Aim that at me, and I'll kill you," Retief said.

"Go on, burn him, Hoany!" Mr. Tony shouted. Behind him the captain appeared, white-faced.

"Put that away, you!" he yelled. "What kind of—"

"Shut up," Mr. Tony said. "Put it away, Hoany. We'll fix this bum later."

"Not on this vessel, you won't," the captain said shakily. "I got my charter to—"

"Ram your charter," Hoany said harshly. "You won't be needing it long—"

"Button your floppy mouth, damn you," Mr. Tony snapped. He looked at the two men on the floor. "Get Marbles out of here. I ought to dump the slobs . . ." He turned and walked away. The captain signaled and two waiters came up. Retief watched as they carted the casualties from the dining room.

The panel opened. "I usta be about your size, when I was your age," Chip said. "You handled them pansies right. I wouldn't give 'em the time o' day."

"How about a fresh cup of coffee, Chip?"

"Sure, mister. Anything else?"

"I'll think of something," Retief said. "This is shaping up into one of those long days."

"They don't like me bringing yer meals to you in yer cabin," Chip said. "But the cap'n knows I'm the best cook in the Merchant Service; they won't mess with me."

"What has Mr. Tony got on the captain, Chip?" Retief asked.

"They're in some kind o' crooked business together. You want some more of that smoked turkey?"

"Sure. What have they got against my going to Jorgensen's Worlds?"

"Dunno; hasn't been no tourists got in there for six or eight months. I sure like a fella that can put it away. I was a big eater when I was yer age."

"I'll bet you can still handle it, old-timer. What are Jorgensen's Worlds like?"

"One of 'em's cold as hell and three of 'em's colder. Most o' the Jorgies live on Svea; that's the least froze up. Man don't enjoy eatin' his own cookin' like he does somebody else's."

"That's where I'm lucky, Chip. What kind of cargo's the captain got aboard for Jorgensen's?"

"Derned if I know. In and out o' there like a grasshopper, ever few weeks. Don't never pick up no cargo.

No tourists any more, like I says. Don't know what we even run in there for."

"Where are the passengers we have aboard headed?"

"To Alabaster; that's nine days' run in-sector from Jorgensen's. You ain't got another one of them cigars, have you?"

"Have one, Chip. I guess I was lucky to get space on this ship."

"Plenty o' space, mister. We got a dozen empty cabins." Chip puffed the cigar alight, then cleared away the dishes, poured out coffee and brandy.

"Them Sweaties is what I don't like," he said.

Retief looked at him questioningly.

"You never seen a Sweaty? Ugly-lookin' devils. Skinny legs, like a lobster; big chest, shaped like the top of a turnip; rubbery-lookin' head; you can see the pulse beatin' when they get riled."

"I've never had the pleasure."

"You'll prob'ly have it perty soon. Them devils board us nigh ever trip out; act like they was the Customs Patrol or somethin'."

There was a distant clang, and a faint tremor ran through the floor.

"I ain't superstitious ner nothin'," said Chip, "but I'll be triple-danged if that ain't them boardin' us now."

Ten minutes passed before bootsteps sounded outside the door, accompanied by a clicking patter. The doorknob rattled, then a heavy knock sounded.

"They got to look you over," Chip whispered. "Nosey damn Sweaties."

"Unlock it, Chip." The chef threw the latch, opened the door.

"Come in, damn you," he said.

A tall and grotesque creature minced into the room, tiny hoof-like feet tapping on the floor. A flaring metal helmet shaded the deep-set compound eyes, and a loose mantle flapped around the knobbed knees. Behind the alien, the captain hovered nervously.

"Yo' papiss," the alien rasped.

"Who's your friend, captain?" Retief said.

"Never mind; just do like he tells you."

"Yo' papiss," the alien said again.

"Okay," Retief said. "I've seen it. You can take it away now."

"Don't horse around," the captain said. "This fellow can get mean."

The alien brought two tiny arms out from the concealment of the mantle, clicked toothed pincers under Retief's nose. "Quick, soft one."

"Captain, tell your friend to keep its distance. It looks brittle, and I'm tempted to test it."

"Don't start anything with Skaw; he can clip through steel with those snappers."

"Last chance," said Retief. Skaw stood poised, open pincers an inch from Retief's eyes.

"Show him your papers, you damned fool," the captain said hoarsely. "I got no control over Skaw."

The alien clicked both pincers with a sharp report, and in the same instant Retief half turned to the left, leaned away from the alien, and drove his right foot against the slender leg above the bulbous knee-joint. Skaw screeched, floundered, greenish fluid spattering from the burst joint.

"I told you he was brittle," Retief said. "Next time you invite pirates aboard, don't bother to call."

"Jesus, what did you do! They'll kill us!" the captain gasped, staring at the figure flopping on the floor.

"Cart poor old Skaw back to his boat," Retief said. "Tell him to pass the word: no more illegal entry and search of Terrestrial vessels in Terrestrial space."

"Hey," Chip said. "He's quit kickin'."

The captain bent over Skaw, gingerly rolled him over. He leaned close, sniffed.

"He's dead." The captain stared at Retief. "We're all dead men. These Soetti got no mercy."

"They won't need it. Tell 'em to sheer off; their fun is over."

"They got no more emotions than a blue crab—"

"You bluff easily, captain. Show a few guns as you hand the body back. We know their secret now."

"What secret? I—"

"Don't be dumber than you gotta, Cap'n," Chip said. "Sweaties dies easy; that's the secret."

"Maybe you got a point," the captain said, looking at Retief. "All they got's a three-man scout. It could work."

He went out, came back with two crewmen. They circled the dead alien, hauled him gingerly into the hall.

"Maybe I can run a bluff on the Soetti," the captain said, looking back from the door. "But I'll be back to see you later."

"You don't scare us, Cap'n," Chip called as the door closed. He grinned at Retief. "Him and Mr. Tony and all his goons. You hit 'em where they live, that time. They're pals o' these Sweaties. Runnin' some kind o' crooked racket."

"You'd better take the captain's advice, Chip. There's no point in your getting involved in my problems."

"They'd of killed you before now, mister, if they had any guts. That's where we got it over these monkeys; they got no guts."

"They act scared, Chip. Scared men are killers."

"They don't scare me none." Chip picked up the tray. "I'll scout around a little and see what's goin' on. If the Sweaties figure to do anything about that Skaw fella they'll have to move fast; they won't try nothin' close to port."

"Don't worry, Chip. I have reason to be pretty sure they won't do anything to attract a lot of attention in this sector just now."

Chip looked at Retief. "You ain't no tourist, mister. I know that much. You didn't come out here for fun, did you?"

"That," said Retief, "would be a hard one to answer."

Retief awoke at a tap on his door.

"It's me, mister: Chip."

"Come on in."

The chef entered the room, locked the door. "You

shoulda had that door locked." He stood by the door, listening, then turned to Retief.

"You want to get to Jorgensen's pretty bad, don't you, mister?"

"That's right, Chip."

"Mr. Tony give the captain a real hard time about old Skaw. The Sweaties didn't say nothin'; didn't even act surprised, just took the remains and pushed off. But Mr. Tony and that other crook they call Marbles— they was fit to be tied. Took the cap'n in his cabin and talked loud at him fer half a hour. Then the cap'n come out and give some orders to the mate."

Retief sat up and reached for a cigar.

"Mr. Tony and Skaw were pals, eh?"

"He hated Skaw's guts. But with him it was business. Mister, you got a gun?"

"A 2mm needler. Why?"

"The orders Cap'n give was to change course fer Alabaster; we're by-passin' Jorgensen's Worlds. We'll feel the course change any minute."

Retief lit the cigar, reached under the mattress and took out a short-barreled pistol. He dropped it in his pocket, looked at Chip.

"Maybe it was a good thought, at that. Which way to the captain's cabin?"

"This is it," Chip said softly. "You want me to keep a eye on who comes down the passage?"

Retief nodded, opened the door, and stepped into the cabin. The captain looked up from his desk, then jumped up. "What do you think you're doing, busting in here—"

"I hear you're planning a course change, captain."

"You've got damn big ears."

"I think we'd better call in at Jorgensen's."

"You do, huh?" The captain sat down. "I'm in command of this vessel. I'm changing course for Alabaster."

"I wouldn't find it convenient to go to Alabaster. So just hold your course for Jorgensen's."

"Not bloody likely." The captain reached for the mike on his desk, pressed the key. "Power Section, this is the captain," he said. Retief reached across the desk, gripped the captain's wrist.

"Tell the mate to hold his present course," he said softly.

"Let go my hand, Buster," the captain snarled. With his eyes on Retief's, he eased a drawer open with his left hand, reached in. Retief kneed the drawer. The captain yelped, dropped the mike.

"You busted my wrist, you—"

"And one to go," Retief said. "Tell him."

"I'm an officer of the Merchant Service—"

"You're a cheapjack who's sold his bridge to a pack of back-alley hoods."

"You can't put it over, hick. The landing—"

"Tell him."

The captain groaned, keyed the mike.

"Captain to Power Section. Hold your present course until you hear from me." He dropped the mike, looked up at Retief. "It's eighteen hours yet before we pick up Jorgensen control; you going to sit here and bend my arm the whole time?"

Retief released the captain's wrist, turned to Chip. "Chip, I'm locking the door. You circulate around, let me know what's going on. Bring me a pot of coffee every so often. I'm sitting up with a sick friend."

"Right, mister. Keep an eye on that jasper; he's slippery."

"What are you going to do?" the captain demanded.

Retief settled himself in a chair.

"Instead of strangling you, as you deserve, I'm going to stay here and help you hold your course for Jorgensen's Worlds."

The captain looked at Retief. He laughed, a short bark. "Then I'll stretch out and have a little nap, farmer. If you feel like dozing off some time during the next eighteen hours, don't mind me."

Retief took out the needler and put it on the desk before him.

"If anything happens that I don't like," he said, "I'll wake you up with this."

"Why don't you let me spell you, mister," Chip said. "Four hours to go yet; you're gonna hafta be on yer toes to handle the landing."

"I'll be all right, Chip. You get some sleep."

"Nope. Many's the time I stood four, five watches runnin', back when I was yer age. I'll make another round."

Retief stood up, stretched his legs, paced the floor, stared at the repeater instruments on the wall. Things had gone quietly so far, but the landing would be another matter. The captain's absence from the bridge during the highly complex maneuvering would be difficult to explain . . .

The desk speaker crackled.

"Captain, Office of the Watch here. Ain't it about time you was getting up here with the orbit figures?"

Retief nudged the captain. He awoke with a start, sat up. "Whazzat?" He looked wild-eyed at Retief.

"Watch Officer wants orbit figures," Retief said, nodding toward the speaker.

The captain rubbed his eyes, shook his head, picked up the mike. Retief released the safety on the needler with an audible click.

"Watch Officer, I'll . . . ah . . . get some figures for you right away. I'm . . . ah . . . busy right now."

"What the hell you talking about, busy?" the speaker blared. "You ain't got the figures ready, you'll have a hell of a hot time getting 'em up in the next three minutes. You fergot your approach pattern or something?"

"I guess I overlooked it," the captain said, looking sideways at Retief. He smiled crookedly. "I've been busy."

"One for your side," Retief said. He reached for the captain.

"I'll make a deal," the captain squalled. "Your life for—"

Retief took aim, slammed a hard right to the captain's jaw. He slumped to the floor.

Retief glanced around the room, yanked wires loose from a motile lamp, trussed the man's hands and feet, stuffed his mouth with paper and taped it.

Chip tapped at the door. Retief opened it and the chef stepped inside, looked at the man on the floor.

"The jasper tried somethin', huh? Figured he would. What we goin' to do now?"

"The captain forgot to set up an approach, Chip. He outfoxed me."

"If we overrun our approach patterns," Chip said, "we can't make orbit at Jorgensen's on automatic, and a manual approach—"

"That's out. But there's another possibility."

Chip blinked. "Only one thing you could mean, mister. But cuttin' out in a lifeboat in deep space is no picnic."

"They're on the port side, aft, right?"

Chip nodded. "Hot damn!" he said. "Who's got the 'tater salad?"

"We'd better tuck the skipper away out of sight."

"In the locker."

The two men carried the limp body to a deep storage chest, dumped it in, closed the lid.

"He won't suffercate; lid's a lousy fit."

Retief opened the door, went into the corridor, Chip behind him.

"Shouldn't oughta be nobody around now," the chef said. "Everybody's mannin' approach stations."

At the D deck companionway Retief stopped suddenly.

"Listen."

Chip cocked his head. "I don't hear nothin'," he whispered.

"Sounds like a sentry posted on the lifeboat deck," Retief said softly.

"Let's take him, mister."

"I'll go down. Stand by, Chip."

Retief started down the narrow steps, half stair, half

ladder. Halfway, he paused to listen. There was a sound of slow footsteps, then silence. Retief palmed the needler, went down the last steps quickly, emerged in the dim light of a low-ceilinged room. The stern of a five-man lifeboat bulked before him.

"Freeze, you!" a cold voice snapped.

Retief dropped, rolled behind the shelter of the lifeboat as the whine of a power pistol echoed off metal walls. A lunge, and he was under the boat, on his feet. He jumped, caught the quick-access handle, hauled it down. The lifeboat's outer port cycled open.

Feet scrambled at the bow of the boat, and Retief whirled, fired. The guard rounded into sight and fell headlong. Above, an alarm bell jangled. Retief stepped on a stanchion, hauled himself into the open port. A yell rang, then the clatter of feet on the stair.

"Don't shoot, mister!" Chip shouted.

"All clear, Chip," Retief called.

"Hang on; I'm comin' with ya!"

Retief reached down, lifted the chef bodily through the port, slammed the lever home. The outer door whooshed, clanged shut.

"Take number two, tie in! I'll blast her off," Chip said. "Been through a hunderd 'bandon ship drills . . ."

Retief watched as the chef flipped levers, pressed a fat red button. The deck trembled under the lifeboat.

"Blew the bay doors," Chip said, smiling happily. "That'll cool them jaspers down." He punched a green button.

"Look out, Jorgensen's . . ." With an ear-splitting blast, the stern rockets fired, a sustained agony of pressure . . .

Abruptly, there was silence, weightlessness. Contracting metal pinged loudly. Chip's breathing rasped in the stillness.

"Pulled nine Gs there for ten seconds," he gasped. "I gave her full emergency kick-off."

"Any armament aboard our late host?"

"A pop-gun; time they get their wind, we'll be clear.

Now all we got to do is set tight till we pick up a R and D from Svea Tower: maybe four, five hours."

"Chip, you're a wonder," Retief said. "This looks like a good time to catch that nap."

"Me too. Mighty peaceful here, ain't it?"

There was a moment's silence.

"Durn!" Chip said softly.

Retief opened one eye. "Sorry you came, Chip?"

"Left my best carvin' knife jammed up 'tween Marbles' ribs," the chef said. "Comes o' doin' things in a hurry."

The blond girl brushed her hair from her eyes and smiled at Retief.

"I'm the only one on duty," she said. "I'm Freya Dahl."

"It's important that I talk to someone in your government, miss," Retief said.

The girl looked at Retief. "The men you want to see are Thor Stahl and Bo Bergman. They will be at the lodge by nightfall."

"Then it looks like we go to the lodge," Retief said. "Lead on, ma'am."

"What about the boat?" Chip asked.

"I'll send someone to see to it tomorrow," the girl said.

"You're some gal," Chip said admiringly. "Dern near six feet, ain't you? And built too, what I mean."

They stepped out of the building into a whipping wind.

"Let's go across to the equipment shed, and get parkas for you," Freya said. "It will be cold on the slopes."

"Yeah," Chip said, shivering. "I've heard you folks don't believe in ridin' ever time you want to go a few miles uphill in a blizzard."

"It will make us hungry," Freya said.

Across the wind-scoured ramp abrupt peaks rose, snow-blanketed. A faint trail led across white slopes, disappeared into low clouds.

"The lodge is above the cloud layer," Freya said. "Up there the sky is always clear."

It was three hours later, and the sun was burning the peaks red, when Freya stopped, pulled off her woolen cap, and waved at the vista below.

"There you see it. Our valley."

"It's a mighty perty sight," Chip gasped. "Anything this tough to get a look at ought to be."

Freya pointed to where gaily painted houses nestled together, a puddle of color in the bowl of the valley. "There," she said. "The little red house by itself; do you see it? It is my father's home-acre."

"I'd appreciate it a dern sight better if my feet was up to that big fire you was talking about, Honey," Chip said.

They climbed on, crossed a shoulder, a slope of broken rock, reached the final slope. Above, the lodge sprawled, a long low structure of heavy logs, outlined against the deep-blue twilight sky. Smoke billowed from stone chimneys at either end, and yellow light gleamed from the narrow windows, reflected on the snow. Men and women stood in groups of three or four, skis over their shoulders. Their voices and laughter rang in the icy air.

Freya whistled shrilly. Someone waved.

"Come," she said. "Meet all my friends."

A man separated himself from the group, walked down the slope to meet them. Freya introduced the guests.

"Welcome," the man said heartily. "Come inside and be warm."

They crossed the trampled snow to the lodge, pushed through a heavy door into a vast low-beamed hall, crowded with people talking, singing, some sitting at long plank tables, others ringed around an eight-foot fireplace at the far side of the room. Freya led the way to a bench near the fire, made introductions, found a stool to prop Chip's feet on near the blaze. He looked around.

"I never seen so many perty gals before," he said delightedly.

A brunette with blue eyes raked a chestnut from the

fire, cracked it, and offered it to Retief. A tall man with arms like oak roots passed heavy beer tankards to the two guests.

"Tell us about the places you've seen," someone called. Chip emerged from a long pull at the mug, heaved a sigh.

"Well," he said. "I tell you I been in some places . . ."

Music started up, ringing above the clamor of talk. Freya rose. "Come," she said to Retief. "Dance with me."

When the music stopped, Retief rejoined Chip, who put down his mug and sighed. "Derned if I ever felt right at home so quick before." He lowered his voice. "They's some kind o' trouble in the air, though. Some o' the remarks they passed sounds like they're lookin' to have some trouble with the Sweaties. Don't seem to worry 'em none, though."

"Chip," Retief said, "how much do these people know about the Soetti?"

"Dunno. We useta touch down here regler, but I always jist set in my galley and worked on ship models or somethin'. I hear the Sweaties been nosin' around here some, though."

Two girls came up to Chip. "I gotta go now, mister," he said. "These gals got a idea I oughta take a hand in the kitchen."

"Smart girls," Retief said. He turned as Freya came up.

"Bo Bergman and Thor aren't back yet," she said. "They stayed to ski after moonrise."

"That moon is something. Almost like daylight."

"They will come soon, now. Shall we go to see the moonlight on the snow?"

Outside, long black shadows fell like ink on silver. The top of the cloud layer below glared white under the immense moon.

"Our sister world, Göta," Freya said. "Nearly as

big as Svea. I would like to visit it someday, although they say it's all stone and ice."

"Freya," Retief said, "how many people live on Jorgensen's Worlds?"

"About fifteen million, most of us here on Svea. There are mining camps and ice-fisheries on Göta. No one lives on Vasa or Skòne, but there are always a few ice-wolf hunters there."

"Have you ever fought a war?"

Freya turned to look at Retief. "Don't be afraid for us, Retief. The Soetti will attack our worlds, and we will fight them. We have fought before. These planets were not friendly ones . . ."

"I thought the Soetti attack would be a surprise to you," Retief said. "Have you made any preparation for it?"

"We have ten thousand merchant ships. When the enemy come, we will meet them."

Retief frowned. "Are there any guns on this planet? Any missiles?"

Freya shook her head. "We have a plan of deployment—"

"Deployment hell! Against a modern assault force you need modern armament."

"Look!" Freya touched Retief's arm. "They're coming now."

Two tall grizzled men came up the slope, skis over their shoulders. Freya went forward to meet them, Retief at her side.

The two came up, embraced the girl, shook hands with Retief.

"He has come to help us," Freya said.

"Welcome to Svea," Thor said. "Let's find a warm corner where we can talk."

Retief shook his head, smiling, as a tall girl with coppery hair offered a vast slab of venison. "I've caught up," he said, "for every hungry day I ever lived."

Bo Bergman poured Retief's beer mug full. "Our captains are the best in space," he said. "Our population is concentrated in half a hundred small cities all across the planet. We know where the Soetti must strike us. We will ram their major vessels with unmanned ships; on the ground, we will hunt them down with small-arms."

"An assembly line turning out penetration missiles would have been more to the point."

"Yes," Bo Bergman said. "If we had known sooner."

"We've seen very few of the Soetti," Thor said. "Their ships have landed and taken on stores. They say little to us, but we've felt their contempt. They envy us our worlds. They come from a cold land."

"Freya says you have a plan of defense," Retief said. "A sort of suicide squadron idea, followed by guerrilla warfare."

"It's the best we can devise, Retief. If there aren't too many of them, it might work."

Retief shook his head. "It might delay matters—but not much."

"Perhaps; but our remote control equipment is excellent; we have plenty of ships, albeit unarmed. And our people know how to live on the slopes—and how to shoot."

"There are too many of them," Retief said. "They breed like flies and, according to some sources, they mature in a matter of months. They've been feeling their way into the sector for years now; set up outposts on a thousand or so minor planets—cold ones, the kind they like. They want your worlds because they need living space."

"Retief must not be trapped here," said Freya to her compatriots. "His small boat is useless now; he must have a ship."

"Of course," Thor said. "And—"

"Retief," a voice called. "A message for you; the operator has phoned it up. A gram . . ."

Retief took the slip of paper, unfolded it. It was short, in verbal code, and signed by Magnan.

"You are recalled herewith," he read. "Assignment canceled. Agreement concluded with Soetti relinquishing all claims so-called Jorgensen system. Utmost importance that under no repeat no circumstances classified intelligence regarding Soetti be divulged to locals. Advise you depart instanter; Soetti occupation imminent."

Retief looked thoughtfully at the scrap of paper, then crumpled it, dropped it on the floor.

"Any answer?" the messenger asked.

"No," Retief said. "As a matter of fact, I didn't even get the message." He turned to Bo Bergman, took a tiny reel of tape from his pocket.

"This contains information," he said. "The Soetti attack plan, a defensive plan worked out at Corps HQ, and instructions for the conversion of a standard antiacceleration unit into a potent weapon. If you have a screen handy, we'd better get started; we have about seventy-two hours."

In the Briefing Room at Svea Tower, Thor snapped off the projector.

"Our plan would have been worthless against that," he said. "We assumed they'd make their strike from a standard in-line formation. This scheme of hitting all our settlements simultaneously, in a random order from all points—we'd have been helpless."

"It's perfect for this defensive plan," Bo Bergman said. "Assuming this antiac trick works."

"It works," said Retief. "I hope you've got plenty of heavy power cable available."

"We export copper," Thor said.

"We'll assign about two hundred vessels to each settlement. Linked up, they should throw up quite a field."

"It ought to be effective up to about fifteen miles, I'd estimate," Retief said.

A red light flashed on the communications panel. Thor went to it, flipped a key.

"Tower, Thor here," he said.

"I've got a ship on the scope, Thor," a voice said.

"There's nothing scheduled; ACI 228 by-passed at 1600 . . ."

"Just one?"

"A lone ship; coming in on a bearing of 291/456/ 653; on manual, I'd say."

"How does this track key in with the idea of ACI 228 making a manual correction for a missed automatic approach?" Retief asked.

Thor talked to the tower, got a reply.

"That's it," he said.

"How long before he touches down?"

Thor glanced at a lighted chart. "Perhaps eight minutes."

"Any guns here?"

Thor shook his head.

"If that's old 228, she ain't got but the one 50mm rifle," Chip said. "She cain't figure on jumpin' the whole planet."

"Hard to say what she figures on," Retief said. "Mr. Tony will be in a mood for drastic measures."

"I wonder what kind o' deal the skunk's got with the Sweaties," Chip said. "Prob'ly he gits to scavenge, after the Sweaties kill off the Jorgensens."

"He's upset about our leaving him without saying goodbye. And you left the door hanging open, too."

Chip cackled. "Old Mr. Tony don't look so good to the Sweaties now, hey, mister?"

Retief turned to Bo Bergman. "Chip's right. A Soetti died on the ship, and a tourist got through the cordon. Tony's out to redeem himself."

"He's on final now," the tower operator said. "Still no contact."

"We'll know soon enough what he has in mind," Thor said.

"Let's take a look."

Outside, the four men watched the point of fire grow, evolve into a ship ponderously settling to rest. The drive faded and cut; silence fell.

Inside the briefing room, the speaker called out. Bo Bergman went inside, talked to the tower, motioned the others in. "This is the tower talking to the ship," he said.

"—over to you," the speaker was saying. There was a crackling moment of silence; then another voice:

"—illegal entry. Send the two of them out, I'll see to it they're dealt with."

Thor flipped a key. "Tower, switch me direct to the ship."

"Right."

"You on ACI 228," he said. "Who are you?"

"What's that to you?" the speaker crackled.

"You weren't cleared to berth here. Do you have an emergency aboard?"

"Never mind that, you," the speaker rumbled. "I tracked this bird in; I got the lifeboat on the screen now. They haven't gone far in six hours. Let's have 'em."

"You're wasting your time."

There was a momentary silence.

"You think so, hah?" the speaker blared. "I'll put it to you straight: I see two guys on their way out in one minute, or I open up."

"He's bluffin'," Chip said. "The pop-gun won't bear on us."

"Take a look out the window," said Retief.

In the white glare of the moonlight a loading cover swung open at the stern of the ship, dropped down, formed a sloping ramp. A squat and massive shape appeared in the opening, trundled down onto the snow-swept tarmac.

Chip whistled. "I told you the captain was slippery," he muttered. "Where the devil'd he git that at?"

"What is it?" Thor asked.

"A tank," Retief said. "A museum piece, by the look of it."

"I'll say," Chip said. "That's a Bolo *Resartus,* Model M. Built mebbe two hunderd years ago in Concordiat times. Packs a wallop too, I'll tell ye."

The tank wheeled, brought a gun muzzle to bear in the base of the tower.

"Send 'em out," the speaker growled. "Or I blast 'em out."

"One round in here, and I've had a wasted trip," Retief said. "I'd better go out."

"Wait a minute, mister. I got the glimmerins of a idear."

"I'll stall them," Thor said. He keyed the mike. "ACI 228, what's your authority for this demand?"

"I know that machine," Chip said. "My hobby, old-time fightin' machines. Built a model of a *Resartus* once, inch to the foot; a beauty. Now lessee . . ."

The icy wind blew snow crystals stingingly against Retief's face. Chip carried a short length of iron bar thrust into his belt. He looked across at the tank. "Useta think that was a perty thing, that *Resartus*," he said. "Looks mean, now."

"You're getting the target's eye view," Retief said. "Sorry you had to get mixed up in this, old timer."

"Mixed myself in. Dern good thing too." Chip sighed. "I like these folks. Them boys didn't like lettin' us come out here, but I'll give 'em credit; they seen it had to be this way, and they didn't set to moanin' about it."

"They're tough people, Chip."

"Funny how it sneaks up on you, ain't it, mister? Few minutes ago we was eatin' high on the hog; now we're right close to bein' dead men."

"They want us alive."

"It'll be a hairy deal. But t'hell with it. If it works, it works."

"That's the spirit."

"I hope I got them fields o' fire right—"

"Don't worry; I'll bet a barrel of beer we make it."

"We'll find out in about ten seconds," Chip said. "Here we go . . ."

As they reached the tank the two men broke stride and jumped. Retief leaped for the gun barrel, swung up astride it, ripped off the fur-lined leather cap he wore, and, leaning forward, jammed it into the bore of

the cannon. The chef sprang for a perch above the fore
scanner antenna. With an angry whuff! anti-personnel
charges slammed from apertures low on the sides of
the vehicle. Retief swung around, pulled himself up on
the hull.

"Okay, mister," Chip called. "I'm goin' under." He
slipped down the front of the tank, disappeared between the treads. Retief clambered up, took a position
behind the turret, lay flat as it whirled angrily, sonar
eyes searching for the tank's tormentors. The vehicle
shuddered, backed, stopped, moved forward, pivoted.

Chip reappeared at the front of the tank.

"It's stuck," he called. He stopped to breathe hard,
clung as the machine lurched forward, spun to the
right, stopped, rocking slightly.

"Take over here," Retief said. He crawled forward,
watched as the chef pulled himself up, slipped down
past him, feeling for the footholds between the treads.
He reached the ground, dropped on his back, hitched
himself under the dark belly of the tank. He groped,
found the handholds, probed with a foot for the tread-
jack lever.

The tank rumbled, backed quickly, turned left and
right in a sine curve. Retief clung grimly, inches from
the clashing treads. He found the lever, braced his
back, pushed. The lever seemed to give minutely. He
set himself again, put both feet against the frozen bar,
and heaved. With a dry rasp it slid back. Immediately,
two heavy rods extended themselves, slid down to grate
against the pavement, drove on irresistibly. The left
track raced as the weight went off it. Retief grabbed
for a hold as the right tread clashed, heaving the fifty-
ton machine forward, jacks screeching as they scored
the tarmac. The tank pivoted, chips of pavement flying.
The jacks lifted the clattering left track clear of the
surface and the tank spun like a hamstrung buffalo.

The tank stopped, sat silent, canted now on the extended jacks. Retief emerged from under the machine,
jumped, pulled himself above the anti-personnel apertures as another charge rocked the tank. He clambered

to the turret, crouched beside Chip. They waited, watching the entry hatch.

Five minutes passed.

"I'll bet old Tony's givin' the chauffeur hell," Chip said.

The hatch moved, cycled open. A head came cautiously into view in time to see the needler in Retief's hand.

"Come on out," Retief said.

The head dropped, and Chip snaked forward, rammed the iron rod under the hatch near the hinge. The hatch began to cycle shut, groaned, stopped. There was a sound of metal failing, and the hatch popped, stood open. Retief half rose, aimed the needler. The walls of the tank rang as the metal splinter ricocheted inside.

"That's one keg o' beer I owe you, mister," Chip said. "Now let's git outa here before the ship lifts and fries us."

"The biggest problem the Jorgensen's people will have is decontaminating the wreckage," Retief said.

Magnan leaned forward. "Amazing," he said. "They just kept coming, did they? Had they no inter-ship communication?"

"They had their orders. And their attack plan. They followed it."

"What a spectacle! Over a thousand ships, plunging out of control one by one as they entered the stress-field."

"Not much of a spectacle. You couldn't see them; too far away. They all crashed back in the mountains."

"Oh." Magnan's face fell. "But it's as well they did; the bacterial bombs—"

"Too cold for bacteria. They won't spread."

"Nor will the Soetti," Magnan said smugly, "thanks to the promptness with which I acted in dispatching you with the requisite data." He looked narrowly at Retief. "By the way, you're sure no . . . ah . . . message reached you after your arrival?"

"I got something," Retief said, looking Magnan in the eye. "It must have been a garbled transmission. It didn't make sense."

Magnan coughed, shuffled papers. "This information you've reported," he said hurriedly. "This rather fantastic story that the Soetti originated in the Cloud, that they're seeking a foothold in the main galaxy because they've literally eaten themselves out of subsistence; how did you get it? The one or two Soetti we attempted to question . . . ah" Magnan coughed again. "There was an accident," he finished. "We got nothing from them."

"The Jorgensens took a Soetti from a wreck, still alive but unconscious. They managed to get the story from him."

"It's immaterial, actually," Magnan said. "The Soetti violated their treaty with us the day after it was signed. Had no intention of fair play. Far from evacuating the agreed areas, they had actually occupied half a dozen additional minor bodies in the *Whate* system."

Retief clucked sympathetically. "You don't know who to trust, these days," he said. Magnan looked at him coldly.

"Spare me your sarcasm, Retief." He picked up a folder from his desk, opened it. "While you're out that way, I have another little task for you. We haven't had a comprehensive wild life census report from Brimstone lately—"

"Sorry," Retief said. "I'll be tied up. I'm taking a month off. Maybe more."

"What's that?" Magnan's head came up. "You seem to forget—"

"I'm trying, Mr. Secretary. Goodbye now." Retief reached out and flipped the key. Magnan's face faded from the screen. Retief stood up.

"Chip, we'll crack that keg when I get back." He turned to Freya.

"Freya," he said, "do you think you could teach me to ski by moonlight?"

"For all its spirit of detachment from petty local issues, the Corps was never slow to interpose its majestic presence in the path of injustice. Under-Secretary Sternwheeler's classic approach to the problem of Aga Kagan aggression at Flamme testified to the efficacy of tried diplomatic procedures backed by the profound prestige of the Corps . . ."

—Vol. XV, Reel 3, 494 AE (AD 2955)

Protest Note

"I'm not at all sure," Under-Secretary Stern-wheeler said, "that I fully understand the necessity of your absenting yourself from your post of duty at this time, Mr. Retief. Surely this matter could have been dealt with in the usual way—assuming any action is necessary."

"I had a sharp attack of writer's cramp, Mr. Secretary," Retief said. "So I thought I'd better come along in person—just to be sure of making my point."

"I seem to recall seeing a despatch or two on the subject," Deputy Under-Secretary Magnan put in. "Unfortunately, this being end-of-the-fiscal-year time, we found ourselves quite inundated with reports. Reports, reports, reports—"

"Not criticizing the reporting system, are you, Mr. Magnan?" the Under-Secretary barked.

"Gracious, no. I love reports—"

"It seems nobody's told the Aga Kagans about fiscal years," Retief said. "They're going right ahead with their program of land-grabbing on Flamme. So far,

I've persuaded the Boyars that this is a matter for the Corps, and not to take matters into their own hands."

The Under-Secretary nodded. "Quite right. Carry on along the same lines. Now, if there's nothing further—"

"Thank you, Mr. Secretary," Magnan said, rising. "We certainly appreciate your guidance—"

"There is a little something further," said Retief, sitting solidly in his chair. "What's the Corps going to do about the Aga Kagans?"

The Under-Secretary turned a liverish eye on Retief. "As Minister to Flamme, you should know that the function of a diplomatic representative is merely to . . . what shall I say . . . ?"

"String them along?" Magnan suggested.

"An unfortunate choice of phrase," the Under-Secretary said.

"However, it embodies certain realities of Galactic politics. The Corps must concern itself with matters of broad policy—"

"Sixty years ago the Corps was encouraging the Boyars to settle Flamme," Retief said. "They were assured of Corps support."

"I don't believe you'll find that in writing," said the Under-Secretary blandly. "In any event, that was sixty years ago. At that time a foothold against Neo-Concordiatist elements was deemed desirable. Now the situation has changed."

"The Boyars have spent sixty years terraforming Flamme," Retief said. "They've cleared jungle, descummed the seas, irrigated deserts, set out forests. They've just about reached the point where they can begin to enjoy it. The Aga Kagans have picked this as a good time to move in. They've landed thirty detachments of 'fishermen'—complete with armored trawlers mounting 40mm infinite repeaters—and two dozen parties of 'homesteaders'—all male and toting rocket launchers."

"Surely there's land enough on the world to afford space to both groups," the Under-Secretary said. "A spirit of co-operation—"

"The Boyars needed some co-operation sixty years ago. They tried to get the Aga Kagans to join in, help them beat back some of the saurian wild life that liked to graze on people. The Aga Kagans didn't want to play. The Corps didn't like the idea either; they wanted to see an undisputed anti-Concordiatist enclave. But now that the world is tamed, the squatters are moving in."

"The exigencies of diplomacy require a flexible policy—"

"I want a firm assurance of Corps support to take back to Flamme," Retief said. "The Boyars are a little naive; they don't understand diplomatic triple-speak. They just want to hold onto the homes they've made out of a wasteland."

"I'm warning you, Retief!" the Under-Secretary snapped, leaning forward, wattles quivering. "Corps policy with regard to Flamme includes no inflammatory actions based on outmoded concepts. The Boyars will have to accommodate themselves to the situation!"

"That's what I'm afraid of," Retief said. "They're not going to sit still and watch it happen. If I don't take back concrete evidence of Corps backing, we're going to have a nice hot little shooting war on our hands."

The Under-Secretary pushed out his lips, drummed his fingers on the desk. "Confounded hot-heads," he muttered. "Very well, Retief. I'll go along to the extent of a Note; but no further."

"A Note? I was thinking of something more like a squadron of Corps Peace Enforcers running through a few routine maneuvers off Flamme—"

"Out of the question. A stiffly worded Protest Note is the best I can do. That's final."

Back in the corridor, Magnan turned to Retief. "When will you learn not to argue with Under-Secretaries? One would think you actively dislike the idea of promotion. I was astonished at the Under-Secretary's restraint. Frankly, I was stunned when he actually agreed to a Note. I, of course, will have to draft it."

Magnan pulled at his lower lip thoughtfully. "Now, I wonder, should I view with deep concern an act of open aggression, or merely point out an apparent violation of technicalities . . ."

"Don't bother," Retief said. "I have a draft all ready to go."

"But how——?"

"I had a feeling I'd get paper instead of action. I thought I'd save a little time all around."

"At times your cynicism borders on impudence."

"At other times it borders on disgust. Now, if you'll run the Note through for signature, I'll try to catch the six o'clock shuttle."

"Leaving so soon? There's an important reception tonight. Some of our biggest names will be there. An excellent opportunity for you to join in the diplomatic give-and-take."

"No, thanks. I want to get back to Flamme and join in something mild, like a dinosaur hunt."

"When you get there, I hope you'll make it clear that this matter is to be settled without violence."

"Don't worry. I'll keep the peace, if I have to start a war to do it."

On the broad veranda at Government House, Retief settled himself comfortably in a lounge chair, accepted a tall glass from a white-jacketed waiter, and regarded the flamboyant Flamme sunset, a gorgeous blaze of vermilion and purple that reflected from a still lake, tinged the broad lawn with color, silhouetted tall poplars among flower beds.

"You've done great things here in sixty years, Georges," said Retief. "Not that natural geological processes couldn't have produced the same results, given a couple of hundred million years."

"Don't belabor the point," the Boyar Chef d'Regime said, "—since we seem to be on the verge of losing it."

"You're forgetting the Note."

"A Note," Georges said, waving his cigar. "What the

purple polluted hell is a Note supposed to do? I've got
Aga Kagan claim-jumpers camped in the middle of
what used to be a fine stand of barley, cooking sheep's
brains over dung fires not ten miles from Government
House—and up-wind at that."

"Say, if that's the same barley you distill your whiskey from, I'd call that a first-class atrocity."

"Retief, on your say-so, I've kept my boys on a short
leash. They've put up with plenty. Last week, while
you were away, these barbarians sailed that flotilla of
armor-plated junks right through the middle of one of
our best oyster breeding beds. It was all I could do to
keep a bunch of our men from going out in private
helis and blasting 'em out of the water."

"That wouldn't have been good for the oysters,
either."

"That's what I told 'em. I also said you'd be back
here in a few days with something from Corps HQ.
When I tell 'em all we've got is a piece of paper, that'll
be the end. There's a strong vigilante organization here
that's been outfitting for the last four weeks. If I hadn't
held them back with assurances that the CDT would
step in and take care of this invasion, they would have
hit them before now."

"That would have been a mistake. The Aga Kagans
are tough customers. They're active on half a dozen
worlds at the moment. They've been building up for
this push for the last five years. A show of resistance by
you Boyars without Corps backing would be an invitation to slaughter—with the excuse that you started it."

"So what are we going to do? Sit here and watch
these goat-herders take over our farms and fisheries?"

"Those goat-herders aren't all they seem. They've
got a first-class modern navy."

"I've seen 'em. They camp in goat-skin tents, gallop
around on animal-back, wear dresses down to their
ankles—"

"The 'goat-skin' tents are a high-polymer plastic,
made in the same factory that turns out those long

flowing bullet-proof robes you mention. The animals are just for show; back home they use helis and ground cars of the most modern design."

The Chef d'Regime chewed his cigar.

"Why the masquerade?"

"Something to do with internal policies, I suppose."

"So we sit tight and watch 'em take our world away from us. That's what I get for playing along with you, Retief. We should have clobbered these monkeys as soon as they set foot on our world."

"Slow down, I haven't finished yet. There's still the Note."

"I've got plenty of paper already; rolls and rolls of it."

"Give diplomatic processes a chance," said Retief. "The Note hasn't even been delivered yet. Who knows? We may get surprising results."

"If you expect me to supply a runner for the purpose, you're out of luck. From what I hear, he's likely to come back with his ears stuffed in his hip pocket."

"I'll deliver the Note personally," Retief said. "I could use a couple of escorts—preferably strong-arm lads."

The Chef d'Regime frowned, blew out a cloud of smoke. "I wasn't kidding about these Aga Kagans," he said. "I hear they have some nasty habits. I don't want to see you operated on with the same knives they use to skin out the goats."

"I'd be against that myself. Still, the mail must go through."

"Strong-arm lads, eh? What have you got in mind, Retief?"

"A little muscle in the background is an old diplomatic custom," Retief said.

The Chef d'Regime stubbed out his cigar thoughtfully. "I used to be a pretty fair elbow-wrestler myself," he said. "Suppose I go along . . . ?"

"That," said Retief, "should lend just the right note of solidarity to our little delegation." He hitched his chair closer. "Now, depending on what we run into, here's how we'll play it . . ."

Eight miles into the rolling granite hills west of the capital, a black-painted official air car flying the twin flags of Chief of State and Terrestrial Minister skimmed along a foot above a pot-holed road. Slumped in the padded seat, the Boyar Chef d'Regime waved his cigar glumly at the surrounding hills.

"Fifty years ago this was bare rock," he said. "We've bred special strains of bacteria here to break down the formations into soil, and we followed up with a program of broad-spectrum fertilization. We planned to put the whole area into crops by next year. Now it looks like the goats will get it."

"Will that scrub-land support a crop?" Retief said, eyeing the lichen-covered knolls.

"Sure. We start with legumes, follow up with cereals. Wait until you see this next section. It's on old flood plain, came into production thirty years ago. One of our finest—"

The air car topped a rise and the Chef dropped his cigar, half rose, with a hoarse yell. A herd of scraggly goats tossed their heads among a stand of ripe grain. The car pulled to a stop. Retief held the Boyar's arm.

"Keep calm, Georges," he said. "Remember, we're on a diplomatic mission. It wouldn't do to come to the conference table smelling of goats."

"Let me at 'em!" Georges roared. "I'll throttle 'em with my bare hands!"

A bearded goat eyed the Boyar Chef sardonically, jaw working.

"Look at that long-nosed son of a—!" The goat gave a derisive bleat and took another mouthful of ripe grain.

"Did you see that?" Georges yelled. "They've trained the son of a—"

"Chin up, Georges," Retief said. "We'll take up the goat problem along with the rest."

"I'll murder 'em—!"

"Hold it, Georges. Look over there . . ."

A hundred yards away a trio of brown-cloaked horsemen topped a rise, paused dramatically against the cloudless pale sky, then galloped down the slope toward the car, rifles bobbing at their backs, cloaks billowing out behind. Side by side they rode, through the brown-golden grain, cutting three narrow swaths that ran in a straight sweep from the ridge to the air car where Retief and the Chef d'Regime hovered, waiting.

Georges scrambled for the side of the car. "Just wait till I get my hands on the son of a—"

Retief pulled him back. "Sit tight and look pleased, Georges. Never give the opposition a hint of your true feelings. Pretend you're a goat lover—and hand me one of your cigars."

The three horsemen pulled up in a churn of chaff and a clatter of pebbles. Georges coughed, batting a hand at the settling dust. Retief peeled the cigar unhurriedly, sniffed at it, thumbed it alight. He drew at it, puffed out a cloud of smoke, and glanced casually at the trio of Aga Kagan cavaliers.

"Peace be with you," he intoned in accent-free Kagan. "May your shadows never grow less."

The leader of the three, a hawk-faced man with a heavy beard, unlimbered his rifle, fingered it, frowning ferociously.

"Have no fear," Retief said, smiling graciously. "He who comes as a guest enjoys perfect safety."

A smooth-faced member of the threesome barked an oath, leveled his rifle at Retief.

"Youth is the steed of folly," Retief said. "Take care that the beardless one does not disgrace his house."

The leader whirled on the youth, snarled an order; he lowered the rifle, muttering. Blackbeard turned back to Retief.

"Begone, interlopers," he said. "You disturb the goats."

"Provision is not taken to the house of the generous,"

Retief said. "May the creatures dine well ere they move on."

"Hah! The goats of the Aga Kaga graze on the lands of the Aga Kaga." The leader edged his horse close, eyed Retief fiercely. "We welcome no intruders on our lands."

"To praise a man for what he does not possess is to make him appear foolish," Retief said. "These are the lands of the Boyars. But enough of these pleasantries. We seek audience with your ruler."

"You may address me as 'Exalted One,' " the leader said. "Now dismount from that steed of Shaitan—"

"It is written, 'If you need anything from a dog, call him "sir," ' " Retief said. "I must decline to impute canine ancestry to a guest. Now you may conduct me to your headquarters."

"Enough of your insolence—!" The bearded man cocked his rifle. "I could blow your heads off—"

"The hen has feathers, but it does not fly," Retief said. "We have asked for escort. A slave must be beaten with a stick; for a free man, a hint is enough."

"You mock me, pale one. I warn you—"

"Only love makes me weep," Retief said. "I laugh at hatred."

"Get out of the car!"

Retief puffed at his cigar, eyed the Aga Kagan cheerfully. The youth in the rear moved forward, teeth bared.

"Never give in to the fool, lest he say, 'He fears me,' " Retief said.

"I cannot restrain my men in the face of your insults," the bearded Aga Kagan roared. "These hens of mine have feathers—and talons as well!"

"When God would destroy an ant, he gives him wings," Retief said. "Distress in misfortune is another misfortune."

The bearded man's face grew purple.

Retief dribbled the ash from his cigar over the side of the car.

"Now I think we'd better be getting on," he said

briskly. "I've enjoyed our chat, but we do have business to attend to."

The bearded leader laughed shortly. "Does the condemned man beg for the axe?" he inquired rhetorically. "You shall be allowed audience with the Aga Kaga, then. Move on—and make no attempt to escape, else my gun will speak you a brief farewell."

The horsemen glowered, then at a word from the leader, took positions around the car. Georges started the vehicle forward, following the leading rider. Retief leaned back and let out a long sigh.

"That was close," he said. "I was out of proverbs."

"You sound as though you'd brought off a coup," Georges said. "From the expression on the whiskery one's face, we're in for trouble. What was he saying?"

"Just a routine exchange of bluffs," Retief said. "Now when we get there, remember to make your flattery sound like insults and your insults sound like flattery, and you'll be all right."

"These birds are armed—and they don't like strangers," Georges said. "Maybe I should have boned up on their habits before I joined this expedition."

"Just stick to the plan. And remember: a handful of luck is better than a camel-load of learning."

The air car followed the escort down a long slope to a dry river bed, across it, through a barren stretch of shifting sand, to a green oasis, set with canopies.

The armed escort motioned the car to a halt before an immense tent of glistening black, before which armed men lounged under a pennant bearing a lion *couchant* in crimson on a field vert.

"Get out," Blackbeard ordered. The guards eyed the visitors, drawn sabers catching sunlight. Retief and Georges stepped from the car onto rich rugs spread on the grass, followed the ferocious gesture of the bearded man through the opening into a perfumed interior of luminous shadows. A heavy odor of incense hung in the air, and the strumming of stringed instruments laid a muted pattern of sound behind the decorations of gold and blue, silver and green. At the far end of the room, among a bevy of female slaves, a large and resplendently clad man with blue-black hair and a clean-shaven chin popped a grape into his mouth, wiped his fingers negligently on a wisp of silk offered by a hand-maiden, belched loudly, and looked the callers over.

Blackbeard cleared his throat. "Down on your faces in the presence of the Exalted One, the Aga Kaga, ruler of the East and West—"

"Sorry," Retief said firmly. "My hay-fever, you know."

The reclining giant waved a hand languidly.

"Never mind the formalities," he said. "Approach."

Retief and Georges crossed the thick rugs. A cold draft blew toward them. The reclining man sneezed violently, wiped his nose on another silken scarf, and held up a hand.

"Night and the horses and the desert know me," he said in resonant tones. "Also the sword and the guest and paper and pen—" He paused, wrinkled his nose, and sneezed again.

"Turn off that damned air-conditioner," he snapped. He settled himself, motioned the bearded man to him; the two exchanged muted remarks. Then the bearded man stepped back, ducked his head, and withdrew to the rear.

"Excellency," Retief said, "I have the honor to present M. Georges Duror, Chef d'Regime of the Planetary government—"

"Planetary government?" The Aga Kaga spat grape seeds on the rug. "My men have observed a few squatters along the shore. If they're in distress, I'll see about a distribution of goat-meat."

"It is the punishment of the envious to grieve at another's plenty," Retief said. "No goat-meat will be required."

"Ralph told me you talk like a page out of Mustapha ben Abdallah Katib Jelebi," the Aga Kaga said. "I

know a few old sayings myself. For example, 'A Bed-
ouin is only cheated once.' "

"We have no such intentions, Excellency," Retief
said. "Is it not written, 'Have no faith in the Prince
whose minister cheats you?' "

"I've had some unhappy experiences with strangers,"
the Aga Kaga said. "It is written in the sands, 'All
strangers are kin.' Still, he who visits rarely is a welcome guest. Be seated."

Hand-maidens brought cushions, giggled, and fled.
Retief and Georges settled themselves comfortably. The
Aga Kaga eyed them in silence.

"We have come to bear tidings from the Corps Diplomatique Terrestrienne," Retief said solemnly. A perfumed slave girl offered grapes.

"Modest ignorance is better than boastful knowledge," the Aga Kaga said. "What brings the CDT into
the picture?"

"The essay of the drunkard will be read in the
tavern," Retief said. "Whereas the words of kings . . ."

"Very well, I concede the point." The Aga Kaga
waved a hand at the serving maids. "Depart, my dears.
Attend me later. You too, Ralph. These are mere
diplomats: men of words, not deeds."

The bearded man glared and departed. The girls hurried after him.

"Now," the Aga Kaga said. "Let's drop the wisdom
of the ages and get down to the issues. Not that I don't
admire your repertoire of platitudes. How do you remember them all?"

"Diplomats and other liars require good memories,"
Retief said. "But, as you point out, small wisdom to
small minds. I'm here to effect a settlement of certain
differences between yourself and the planetary authorities. I have here a Note, which I'm conveying on behalf
of the Sector Under-Secretary. With your permission,
I'll read it."

"Go ahead." The Aga Kaga kicked a couple of
cushions onto the floor, eased a bottle from under
the couch, and reached for glasses.

"The Under-Secretary for Sector Affairs presents his compliments to his Excellency the Aga Kaga of the Aga Kaga, Primary Potentate, Hereditary Sheik, Emir of the—"

"Yes, yes; skip the titles."

Retief flipped over two pages.

". . . and with reference to the recent relocation of persons under the jurisdiction of his Excellency, has the honor to point out that the territories now under settlement comprise a portion of that area, designated as Sub-sector Alpha, which, under terms of the Agreement entered into by his Excellency's predecessor, and as referenced in Sector Ministry's Notes numbers G-1758-46573957-b and X-7584736 c-1, with particular pertinence to that body designated in the Revised Galactic Catalogue, tenth edition, as amended, Volume Nine, reel 43, as 54 Cygni Alpha, otherwise referred to hereinafter as Flamme—"

"Come to the point," the Aga Kaga cut in. "You're here to lodge a complaint that I'm invading territories to which someone else lays claim, is that it?" He smiled broadly, offered dope-sticks, and lit one. "Well, I've been expecting a call. After all, it's what you gentlemen are paid for. Cheers."

"Your Excellency has a lucid way of putting things," Retief said.

"Call me Stanley," the Aga Kaga said. "The other routine is just to please some of the old fools—I mean the more conservative members of my government. They're still gnawing their beards and kicking themselves because their ancestors dropped science in favor of alchemy and got themselves stranded in a cultural dead-end. This charade is supposed to prove they were right all along. However, I've no time to waste in neurotic compensations. I have places to go and deeds to accomplish."

"At first glance," Retief said, "it looks as though the places are already occupied and the deeds are illegal."

The Aga Kaga guffawed. "For a diplomat, you speak

plainly, Retief. Have another drink." He poured, eyeing Georges. "What of M. Duror? How does he feel about it?"

Georges took a thoughtful swallow of whiskey. "Not bad," he said. "But not quite good enough to cover the odor of goats."

The Aga Kaga snorted. "I thought the goats were over-doing it a bit myself," he said. "Still, the grey-beards insisted. And I need their support."

"Also," Georges said distinctly, "I think you're soft. You lie around letting women wait on you, while your betters are out doing an honest day's work."

The Aga Kaga looked startled. "Soft? I can tie a knot in an iron bar as thick as your thumb." He popped a grape into his mouth. "As for the rest, your pious views as to the virtues of hard labor are as childish as my advisors' faith in the advantages of primitive plumbing. As for myself, I am a realist. If two monkeys want the same banana, in the end one will have it, and the other will cry morality. The days of my years are numbered, praise be to God. While they last, I hope to eat well, hunt well, fight well, and take my share of pleasure. I leave to others the arid satisfactions of self-denial and other perversions."

"You admit you're here to grab our land then," Georges said. "That's the damnedest piece of bare-faced aggression—"

"Ah, ah"; the Aga Kaga held up a hand; "watch your vocabulary, my dear sir. I'm sure that 'justifiable yearnings for territorial self-realization' would be more appropriate to the situation. Or possibly 'legitimate aspirations for self-determination of formerly exploited peoples' might fit the case. Aggression is, by definition, an activity carried on only by those who have inherited the mantle of 'Colonial Imperialism.'"

"Imperialism! Why, you Aga Kagans have been the most notorious planet-grabbers in Sector history, you—you—"

"Call me Stanley." The Aga Kaga munched a grape. "I merely face the realities of popular folk lore. Let's be pragmatic; it's a matter of historical association. Some people can grab land and pass it off lightly as a moral duty; others are dubbed imperialist merely for holding onto their own. Unfair, you say. But that's life, my friends. And I shall continue to take every advantage of it."

"We'll fight you!" Georges bellowed. He took another gulp of whiskey and slammed the glass down. "You won't take this world without a struggle—"

"Another?" the Aga Kaga said, offering the bottle. Georges glowered as his glass was filled. The Aga Kaga held the glass up to the light. "Excellent color, don't you agree?" He turned his eyes on Georges.

"It's pointless to resist," he said. "We have you outgunned and outmanned. Your small nation has no chance against us. But we're prepared to be generous. You may continue to occupy such areas as we do not immediately require until such time as you're able to make other arrangements."

"And by the time we've got a crop growing out of what was bare rock, you'll be ready to move in," the Boyar Chef d'Regime snapped. "But you'll find we aren't alone!"

"Quite alone," the Aga Kaga said. He nodded sagely. "Yes, one need but read the lesson of history. The Corps Diplomatique Terrestrienne will make expostulatory noises, but it will accept the *fait accompli*. You, my dear sir, are but a very small nibble. We won't make the mistake of excessive greed; we shall inch our way to empire—and those who stand in our way shall be dubbed warmongers."

"I see you're quite a student of history, Stanley," Retief said. "I wonder if you recall the eventual fate of most of the would-be empire nibblers of the past?"

"Ah, but they grew incautious; they went too far, too fast."

"The confounded impudence," Georges rasped. "Tells us to our face what he has in mind . . ."

"An ancient and honorable custom, from the time of *Mein Kampf* and the *Communist Manifesto* through the

Porcelain Wall of Leung. Such declarations have a legendary quality; it's traditional that they're never taken at face value."

"But always," Retief said, "there was a critical point at which the man on horseback could have been pulled from the saddle—"

"COULD have been," the Aga Kaga chuckled. He finished the grapes and began peeling an orange. "But they never were. Hitler could have been stopped by the Czech Air Force in 1938; Stalin was at the mercy of the primitive atomics of the West in 1946; Leung was grossly over-extended at Rangoon. But the onus of that historic role could not be overcome. It has been the fate of your spiritual forebears to carve civilizations from the wilderness, and then, amid tearing of garments and the heaping of ashes of self-accusation on your own confused heads, to withdraw, leaving the spoils for local political opportunists and mob leaders, clothed in the mystical virtue of native birth. Have a banana."

"You're stretching your analogy a little too far," Retief said. "You're banking on the inaction of the Corps. You could be wrong."

"I shall know when to stop," the Aga Kaga said.

"Tell me, Stanley," Retief said, rising. "Are we quite private here?"

"Yes, perfectly so. None would dare to intrude in my council." He cocked an eyebrow at Retief. "You have a proposal to make in confidence? But what of our dear friend Georges? One would not like to see him disillusioned . . ."

"Don't worry about Georges. He's a realist, like you. He's prepared to deal in facts. Hard facts, in this case."

The Aga Kaga nodded thoughtfully. "What are you getting at?"

"You're basing your plan of action on the certainty that the Corps will sit by, wringing its hands, while you embark on a career of interplanetary piracy—"

"Isn't it the custom?" the Aga Kaga smiled complacently.

"I have news for you, Stanley. In this instance, neck-wringing seems more in order than hand-wringing . . ."

The Aga Kaga frowned. "Your manner—"

"Never mind our manners!" Georges blurted, standing. "We don't need any lessons from goat-herding land-thieves!"

The Aga Kaga's face darkened. "You dare to speak thus to me, pig of a muck-grubber—"

With a muffled curse Georges launched himself at the potentate. The giant rolled aside, grunted as the Boyar's fist thumped in his short ribs, then chopped down on Georges' neck. The Chef d'Regime slid off onto the floor as the Aga Kaga bounded to his feet, sending fruit and silken cushions flying.

"I see it now!" he hissed. "An assassination attempt!" He stretched his arms, thick as tree-roots—a grizzly in satin robes. "Your heads will ring together like gongs before I have done with you . . . !" He lunged for Retief. Retief came to his feet, feinted with his left, and planted a short right against the Aga Kaga's jaw with a solid smack. The potentate stumbled, grabbed; Retief slipped aside. The Aga Kaga whirled to face Retief.

"A slippery diplomat, by all the houris in Paradise!" he grated, breathing hard. "But a fool. True to your medieval code of chivalry, you attacked singly, a blunder I would never have made. And you shall die for your idiocy!" He opened his mouth to bellow—

"You sure look foolish, with your fancy hair-do down in your eyes," Retief said. "The servants will get a big laugh out of that—"

With a choked yell, the Aga Kaga dived for Retief, missed as he leaped aside. The two went to the mat together, rolled, sending a stool skittering. Grunts and curses were heard as the two big men strained, muscles popping. Retief groped for a scissors hold; the Aga Kaga seized his foot, bit hard. Retief bent nearly double, braced himself, and slammed the potentate against the rug. Dust flew. Then the two were on their feet, circling.

"Many times have I longed to broil a diplomat over

a slow fire," the Aga Kaga snarled. "Tonight will see it come to pass . . ."

"I've seen it done often at staff meetings," said Retief. "It seems to have no permanent effect—"

The Aga Kaga reached for Retief, who feinted left, hammered a right to the chin. The Aga Kaga tottered. Retief measured him, brought up a haymaker. The potentate slammed to the rug—out cold.

Georges rolled over, sat up. "Let me at the son of a—" he muttered.

"Take over, Georges," Retief said, panting. "Since he's in a mood to negotiate now, we may as well get something accomplished."

Georges eyed the fallen ruler, who stirred, groaned lugubriously. "I hope you know what you're doing. But I'm with you in any case." Georges straddled the prone body, plucked a curved knife from the low table, prodded the Aga Kaga's Adam's apple. He groaned again and opened his eyes.

"Make one little peep and your wind-bag will spring a leak," Georges said. "Very few historical figures have accomplished anything important after their throats were cut."

"Stanley won't yell," Retief said. "We're not the only ones who're guilty of cultural idiocy. He'd lose face something awful if he let his followers see him like this." Retief settled himself on a tufted ottoman. "Right, Stanley?"

The Aga Kaga snarled.

Retief selected a grape, ate it thoughtfully. "These aren't bad, Georges. You might consider taking on a few Aga Kagan vine-growers—purely on a yearly contract basis, of course."

The Aga Kaga groaned, rolling his eyes.

"Well, I believe we're ready to get down to diplomatic proceedings now," Retief said. "Nothing like dealing in an atmosphere of realistic good-fellowship. First, of course, there's the matter of the presence of aliens lacking visas." He opened his briefcase, withdrew a heavy sheet of parchment. "I have the document here, drawn up and ready for signature. It provides for the prompt deportation of such persons, by Corps Transport, all expenses to be borne by the Aga Kagan government. That's agreeable, I think?" Retief looked expectantly at the purple face of the supine potentate. The Aga Kaga grunted a strangled grunt.

"Speak up, Stanley," Retief said. "Give him plenty of air, Georges."

"Shall I let some in through the side?"

"Not yet. I'm sure Stanley wants to be agreeable."

The Aga Kaga snarled.

"Maybe just a little then, Georges," Retief said judiciously. Georges jabbed the knife in far enough to draw a bead of blood. The Aga Kaga grunted.

"Agreed!" he snorted. "By the beard of the Prophet, when I get my hands on you . . ."

"Second item: certain fields, fishing grounds, et cetera, have suffered damage due to the presence of the aforementioned illegal immigrants. Full compensation will be made by the Aga Kagan government. Agreed?"

The Aga Kaga drew a breath, tensed himself; Georges jabbed with the knife point. His prisoner relaxed with a groan. "Agreed!" he grated. "A vile tactic! You enter my tent under the guise of guests, protected by diplomatic immunity—"

"I had the impression we were herded in here at sword point," said Retief. "Shall we go on? Now, there's the little matter of restitution for violation of sovereignty, reparations for mental anguish, payment for damaged fences, roads, drainage canals, communications, et cetera, et cetera. Shall I read them all?"

"Wait until the news of this outrage is spread abroad—"

"They'd never believe it. History would prove it impossible. And on mature consideration, I'm sure you won't want it noised about that you entertained visiting dignitaries flat on your back."

"What about the pollution of the atmosphere by goats?" Georges put in. "And don't overlook the muddying of streams, the destruction of valuable timber for camp fires, and—"

"I've covered all that sort of thing under a miscellaneous heading," Retief said. "We can fill it in at leisure when we get back."

"Bandits!" the Aga Kaga hissed. "Thieves! Dogs of unreliable imperialists!!"

"It's disillusioning, I know," Retief said. "Still, of such little surprises is history made. Sign here." He held the parchment out and offered a pen. "A nice clear signature, please. We wouldn't want any quibbling about the legality of the treaty, after conducting the negotiation with such scrupulous regard for the niceties."

"Niceties! Never in history has such an abomination been perpetrated!"

"Oh, treaties are always worked out this way, when it comes right down to it. We've just accelerated the process a little. Now, if you'll just sign like a good fellow, we'll be on our way. Georges will have his work cut out for him, planning how to use all this reparations money."

The Aga Kaga gnashed his teeth; Georges prodded. The Aga Kaga seized the pen and scrawled his name. Retief signed with a flourish. He tucked the treaty away in his briefcase, took out another paper.

"This is just a safe-conduct, to get us out of the door and into the car," he said. "Probably unnecessary, but it won't hurt to have it, in case you figure out some way to avoid your obligations as a host."

The Aga Kaga signed the document after another prod from Georges.

"One more paper, and I'll be into the jugular," he said.

"We're all through now," said Retief. "Stanley, we're going to have to run now. I'm going to strap up your hands and feet a trifle; it shouldn't take you more than ten minutes or so to get loose, stick a band-aid over that place on your neck, and get back in your grape-eating pose."

"My men will cut you down for the rascals you are!"

"—By that time, we'll be over the hill," Retief continued. "At full throttle, we'll be at Government House in an hour, and of course I won't waste any time transmitting the treaty to Sector HQ. And the same concern for face that keeps you from yelling for help will ensure that the details of the negotiation remain our secret."

"Treaty! That scrap of paper—"

"I confess the Corps is a little sluggish about taking action at times," Retief said, whipping a turn of silken cord around the Aga Kaga's ankles. "But once it's got signatures on a legal treaty, it's extremely stubborn about all parties' adhering to the letter. It can't afford to be otherwise, as I'm sure you'll understand." He cinched up the cord, went to work on the hands. The Aga Kaga glared at him balefully.

"To the Pit with the Corps! The ferocity of my revenge—"

"Don't talk nonsense, Stanley. There are several squadrons of Peace Enforcers cruising in the Sector just now. I'm sure you're not ready to make any historical errors by taking them on." Retief finished and stood up.

"Georges, just stuff a scarf in Stanley's mouth. I think he'd prefer to work quietly until he recovers his dignity." Retief buckled his briefcase, selected a large grape, and looked down at the Aga Kaga.

"Actually, you'll be glad you saw things our way, Stanley," he said. "You'll get all the credit for the generous settlement. Of course, it will be a striking precedent for any other negotiations that may become necessary if you get grabby on other worlds in this region. And if your advisors want to know why the sudden change of heart, just tell them you've decided to start from scratch on an unoccupied world. Mention the virtues of thrift and hard work. I'm confident you can find plenty of historical examples to support you."

"Thanks for the drink," said Georges. "Drop in on

me at Government House some time and we'll crack another bottle."

"And don't feel bad about your project's going awry," said Retief. "In the words of the Prophet, 'Stolen goods are never sold at a loss.'"

"A remarkable about-face, Retief," Magnan said. "Let this be a lesson to you. A stern Note of Protest can work wonders."

"A lot depends on the method of delivery," Retief said.

"Nonsense. I knew all along the Aga Kagans were a reasonable, peace-loving people. One of the advantages of senior rank, of course, is the opportunity to see the big picture. Why, I was saying only this morning—"

The desk screen broke into life. The mottled jowls of Under-Secretary Sternwheeler appeared.

"Magnan! I've just learned of the Flamme affair. Who's responsible?"

"Why, ah . . . I suppose that I might be said—"

"This is your work, is it?"

"Well . . . Mr. Retief did play the role of messenger—"

"Don't pass the buck, Magnan!" the Under-Secretary barked. "What the devil went on out there?"

"Why, just a routine Protest Note. Everything is quite in order—"

"Bah! Your over-zealousness has cost me dear. I was feeding Flamme to the Aga Kaga to consolidate our position of moral superiority for use as a lever in a number of important negotiations. Now they've backed out. The Aga Kaga emerges from the affair wreathed in virtue. You've destroyed a very pretty finesse in power politics, Mr. Magnan! A year's work down the drain!"

"But I thought—"

"I doubt that, Mr. Magnan. I doubt that very much!" The Under-Secretary rang off.

"This is a fine turn of events," Magnan groaned. "Retief, you know very well Protest Notes are merely intended for the historical record; no one ever takes them seriously."

"You and the Aga Kaga ought to get together," said Retief. "He's a great one for citing historical parallels. He's not a bad fellow, as a matter of fact. I have an invitation from him to visit Kaga and go mud-pig hunting. He was so impressed by Corps methods that he wants to be sure we're on his side next time. Why don't you come along?"

"Mmmm. Perhaps I should cultivate him. A few high-level contacts never do any harm. On the other hand, I understand he lives in a very loose way, feasting and merry-making. Frivolous in the extreme. No wife, I understand, but hordes of lightly-clad women about. And in that connection, the Aga Kagans have some very curious notions as to what constitutes proper hospitality to guests."

Retief rose, pulled on the powder blue cloak and black velvet gauntlets of a Career Minister.

"Don't let it worry you," he said. "You'll have a great time. And as the Aga Kaga would say, 'Ugliness is the best safeguard of virginity.'"

Truce or Consequences

First Secretary Jame Retief of the Terran Embassy pushed open the conference room door and ducked as a rain of plaster chips clattered down from the ceiling. The chandelier, a baroque construction of Yalcan glasswork, danced on its chain, fell with a crash on the center of the polished greenwood table. Across the room, drapes fluttered at glassless windows which rattled in their frames in resonance with the distant *crump-crump!* of gunfire.

"Mr. Retief, you're ten minutes late for staff meeting!" a voice sounded from somewhere. Retief stooped, glanced under the table. A huddle of eyes stared back.

"Ah, there you are, Mr. Ambassador, gentlemen," Retief greeted the Chief of Mission and his staff. "Sorry to be tardy, but there was a brisk little aerial dogfight going on just over the Zoological Gardens. The Gloys are putting up a hot resistance to the Blort landings this time."

"And no doubt you paused to hazard a wager on the outcome," Ambassador Biteworse snapped. "Your mission, sir, was to deliver a sharp rebuke to the Foreign Office regarding the latest violations of the Embassy! What have you to report?"

"The Foreign Minister sends his regrets. He was just packing up to leave. It looks as though the Blorts will be reoccupying the capital about dinnertime."

"What, again? Just as I'm on the verge of re-establishing a working rapport with His Excellency?"

"Oh, but you have a dandy rapport with His Blortian Excellency, too," the voice of Counsellor of Embassy Magnan sounded from his position well to the rear. "Remember, you were just about to get him to agree to a limited provisional preliminary symbolic partial cease-fire covering left-handed bloop guns of calibre .25 and below!"

"I'm aware of the status of the peace talks!" Biteworse cut him off. The peppery diplomat emerged, rose and dusted off the knees of his pink- and green-striped satin knee-breeches, regulation early afternoon semi-informal dress for top three graders of the *Corps Diplomatique Terrestrienne* on duty on prenuclear worlds.

"Well, I suppose we must make the best of it." He glared at his advisors as they followed his lead, ranging themselves at the table around the shattered remains of the chandelier as the chatter and rumble of gunfire continued outside. "Gentlemen, in the nine months since this Mission was accredited here on Plushnik II, we've seen the capital change hands four times. Under such conditions, the shrewdest diplomacy is powerless to bring to fruition our schemes for the pacification of the system. Nevertheless, today's despatch from Sector indicates that unless observable results are produced prior to the upcoming visit of the Inspectors, a drastic reassessment of the personnel requirements may result—and I'm sure you know what that means!"

"Ummm. We'll all be fired." Magnan brightened at a thought. "Unless, perhaps, Your Excellency points out that after all, as Chief of Mission, you're the one"—he paused as he noted the expression on the Biteworse features—"the one who suffered most," he finished weakly.

"I need not remind you," the Ambassador bored on relentlessly, "that alibis fail to impress visiting inspection teams! Results, gentlemen! Those are what count! Now, what proposals do I hear for new approaches to the problem of ending this fratricidal war which even now . . ."

The ambassadorial tones were drowned by the deep-throated snarl of a rapidly approaching internal-combustion engine. Glancing out the window, Retief saw a bright blue twin-winged aircraft coming in from the northwest at treetop level, outlined against the sky-filling disk of the planet's sister world, Plushnik I. The late-afternoon sun glinted from the craft's polished wooden propellor blades; its cowl-mounted machine guns sparkled as they hosed a stream of tracers into the street below.

"Take cover!" the Military Attaché barked and dived for the table. At the last instant, the fighter plane banked sharply up, executed a flashy slow roll and shot out of sight behind the chipped tile dome of the Temple of Erudition across the park.

"This is too much!" Biteworse shrilled from his position behind a bullet-riddled filing cabinet. "That was an open, overt attack on the Chancery! A flagrant violation of interplanetary law!"

"Actually, I think he was after a Gloian armored column in the park," Retief said. "All we got was the overkill."

"Inasmuch as you happen to be standing up, Mr. Retief," Biteworse called, "I'll thank you to put a call through on the hot line to Lib Glip at the Secretariat. I'll lodge a protest that will make his caudal cilia stand on end!"

Retief pressed buttons on the compact CDT issue field rig which had been installed to link the Embassy to the local governmental offices. Behind him, Ambassador Biteworse addressed the staff:

"Now, while it's necessary to impress on the Premier the impropriety of shooting up a Terran Mission, we must hold something in reserve for future atrocities. I think we'll play the scene using a modified Formula Nine image: Kindly Indulgence tinged with Latent Firmness, which may at any moment crystallize into Reluctant Admonition, with appropriate overtones of Gracious Condescension."

"How would you feel about a dash of Potential Impatience, with maybe just a touch of Appropriate Reprisals?" the Military Attaché suggested.

"We don't want to antagonize anyone with premature sabre-rattling, Colonel," Biteworse frowned a rebuke.

"Hmmm." Magnan pulled at his lower lip. "A masterful approach as you've outlined it, Your Excellency. But I wonder if we mightn't add just the teeniest hint of Agonizing Reappraisal?"

Biteworse nodded approvingly. "Yes—an element of the traditional might be quite in order."

A moment later the screen cleared to reveal a figure lolling in an easy chair, splendidly clad in an iridescent Bromo Seltzer blue tunic, open over an exposed framework of leathery-looking ribs from which gaily bejeweled medals dangled in rows. From the braided collar, around which a leather strap was slung supporting a pair of heavy Japanese-made binoculars, a stout neck extended, adorned along its length with varicolored patches representing auditory, olfactory, and radar organs, as well as a number of other senses the nature of which was still unclear to Terran physiologists. At the tip of the stem, a trio of heavy-lidded eyes stared piercingly at the diplomats.

"General Barf!" Biteworse exclaimed. "But I was calling the Premier! How—what—"

"Evening, Hector," the general said briskly. "I made it a point to seize the Secretariat first, this trip." He brought his vocalizing organ up on the end of its tentacle to place it near the audio pick-up. "I've been meaning to give you a ring, but I'll be damned if I could remember how to operate this thing."

"General," Biteworse cut in sharply, "I've grown accustomed to a certain amount of glass breakage during these, ah, readjustment periods, but—"

"I warned you against flimsy construction," the general countered. "And I assure you, I'm always careful to keep that sort of thing at a minimum. After all, there's no telling who'll be using the facilities next, eh?"

". . . but this is an entirely new category of outrage!" Biteworse bored on. "I've just been bombed and strafed

by one of your aircraft! The scoundrel practically flew
into the room! It's a miracle I survived!"

"Now, Hector, you know there are no such things as
miracles," the Blortian officer chuckled easily. "There's
a perfectly natural explanation of your survival, even if
it does seem a bit unreasonable at first glance."

"This is no time to haggle over metaphysics!" Biteworse shook a finger at the screen. "I demand an
immediate apology, plus assurances that nothing of the
sort will occur again until after my transfer!"

"Sorry, Hector," the general said calmly. "I'm afraid
I can't guarantee that a few wild rounds won't be
coming your way during the course of the night. This
isn't a mere commando operation this time; now that
I've secured my beachhead, I'm ready to launch my
full-scale Spring Offensive for the recovery of our glorious homeland. Jump-off will be in approximately eight
hours from now; so if you'd care to synchronize chro-
nometers—"

"An all-out offensive? Aimed at this area?"

"You have a fantastic grasp of tactics," Barf said
admiringly. "I intend to occupy the North Continent
first, after which I'll roll up the Gloian Divisions like
carpets in all directions!"

"But—my Chancery is situated squarely in the center
of the capital! You'll be carrying your assault directly
across the Embassy grounds!"

"Well, Hector, I seem to recall it was you who
selected the site for your quarters—"

"I asked for neutral ground!" Biteworse shrilled. "I
was assigned the most fought-over patch on the planet!"

"What could be more neutral than no-man's-land?"
General Barf inquired in a reasonable tone.

"Gracious," Magnan whispered to Retief. "Barf
sounds as though he may be harboring some devious
motivation behind that open countenance."

"Maybe he has a few techniques of his own," Retief
suggested. "This might be his version of the Number
Twenty-three Leashed Power gambit, with a side order
of Imminent Spontaneous Rioting."

"Heavens, do you suppose . . . ? But he hasn't had time to learn the finer nuances; he's only been in the business for a matter of months."

"Perhaps it's just a natural aptitude for diplomacy."

"That's possible; I've observed the intuitive fashion in which he distinguishes the bonded whiskey at cocktail parties."

". . . immediate cessation of hostilities!" the Ambassador was declaring. "Now, I have a new formula, based on the battle lines of the tenth day of the third week of the Moon of Limitless Imbibing, as modified by the truce team's proposals of the second week of the Moon of Ceaseless Complaining, up-dated in accordance with Corps Policy Number 746358-b, as amended—"

"That's thoughtful of you, Hector," Barf held up a tactile member in a restraining gesture. "But as it happens, inasmuch as this will be the final campaign of the War for Liberation of the Homeland, peacemaking efforts become nugatory."

"I seem to recall similar predictions at the time of the Fall Campaign, the pre-Winter Offensive, the Winter Counteroffensive, the post-Winter Anschluss, and the pre-Spring Push," Biteworse retorted. "Why don't you reconsider, General, before incurring a new crop of needless casualties?"

"Hardly needless, Hector. You need a few casualties to sharpen up discipline. And in any case, this time things will be different. I'm using a new technique of saturation leaflet bombing followed by intensive victory parades, guaranteed to crumble all resistance. If you'll just sit tight—"

"Sit tight, and have the building blown down about my ears?" Biteworse cut in. "I'm leaving for the provinces at once—"

"I think that would be unwise, Hector, with conditions so unsettled. Better stay where you are. In fact, you may consider that an order, under the provisions of martial Law. If this seems a trifle harsh, remember, it's all in a good cause. And now I have to be moving along, Hector. I have a new custom-built VIP-model armored car with air and music that I'm dying to test drive. Ta-ta." The screen blanked abruptly.

"This is fantastic!" The Ambassador stared around at his staff for corroboration of his assessment of the situation. "In the past, the opposing armies have at least made a pretense of respecting diplomatic privilege; now they're openly proposing to make us the center of a massive combined land, sea, and air strike!"

"We'll have to contact Lib Glip at once," the Political Officer said urgently. "Perhaps we can convince him that the capital should be declared an open city!"

"Sound notion, Oscar," the Ambassador agreed. He mopped at his forehead with a large monogrammed tissue. "Retief, keep trying until you reach him."

Half a minute later, the circular visage of the Gloian Foreign Minister appeared on the screen, against a background of passing shopfronts seen through a car window. Two bright black eyes peered through a tangle of thick tendrils not unlike a tangerine-dyed oil mop capped by a leather Lindy cap with goggles.

"Hi, fellows," he greeted the Terrans airily. "Sorry to break our lunch date, Biteworse, but you know how foreign affairs are: Here today and gone to dinner, as the saying goes, I think. But never mind that. What I really called you about was—"

"It was I who called *you!*" the Ambassador broke in. "See here, Lib Glip; a highly placed confidential source has advised me that the capital is about to become the objective of an all-out Blort assault. Now, I think it only fair that your people should relinquish the city peaceably, so as to avoid a possible interplanetary incident—"

"Oh, that big-mouth Barf has been at you again, eh? Well, relax, fellows; everything's going to be OK. I have a surprise in store for those indigo indigents."

"You've decided to propose a unilateral cease-fire?" Biteworse blurted. "A munificent gesture—"

"Are you kidding, Biteworse? Show the white feather while those usurpers are still in full possession of our hallowed mother world?" The Gloian leaned into the screen. "I'll let you in on a little secret. The retreat is just a diversionary measure to suck Barf into over-extending his lines. As soon as he's poured all his available reinforcements into this dry run—whammo! I hit him with a nifty hidden-ball play around left end and land a massive expeditionary force on Blort! At one blow, I'll regain the cradle of the Gloian race and end the war once and for all!"

"I happen to be directly in the path of your proposed dry run!" Biteworse keened. "I remind you, sir, this compound is neither Gloian nor Blortian soil, but Terran!" A patch of plaster fell with a clatter as if to emphasize the point.

"Oh, we won't actually bombard the Chancery it-self—at least not intentionally—unless, that is, Barf's troops try to use it as a sanctuary. I suggest you go down into the subbasement; some of you may come through with hardly a scratch."

"Wait! We'll evacuate! I hereby call upon you for safe-conduct—"

"Sorry; I'll be too busy checking out on the controls of my new hand-tooled pursuit craft to arrange trans-port to the South Pole just now. However, after the offensive—"

"You'll be manning a fighter?"

"Yes, indeed! A beaut. Everything on it but a flush john. I handle the portfolio of Defense Minister in the War Cabinet personally, you know. And a leader's place is with his troops at the front. Maybe not actually *at* the front," he amended. "But in the general area, you know."

"Isn't that a little dangerous?"

"Not if my G-2 reports are on the ball. Besides, I said this was an all-out effort."

"But that's what you said the last time, when you were learning how to operate that leather-upholstered tank you had built!"

"True—but this time it will be all-out all-out. And now I have to scoot or I'll have to flip my own prop.

You won't hear from me again until after the victory, since I'm imposing total communications silence now for the duration. Chou." The alien broke the connection.

"Great galloping Galaxies." Biteworse sank into a plaster-dusted chair. "This is catastrophic! The Embassy will be devastated, and we'll be buried in the rubble."

There was a discreet tap at the conference room door; it opened and an apologetic junior officer peered in. "Ah . . . Mr. Ambassador; a person is here, demanding to see you at once. I've explained to him—"

"Step aside, junior," a deep voice growled. A short, thick-set man in wrinkled blues thrust through the door.

"I've got an Operational Instantaneous Utter Top Secret despatch for somebody." He stared around at the startled diplomats. "Who's in charge?"

"I am," Biteworse barked. "These are my staff, Captain. What's this despatch all about?"

"Beats me. I'm Merchant Service. Some Navy brass hailed me and asked me to convoy it in. Said it was important." He extracted a pink emergency message form from a pouch and passed it across to Biteworse.

"Captain, perhaps you're unaware that I have two emergencies and a crisis on my hands already!" Biteworse looked at the envelope indignantly.

The sailor glanced around the room. "From the looks of this place, I'd say you had a problem, all right, Mister," he agreed. "I ran into a few fireworks myself, on the way in here. Looks like Chinese New Year out there."

"What's the nature of the new emergency?" Magnan craned to read the paper in Biteworse's hand.

"Gentlemen, this is the end," Biteworse said hollowly, looking up from the message form. "They'll be here first thing in the morning."

"My, just in time to catch the action," Magnan said.

"Don't sound so complacent, you imbecile!" Biteworse yelped. "That will be the final straw! An inspection team, here to assess the effectiveness of my pacification efforts, will be treated to the sight of a full-scale battle raging about my very doorstep!"

"Maybe we could tell them it's just the local Water Festival—"

"Silence!" Biteworse screeched. "Time is running out, sir! Unless we find a solution before dawn our careers will end in ignominy."

"If you don't mind sharing space with a cargo of Abalonian Glue-fish eggs, you can come with me," the merchantman offered over a renewed rumble of artillery. "It will only be for a couple of months, until I touch down at Adobe. I hear they've got a borax mining camp there where you can work out your board until the Spring barge convoy shows up."

"Thank you," Biteworse said coldly. "I shall keep your offer in mind."

"Don't wait too long. I'm leaving as soon as I've off-loaded."

"All right, gentlemen," the Ambassador said in an ominous tone as the captain departed in search of coffee. "I'm ordering the entire staff to the cellars for the duration of the crisis. No one is to attempt to leave the building, of course. We must observe Barf's curfew. We'll be burning the midnight fluorescents tonight— and if by sunrise we haven't evolved a brilliant scheme for ending the war, you may all compose suitable letters of resignation—those of you who survive!"

2

In the corridor, Retief encountered his local clerk-typist, just donning a floppy beret dyed a sour orange as an expression of his political alignment.

"Hi, Mr. Retief," he greeted the diplomat glumly. "I was just leaving. I guess you know the Blorts are back in town."

"So it appears, Dil Snop. How about a stirrup cup before you go?"

"Sure; they won't have the streets cordoned off for a while yet."

In Retief's office, the clerk parked his bulging brief-case and accepted a three-finger shot of black Bacchus brandy, which he carefully poured into a pocket like a miniature marsupial's pouch.

He heaved a deep sigh. "Say, Mr. Retief, when that Blue incompetent shows up, tell him not to mess with the files. I've just gotten them straightened out from the last time."

"I'll mention your desires," Retief said. "You know, Snop, it seems strange to me that you Gloians haven't been able to settle your differences with the Blorts peaceably. This skirmishing back and forth has been going on for quite a while now, with no decisive results."

"Hundreds of years, I guess," Snop nodded. "But how can you settle your differences with a bunch of treacherous, lawless, immoral, conscienceless, crooked, planet-stealing rogues like those Blorts?" Dil Snop looked amazed, an effect he achieved by rapidly inter-twining the tendrils around his eyes.

"They seem harmless enough to me," Retief commented. "Just what did they do that earns them that description?"

"What haven't they done?" Dil Snop waved a jointed member. "Look at this office—a diplomatic mission! Bullet holes all over the place, shrapnel scars on the walls—"

"The shrapnel scars were made by your boys in orange the last time they took over," Retief reminded him.

"Oh. Well, these little accidents will happen in the course of foiling the enemy's efforts to ravish our foster home—and this, mind you, sir, after they've invaded the hallowed soil of Plushnik I, swiped the entire planet, and left us to scrabble for ourselves on this lousy world!"

"Seems like a pretty fair planet to me," Retief said. "And I was under the impression this was your home-land."

"Heck, no! This place? Pah! That"—Dil Snop

pointed through window at the looming disk of the nearby sister planet—"is my beloved ancestral stamping ground."

"Ever been there?"

"I've been along on a few invasions, during summer vacations. Just between us," he lowered his voice, "it's a little too cold and wet for my personal taste."

"How did the Blorts manage to steal it?"

"Carelessness on our part," Snop conceded. "Our forces were all over here, administering a drubbing to them, and they treacherously slipped over behind our backs and entrenched themselves."

"What about the wives and little ones?"

"Oh, an exchange was worked out. After all, they'd left their obnoxious brats and shrewish mates here on Plushnik II."

"What started the feud in the first place?"

"Beats me. I guess that's lost in the mists of antiquity or something." The Gloian put down his glass and rose. "I'd better be off now, Mr. Retief. My reserve unit's been called up, and I'm due at the armory in half an hour."

"Well, take care of yourself, Dil Snop. I'll be seeing you soon, I expect."

"I wouldn't guarantee it. Old Lib Glip's taken personal command, and he burns troops like joss sticks." Snop tipped his beret and went out. A moment later, the narrow face of Counsellor Magnan appeared at the door.

"Come along, Retief. The Ambassador wants to say a few words to the staff; everyone's to assemble in the commissary in five minutes."

"I take it he feels that darkness and solitude will be conducive to creative thinking."

"Don't disparage the efficacy of the Deep-think technique. Why, I've already evolved half a dozen proposals for dealing with the situation."

"Will any of them work?"

Magnan looked grave. "No—but they'll look quite impressive in my personnel file during the hearings."

"A telling point, Mr. Magnan. Well, save a seat for me in a secluded corner. I'll be along as soon as I've run down a couple of obscure facts."

Retrief employed the next quarter hour in leafing through back files of classified despatch binders. As he finished, a Blort attired in shapeless blues and a flak helmet thrust his organ cluster through the door.

"Hello, Mr. Retief," he said listlessly. "I'm back."

"So you are, Kark," Retief greeted the lad. "You're early. I didn't expect you until after breakfast."

"I got shoved on the first convoy; as soon as we landed I sneaked off to warn you. Things are going to be hot tonight."

"So I hear, Kark—" A deafening explosion just outside bathed the room in green light. "Is that a new medal you're wearing?"

"Yep." The youth fingered the turquoise ribbon anchored to his third rib. "I got it for service above and beyond the call of nature." He went to the table at the side of the room, opened the drawer.

"Just what I expected," he said. "That Gloian creep didn't leave any cream for the coffee. I always leave a good supply, but does he have the same consideration? Not him. Just like an Oranger."

"Kark, what do you know about the beginning of the war?"

"Eh?" The new clerk looked up from his coffee preparations. "Oh, it has something to do with the founding fathers. Care for a cup? Black, of course."

"No thanks. How does it feel to be back on good old Plushnik II again?"

"Good old? Oh, I see what you mean. OK, I guess. Kind of hot and dry, though." The building trembled to a heavy shock. The snarl of heavy armor passing in the street shook the pictures on the walls.

"Well, I'd better be getting to work, sir. I think I'll start with the Breakage Reports. We're three invasions behind."

"Better skip the paperwork for now, Kark. See if you can round up a few members of the sweeping staff and get some of this glass cleaned up. We're expecting several varieties of VIP about daybreak, and we wouldn't want them to get the impression we throw wild parties."

"You're not going out, sir?" Kark looked alarmed. "Better not try it; there's a lot of loose metal flying around out there, and it's going to get worse!"

"I thought I'd take a stroll over toward the Temple of Higher Learning."

"But—that's forbidden territory to any non-Plushnik. . . ." Kark looked worried, as evidenced by the rhythmic waving of his eyes.

Retief nodded. "I suppose it's pretty well guarded?"

"Not during the battle. The Gloians have called up everybody but the inmates of the amputees ward. They're planning another of their half-baked counter-invasions. But Mr. Retief—if you're thinking what I think you're thinking, I don't think—"

"I wouldn't think of it, Kark." Retief gave the Blortian a cheery wave and went out into the deserted hall.

3

In the twilit street, Retief glanced up at the immense orb of Plushnik I, barely a thousand miles distant, a celestial relief map occluding half the visible sky. A slim crescent of the nearby world sparkled in full sunlight; the remainder was a pattern of lighted cities gleaming in the murk of the shadow cast as its twin transited between it and the primary. The route of the Blortian invasion fleet was clearly visible as a line of tiny, winking fires stretching in a loose catenary curve from the major staging areas on the neighbor world across the not-quite-airless void. As Retief watched, the giant disk sank visibly toward the horizon, racing in its two-hour orbit around the system's common center.

A quarter of a mile distant across the park, the high, peach-colored dome of the university library pushed up into the evening sky. The darting forms of fighter planes were silhouetted beyond it, circling each other with the agility of combative gnats. At the far end of the street, a column of gaily caparisoned Gloian armored cars raced past, in hot pursuit of a troop of light tanks flying the Blort pennant. The sky to the north and west winked and flickered to the incessant dueling of Blue and Orange artillery. There was a sharp, descending whistle as a badly aimed shell dropped half a block away, sending a gout of pavement chips hurtling skyward. Retief waited until the air was momentarily clear of flying fragments to cross the street and head across the park.

The high walls of the Center of Learning, inset with convoluted patterns in dark-colored mosaic tile, reared up behind a dense barrier of wickedly thorned shark trees. Retief used a small pocket beamer to slice a narrow path through into the grounds, where a flat expanse of deep green lawn extended a hundred yards to the windowless structure. Retief crossed it, skirted a neatly trimmed rose bed where a stuffed dustowl lay staring up into the night with red glass eyes. Above, a ragged scar showed in the brickwork of the sacrosanct edifice. There were dense vines on the wall at that point.

It was an easy two-minute climb to the opening, beyond which shattered glass cases and a stretch of hall were visible. Retief gave a last glance at the searchlight-swept sky and stepped inside. Dim light glowed in the distance. He moved silently along the corridor, pushed through a door into a vast room filled with racks containing the fan-shaped books favored by both Gloians and Blorts. As he did, a light stabbed out and flicked across his chest, fixed on the center button of his dark green early-evening blazer.

"Don't come any farther," a reedy voice quavered. "I've got this light right in your eye, and a bloop gun aimed at where I estimate your vitals to be."

"The effect is blinding," Retief said. "I guess you've got me." Beyond the feeble glow, he made out the fragile figure of an aged Gloian draped in zebra-striped academic robes.

"I suppose you sneaked in here to make off with a load of Plushniki historical treasures," the oldster charged.

"Actually I was just looking for a shady spot to load my Brownie," Retief said soothingly.

"Ah-hah, photographing Cultural Secrets, eh? That's two death penalties you've earned so far. Make a false move, and it's three and out."

"You're just too sharp for me, Professor," Retief conceded.

"Well, I do my job." The ancient snapped off the light. "I think we can do without this. It gives me a splitting flurgache. Now, you better come along with me to the bomb shelter. Those rascally Blorts have been dropping shells into the Temple grounds, and I wouldn't want you to get hurt before the execution."

"Certainly. By the way, since I'm to be nipped in the bud for stealing information, I wonder if it would be asking too much to get a few answers before I go?"

"Hmmm. Seems only fair. What would you like to know?"

"A number of things," Retief said. "To start with, how did this war begin in the first place?"

The curator lowered his voice. "You won't tell anybody?"

"It doesn't look as though I'll have the chance."

"That's true. Well, it seems it was something like this . . ."

4

". . . and they've been at it ever since," the ancient Gloian concluded his recital. "Under the circumstances, I guess you can see that the idea of a cessation of hostilities is unthinkable."

"This has been very illuminating," Retief agreed. "By the way, during the course of your remarks, I happened to think of a couple of little errands that need attending to. I wonder if we couldn't postpone the execution until tomorrow?"

"Well—it's a little unusual. But with all this shooting going on outside, I don't imagine we could stage a suitable ceremony in any case. I suppose I could accept your parole; you seem like an honest chap, for a foreigner. But be back by lunchtime, remember. I hate these last-minute noose adjustments." His hand came up suddenly; there was a sharp *zopp!* and a glowing light bulb across the room *poof*ed and died.

"All the same, it's a good thing you asked," the old curator blew across the end of his pistol barrel and tucked the weapon away.

"I'll be here," Retief assured the elder. "Now if you'd just show me the closest exit, I'd better be getting started."

The Gloian tottered along a narrow passage, opened a plank door letting onto the side garden. "Nice night," he opined, looking at the sky where the glowing vapor trails of fighter planes looped across the constellations. "You couldn't ask for a better one for—say, what *are* these errands you've got to run?"

"Cultural secrets," Retief laid a finger across his lips and stepped out into the night.

It was a brisk ten-minute walk to the Embassy garages, where the small official fleet of high-powered CDT vehicles were stored. Retief selected a fast-moving one-man courier boat; a moment later the lift deposited the tiny craft on the roof. He checked over the instruments, took a minute to tune the tight-beam finder to the personal code of the Gloian Chief of State, and lifted off.

5

Rocketing along at fifteen hundred feet, Retief had a superb view of the fireworks below. The Blortian beachhead north of town had been expanded into a wide curve of armored units poised ready for the dawn assault that was to sweep the capital clear. To the west, Gloian columns were massing for the counterstrike. At the point of juncture of the proposed assault lines, the lights of the Terran Embassy glowed forlornly.

Retief corrected course a degree and a half, still climbing rapidly, watching the quivering needles of the seek-and-find beam. The emerald and ruby glow of a set of navigation lights appeared a mile ahead, moving erratically at an angle to his course. He boosted the small flier to match altitudes, swung in on the other craft's tail. Close now, he could discern the bright-doped fabric-covered wings, the taut rigging wires, the brilliant orange blazon of the Gloian national colors on the fuselage, above the ornate personal emblem of Marshal Lib Glip. He could even make out the goggled features of the warrior Premier gleaming faintly in the greenish light from the instrument faces, his satsuma-toned scarf streaming bravely behind him.

Retief maneuvered until he was directly above the unsuspecting craft, then peeled off and hurtled past it on the left close enough to rock the light airplane violently in the buffeting slip stream. He came around in a hairpin turn, shot above the biplane as it banked right, did an abrupt left to pass under it, and saw a row of stars appear across the plastic canopy beside his head as the Gloian ace turned inside him, catching him with a burst from his machine guns.

Retief put the nose of the flier down, dived clear of the stream of lead, swung back and up in a tight curve, rolled out on the airplane's tail. Lib Glip, no mean pilot, put his ship through a series of vertical eights, snaprolls, immelmans, and falling leaves, to no avail. Retief held the courier boat glued to his tail almost close enough to brush the wildly wig-wagging control surfaces.

After fifteen minutes of frantic evasive tactics, the Gloian ship settled down to a straight speed run. Retief loafed alongside, pacing the desperate flier. When Lib Glip looked across at him, Retief made a downward motion of his hand and pointed at the ground. Then he eased over, placed himself directly above the bright-painted plane, and edged downward.

Below, he could see Lib Glip's face, staring upward. He lowered the boat another foot. The embattled Premier angled his plane downward. Retief stayed with him, forcing him down until the craft was racing along barely above the tops of the celery-shaped trees. A clearing appeared ahead. Retief dropped until his keel almost scraped the fuel tank atop Lib Glip's upper wing. The Gloian, accepting the inevitable, throttled back, settled his ship into a bumpy landing, rolled to a stop just short of a fence. Retief dropped in and skidded to a halt beside him.

The enraged Premier was already out of his cockpit, waving a large clip-fed hand gun, as Retief popped the hatch of the boat.

"What's the meaning of this?" the Gloian yelled. "Who are you! How . . ." he broke off. "Hey, aren't you What's-his-name, from the Terry Embassy?"

"Correct," Retief nodded. "I congratulate Your Excellency on your acute memory."

"What's the idea of this piece of unparalleled audacity?" the Gloian leader barked. "Don't you know there's a war on? I was in the middle of leading a victorious air assault on those Blortian blue-bellies—"

"Really? I had the impression your squadrons were several miles to the north, tangling with an impressive armada of Blortian bombers and what seemed to be a pretty active fighter cover."

"Well, naturally I have to stand off at a reasonable distance in order to get the Big Picture," Lib Glip explained. "That still doesn't tell me why a Terry diplomat had the unvarnished gall to interfere with my movements! I've got a good mind to blast you full of holes and leave the explanations to my Chief of Propaganda!"

"I wouldn't," Retief suggested. "This little thing in my hand is a tight-beam blaster—not that there's any need for such implements among friendly associates."

"Armed diplomacy?" Lib Glip choked. "I've never heard of such a thing!"

"Oh, I'm off duty," Retief said. "This is just a personal call. There's a little favor I'd like to ask of you."

"A . . . favor? What is it?"

"I'd like a ride in your airplane."

"You mean you forced me to the ground just to . . . to . . ."

"Right. And there's not much time, so I think we'd better be going."

"I've heard of airplane fanciers, but this is fantastic! Still, now that you're here, I may as well point out to you she has a sixteen-cylinder V-head mill, swinging a twenty-four lamination sword-wood prop, synchronized 9mm lead-spitters, twin spotlights, low-pressure tires, foam-rubber seats, real instruments—no idiot lights—and a ten-coat hand-rubbed lacquer job. Sharp, eh? And wait till you see the built-in bar."

"A magnificent craft, Your Excellency," Retief admired the machine. "I'll take the rear cockpit and tell you which way to steer."

"You'll tell *me*—"

"I have the blaster, remember?"

Lib Glip grunted and climbed into his seat. Retief strapped in behind him. The Premier started up, taxied to the far end of the field, gunned the engine, and lifted off into the tracer-streaked sky.

6

"That's him," Retief pointed to a lone vehicle perched on a hilltop above a lively fire-fight, clearly visible now against a landscape bathed in the bluish light of the newly risen crescent of Plushnik I, the lower curve of which was at the horizon, the upper almost at Zenith.

"See here, this is dangerous," Lib Glip called over the whine of air thrumming the rigging wires as the plane glided down in a wide spiral. "That car packs plenty of firepower, and—" he broke off and banked sharply as vivid flashes of blue light stuttered suddenly from below. The brilliant light of Plushnik I glinted from the armored car's elevated guns as they tracked the descending craft.

"Put a short burst across his bow," Retief said. "But be careful not to damage him."

"Why, that's Barf's personal car!" the Gloian burst out. "I can't fire on him, or he might—that is, we have a sort of gentleman's agreement—"

"Better do it," Retief said, watching the stream of tracers from below arc closer as Barf found the range. "Apparently he feels that at this range, the agreement's not in effect."

Lib Glip angled the nose of the craft toward the car, and activated the twin lead-spitters. A row of pockmarks appeared in the turf close beside the car as the plane shot low over it.

"That'll teach him to shoot without looking," Lib Glip commented.

"Circle back and land," Retief called. The Premier grumbled but complied. The plane came to a halt a hundred feet from the armored car which turned to pin the craft down in the beams of its headlights. Lib Glip rose, holding both hands overhead, and jumped down.

"I hope you realize what you're doing," he said bitterly. "Forcing me to place myself in the hands of this barbarian is flagrant interference in Plushniki internal affairs! So here, if he's been crooked enough to offer you a bribe, I give you my word as a statesman that I'm crookeder. I'll up his offer—"

"Now, now, Your Excellency, this is merely a friendly get-together. Let's go over and relieve the general's curiosity before he decides to clear his guns again."

As Retief and the Gloian came up, a hatch opened at the top of the heavy car and the ocular stalk of the Blortian generalissimo emerged cautiously. The three eyes looked over the situation; then the medal-hung chest of the officer appeared.

"Here, what's all this shooting?" he inquired in an irritated tone. "Is that you, Glip? Come out to arrange surrender terms, I suppose. Could have gotten yourself hurt—"

"Surrender my maternal great-aunt Bunny!" the

Gloian shrilled. "I was abducted by armed force and brought here at gunpoint!"

"Eh?" Barf peered at Retief. "I thought you'd brought Retief along as an impartial witness to the very liberal amnesty terms I'm prepared to offer—"

"Gentlemen, if you'll suspend hostilities for just a moment or two," Retief put in, "I believe I can explain the purpose of this meeting. I confess the delivery of invitations may have been a trifle informal, but when you hear the news, I'm sure you'll agree it was well worth the effort."

"What news?" both combatants echoed.

Retief drew a heavy, fan-shaped paper from an inner pocket. "The war news," he said crisply. "I happened to be rummaging through some old papers, and came across a full account of the story behind the present conflict. I'm going to give it to the press first thing in the morning, but I felt you gentlemen should get the word first, so that you can realign your war aims accordingly."

"Realign?" Barf said cautiously.

"Story?" Lib Glip queried.

"I assume, of course, that you gentlemen are aware of the facts of history?" Retief paused, paper in hand.

"Why, ah, as a matter of fact—" Barf said.

"I don't believe I actually, er . . ." the Gloian Premier harrumphed.

"But of course, we Blort don't need to delve into the past to find cause for the present crusade for the restoration of the national honor," Barf pointed out.

"Gloy has plenty of up-to-date reasons for her determination to drive the invaders from the fair soil of her home planet," Lib Glip snorted.

"Of course—but this will inspire the troops," Retief pointed out. "Imagine how morale will zoom, Mr. Premier," he addressed the Gloian, "when it becomes known that the original Blortians were a group of government employees from Old Plushnik, en route to the new settlements here on Plushnik I and II."

"Government employees, eh?" Barf frowned. "I

suppose they were high-ranking civil servants, that sort of thing?"

"No," Retief demurred. "As a matter of fact, they were prison guards, with a rank of GB 19."

"Prison guards? GB 19?" Barf growled. "Why, that was the lowest rank in the entire Old Plushniki government payroll!"

"Certainly there can be no charge of snobbery there," Retief said in tones of warm congratulation.

A choking sound issued from Lib Glip's speaking aperture. "Pardon my mirth," he gasped. "But after all the tripe we've heard—eek-eek—about the glorious past of Blort . . ."

"And that brings us to the Gloians," Retief put in smoothly. "They, it appears, were traveling on the same vessel at the time of the outbreak—or should I say break-out?"

"Same vessel?"

Retief nodded. "After all, the guards had to have something to guard."

"You mean . . . ?"

"That's right," Retief said cheerfully. "The Gloian founding fathers were a consignment of criminals sentenced to transportation for life."

General Barf uttered a loud screech of amusement and slapped himself on the thigh.

"I don't know why I didn't guess that intuitively!" he chortled. "How right you were, Retief, to dig out this charming intelligence!"

"See here!" Lib Glip shrilled. "You can't publish defamatory information of that sort! I'll take it to court—"

"And give the whole Galaxy a good laugh over the breakfast trough," Barf agreed. "A capital suggestion, my dear Glip!"

"Anyway, I don't believe it! It's a tissue of lies! A bunch of malarkey! A dirty, lousy falsehood and a base canard!"

"Look for yourself." Retief offered the documents.

Lib Glip fingered the heavy parchment, peered at the complicated characters.

"It seems to be printed in Old Plushnik," he grumbled. "I'm afraid I never went in for dead languages."

"General?" Retief handed over the papers. Barf glanced at them and handed them back, still chuckling. "No, sorry, I'll have to take your word for it—and I do."

"Fine, then," Retief said. "There's just one other little point. You gentlemen have been invading and counterinvading now for upward of two centuries. Naturally, in that length of time the records have grown a trifle confused. However, I believe both sides are in agreement that the original home planets have changed hands, and that the Blortians are occupying Gloy territory while the Gloians have taken over the original Blort world."

Both belligerents nodded, one smiling, one glumly.

"That's nearly correct," Retief said, "with just one minor correction. It isn't the planets that have changed hands; it's the identities of the participants in the war."

"Eh?"

"What did you say?"

"It's true, gentlemen," Retief said solemnly. "You, and your troops, General, are descendants of the original Gloians; and your people," he inclined his head to the Gloian Premier, "inherit the mantle of Blortship."

7

"But this is ghastly," General Barf groaned. "I've devoted half a lifetime to instilling a correct attitude toward Gloians in my chaps. How can I face them now!"

"Me, a Blort?" Lib Glip shuddered. "Still," he said as if to himself, "we *were* the guards, not the prisoners. I suppose on the whole we'll be able to console ourselves with the thought that we aren't representatives of the criminal class—"

"Criminal class!" Barf snorted. "By Pud, sir, I'd rather trace my descent from an honest victim of the

venal lackeys of a totalitarian regime than to claim
kinship with a pack of hireling turnkeys!"

"Lackeys, eh? I suppose that's what a pack of butter-
fingered pickpockets would think of a decent servant of
law and order!"

"Now, gentlemen, I'm sure these trifling differences
can be settled peaceably—"

"Ah-hah, so *that's* it!" Barf crowed. "You've dug
the family skeletons out of the closet in the mistaken
belief it would force us to suspend hostilities!"

"By no means, General," Retief said blandly. "Naturally, you'll want to exchange supplies of propaganda
leaflets and go right on with the crusade. But of course
you'll have to swap planets, too."

"How's that?"

"Certainly. The CDT can't stand by and see the
entire populations of two worlds condemned to live
on in exile on a foreign planet. I'm sure I can arrange
for a fleet of Corps transports to handle the transfer
of population—"

"Just a minute," Lib Glip cut in. "You mean you're
going to repatriate all us, er, Blortians to Plushnik I,
and give Plushnik II to these rascally, ah, Gloians?"

"Minus the slanted adjectives, a very succinct state-
ment of affairs."

"Now, just a minute," Barf put in. "You don't expect me to actually settle down on this dust-ball full
time, do you? With *my* sinus condition?"

"Me, live in the midst of *that* swamp?" Lib Glip
hooked a thumb skyward at the fully risen disk of the
gibbous planet, where rivers and mountains, continents
and seas gleamed cheerfully, reflecting the rays of the
distant sun. "Why, my asthma would kill me in three
weeks! That's why I've alway stuck to lightning raids
instead of long, drawn-out operations!"

"Well, gentlemen, the CDT certainly doesn't wish
to be instrumental in undermining the health of two
such cooperative statesmen. . . ."

"Ah . . . how do you mean, cooperative?" Barf
voiced the question cautiously.

"You know how it is, General," Retief said. "When one has impatient superiors breathing down one's neck, it's a little hard to really achieve full rapport with even the most laudable aspirations of others. However, if Ambassador Biteworse were in a position to show the inspectors a peaceful planet in the morning, it might very well influence him to defer the evacuation until further study of the question."

"But . . . my two-pronged panzer thrust," the general faltered. "The crowning achievement of my military career . . . !"

"My magnificently coordinated one-two counterstrike!" Lib Glip wailed. "It cost me two months' golf to work out those logistics!"

"I might even go so far as to hazard a guess," Retief pressed on, "that in the excitement of the announcement of the armistice, I might even forget to publish my historical findings."

"Hmmm," Barf eyed his colleague. "It might be a trifle tricky, at that, to flog up the correct degree of anti-Blort enthusiasm on such short notice."

"Yes; I can foresee a certain amount of residual sympathy for Gloian institutions lingering on for quite some time," Lib Glip nodded.

"I'd still have the use of my car, of course," the general mused. "As well as my personal submarine, my plushed-up transport, and my various copters, hoppers, unicycles, and sedan chairs for use on rough terrain."

"I suppose it would be my duty to keep the armed forces at the peak of condition with annual War Games," Lib Glip commented. He glanced at the general. "In fact, we might even work out some sort of scheme for joint maneuvers, just to keep the recruits sharpened up."

"Not a bad idea, Glip. I might try for the single-engine pursuit trophy myself."

"Ha! Nothing you've got can touch my little beauty when it comes to close-in combat work."

"I'm sure we can work out the details later, gentlemen," Retief said. "I must be getting back to the Embassy now. I hope your formal joint announcement will be along well before presstime."

"Well . . ." Barf looked at Lib Glip. "Under the circumstances . . ."

"I suppose we can work out something," the latter assented glumly.

"I'll give you a lift back in my car, Retief," General Barf offered. "Just wait till you see how she handles on flat ground, my boy. . . ."

8

In the pink light of dawn, Ambassador Biteworse and his staff waited on the breeze-swept ramp to greet the party of portly officials descending from the Corps lighter.

"Well, Hector," the senior member of the inspection team commented, looking around the immaculate environs of the port. "It looks as though perhaps some of those rumors we heard as to a snag in the disarmament talks were a trifle exaggerated."

Biteworse smiled blandly. "A purely routine affair. It was merely necessary for me to drop a few words in certain auditory organs, and the rest followed naturally. There aren't many of these local chieftains who can stand up to the veiled hint of a Biteworse."

"Actually, I think it's about time we began considering you for a more substantive post, Hector. I've had my eye on you for quite some time. . . ." The great men moved away, fencing cautiously. Beside Retief, a tiny, elderly local in striped robes shook his head sadly.

"That was a dirty trick, Retief, getting a pardon directly from young Lib Glip. I don't get much excitement over there in the stacks, you know."

"Things will be better from now on," Retief assured the oldster. "I think you can expect to see the library opened to the public in the near future."

"Oh, boy," the curator exclaimed. "Just what I've been wishing for, for years now! Plenty of snazzy young co-eds coming in, eager to butter an old fellow up in return for a guaranteed crib sheet! Thanks, lad! I can see brighter days a-coming!" He hurried away.

"Retief," Magnan plucked at his sleeve. "I've heard a number of fragmentary rumors regarding events leading up to the truce; I trust your absence from the Chancery for an hour or two early in the evening was in no way connected with the various kidnappings, thefts, trespasses, assaults, blackmailings, breakings and enterings, and other breaches of diplomatic usage said to have occurred."

"Mr. Magnan, what a suggeston." Retief took out a fan-folded paper, began tearing it into strips.

"Sorry, Retief. I should have known better. By the way, isn't that an Old Plushniki manuscript you're destroying?"

"This? Why, no. It's an old Chinese menu I came across tucked in the classified despatch binder." He dropped the scraps in a refuse bin.

"Oh. Well, why don't you join me in a quick bite before this morning's briefing for the inspectors? The Ambassador plans to give them his standard five-hour introductory chat, followed by a quick run-through of the voucher files. . . ."

"No thanks. I have an appointment with Lib Glip to check out in one of his new model pursuit ships. It's the red one over there, fresh from the factory."

"Well, I suppose you have to humor him, inasmuch as he's premier." Magnan cocked an eye at Retief. "I confess I don't understand how it is you get on such familiar terms with these bigwigs, restricted as your official duties are to preparation of reports in quintuplicate."

"I think it's merely a sort of informal manner I adopt in meeting them," Retief said. He waved and headed across the runway to where the little ship waited, sparkling in the morning sun.

The Secret

"Tell him!" Ambassador Smallfrog said in a choked voice. "Tell his Excellency to get down off that chandelier at once!" He plucked at Magnan's sleeve appealingly. "But in a nice way, of course," he added.

Magnan nodded and rose briskly, glancing up in surprise at the amoeboid form of the Minister of Foreign Affairs of Grote, richly garbed in scarlet satin and gold braid, which clung to the ornate crystal lighting fixture above the table where the four diplomats had been lunching on the Embassy terrace.

"Heavens! How did he get up there?" he murmured. "He didn't seem the athletic type. Retief!" He whispered sharply to the broad-shouldered diplomat seated to his right. "Do something! But use no force, of course."

Retief rose, studying the manner in which the short, digitless limbs of the alien were entwined among the branching arms of the chandelier. He drew on his Jorgenson cigar to bring it to a cherry-red glow, then held the hot end close to the purple-pink hide of the alien's exposed elbow, or possibly knee. The limb, immediately contracted, scrambling for new purchase farther from the source of discomfort. Retief continued to apply heat to exposed portions of the Grotian's hide until the alien had retracted his pseudopods and contracted his bulk into a gourd-shaped form dangling by a single jointless limb and quivering nervously.

"Dearie me, Retief," Magnan chirped. "I'm not at all sure Terran-Grote relations are being cemented by your somewhat drastic technique. You'd better let well enough alone now."

"Actually, I haven't touched him," Retief said. "And I doubt that his Excellency would pay any attention to a simple request. He seems pretty much wrapped up in himself."

"Retief, shhh," Magnan interposed hastily, "that came very close to being a racially biased remark!"

"I'm not sure where he keeps his IQ," Retief reassured his senior, "but by now it must be squeezed pretty flat."

"Retief, hush! He's listening—see how he has his ear cocked."

"Actually," Retief said, studying the puckered organ on the undercurve of the alien's bulk, "I think you'll find that's more of a navel."

"Correct, my boy," said a mellow voice which seemed to issue from the general direction of the dangling diplomat. "Pray excuse my probably unconventional act in retreating to this convenient perch. I'll be glad to descend now, since it seems Freddy's upset about it."

"But Mr. Minister, we heard you didn't speak Terry," Magnan wailed. "That's why Ambassador Smallfrog has been communicating with you in sign-language all week."

"Indeed? I assumed poor Freddy was merely afflicted of Oompah, praised be his name."

Magnan resumed his seat and picked at his shrimp cocktail, which consisted of a glass goblet half full of ketchup, with half-a-dozen medium-sized boiled shrimp arranged about its rim. He glanced up as the alien official, once again equipped with various arms and legs, all neatly fitted to the appropriate sleeves and legs of his Terran-tailored satin finery, settled himself in his seat.

"Why, Mr. Ambassador, you fair gave me a turn," Magnan exclaimed. "I didn't even notice you climbing down. In which connection," he went on, "may I inquire just why Your Excellency found it expedient to take up a position on the chandelier just at that time?"

"Doubtless bad protocol on my part, Ben," Foreign Minister D'ong replied apologetically. "But I was quite upset to find that a number of small innocent creatures had crept into my pudding and expired there. Alas, how melancholy." He dabbed with his CDT-crested paper napkin at an eye-like organ from which a large tear was welling.

"Pudding?" Magnan echoed in a puzzled tone. "But dessert hasn't been served yet."

"He means his shrimp cocktail," Retief pointed out quietly. Magnan glanced at the glass cup half filled with red shrimp sauce before the alien.

"I don't er . . . quite . . . ah . . . understand, Your Excellency," he murmured. "Creatures? Do you suggest that you found a . . . er . . . cockroach, or some sort of vermin in your cocktail?"

"Not at all, my dear Ben," D'ong replied. "I simply noted that some charming little fellows, doubtless household pets, had crept over the rim of my cup to steal a bit of the tasty red pudding and had slipped and fallen in and there perished, poor little ones; how too, too sad."

"Retief, he thinks shrimp are pets," Magnan whispered urgently. "Tell him."

"Better not," Retief said. "It might not be diplomatic."

"To be sure, to be sure," Magnan concurred.

"By the way, Mr. Minister," he went on, "how *did* you get down from that chandelier? I was sitting right here, and it seemed as if one second you were up there, and the next you were sitting beside me."

"I whiffled, of course," the Grotian said calmly, as he stared mournfully at his cockail cup.

"How exactly does one whiffle?" Magnan leaned forward to inquire.

"First, one must cinch up the sphincters nice and tight," D'ong said mildly. "Then it's essential to take care not to cogitate on trivia, diplomacy, for example. Having thus placed oneself in the proper spiritual frame of reference, one simply concentrates on the desired destination, and whiffles."

"Gosh, sir, it sounds simple," Magnan gushed. "Retief, just think of staff meetings . . . just when you think you can't stand it another second—just tighten up the old sphincters, think of a comfy park bench—and you're off!"

"Sounds OK," Retief agreed.

"I can't wait to try." Magnan said.

"You'll never whiffle while thinking of staff meetings," D'ong sighed. "Now I must put the concept out of mind or I won't even be able to twaffle."

"Twaffle, sir? What's that?" Magnan cried. "Is it anything like whiffle?"

"Not in the least, Ben," D'ong said coolly.

"What the devil's *this?*" the voice of Ambassador Smallfrog boomed out abruptly.

"Gracious, that's his 4-c Bellow," Magnan whispered, looking anxiously at Retief.

"Wrong, Ben!" Smallfrog roared, "That was my 4-z, and I've heard tell I have one of the finest 4-z's in the corps! Two demerits! Now," he proceeded more calmly, "what's the meaning of this?" He held up a small, greenish crustacean whose long antennae waved aimlessly. At that moment Magnan yelped and groped in his lap.

"Well, Ben," Smallfrog said sternly, "I trust you have some compelling explanation for that outburst."

"Sure, sir. This . . . bug . . . or whatever . . ." He held up a duplicate of the creature the Ambassador was displaying. "It landed in my lap. It just sort of sprang at me."

"Keep cool, Ben," Smallfrog commanded. "I'll soon get to the bottom of this." He glared at the small twitching creature in his hand. It gave a sudden leap and flew across the white-linened table. Other small creatures were twitching and leaping among the crystal and silver.

"Serving live shrimp at table," Smallfrog boomed. "Possibly the chef's idea of a capital jape." His tone indicated that he did not share the cook's taste in practical humor.

"Excuse me, Mr. Ambassador, gentlemen," Magnan said, rising purposefully and moving off toward the door.

"You, too, are grieved by the plight of the little fellows?" D'ong called solicitously after him. "Lost your appetite at the thought of such misfortune, eh? By the way, Retief, I note that a number of their fellows have suffered a similar unhappy fate in *your* pudding." He indicated Retief's untouched shrimp cocktail.

"Yoo-hoo," Magnan carolled from across the room, hesitating at the kitchen door. The portal burst open and a tall, wide, well-muscled fellow in dirty whites, with an apron and chef's toque to match, emerged, folded arms like ham hocks and stared at Magnan.

"You yodeling for me, mister?" he demanded. "What's the beef?"

"Ah, yes, the beef. You may serve it any time you're ready," Magnan improvised, as Retief joined him.

"Too right, Jack. But I don't like civilians hanging around my kitchen giving me hints, get it?"

"Got it," Magnan agreed hastily. "Now, as for your rather unusual, er, appetizer . . ."

"Whatta ya talking, appetizer? You got no appetite, whatta ya eating for? You could afford to drop a little weight, you know, chum. You're skinny, but you got a nice little pot coming along there. Now I got to go water the wine."

"Sir, you are insolent," Magnan observed tartly.

"Whatsa matter, chum, you can't get along with the help?" the cook inquired tonelessly, and made a note on his cuff.

"Why, gracious, no, I mean, yes," Magnan babbled. "Shucks, I'm known throughout the corps for my ability to absorb insolence from menials. One of my strongest suits, actually."

"Called me a menial," the cook muttered, jotting.

"OK, chum, that's it for today. Come around lots." He turned away. Retief followed him into the kitchen.

Magnan was waiting nervously when Retief emerged five minutes later. "Well?" he demanded, "What's his explanation?"

"He didn't have one."

"In that case we'll have to improvise. Suppose we tell their Excellencies live shrimp cocktails are all the rage back on Terra. You know how the great adore novel modes."

"Why not tell them the truth?"

"Whatever for, Retief? I mean, how can we, since George didn't choose to explain?"

"George had nothing to do with it. He boiled the shrimp like he always does."

Back at the table, the two junior officers resumed their chairs, ignored by D'ong and Smallfrog, deep in conversation. The leaping shrimp were no longer in evidence.

"Of course, Mr. Minister," the Terran Ambassador Extraordinary and Minister Plenipotentiary was saying in the tone of Warm Congratulation (271-C) he always employed when addressing aliens. "I adore tea—but alas, none was included in our stores. Perhaps a nip of brandy instead . . . ?"

"If I might request a pot of hot water," D'ong said diffidently, "I think I can offer a solution."

Magnan trotted away to deliver the requisition.

"Hot water? Hmmph!" Smallfrog muttered as Magnan returned.

"Gracious," Magnan murmured behind his hand to Retief. "All this fuss over what was intended to be a cosy little tête-à-tête, to make some mileage with the Grotes before that sneaky little Ambassador Shiss has a chance to start toadying up to poor dear D'ong. He's such an innocent, really. A shrewd interplanetary negotiator, of course, but so naive in practical matters. And now this question of drowned pets has him all upset. And Ambassador Smallfrog is never at his best when faced with the paradoxical. I suggest we slip out and keep an eye on the Groaci Embassy. Perhaps Shiss has something to do with this foolish practical joke."

"Just put it down, my man," the Grotian Foreign Minister said quietly as George loomed, pot in hand. "Leave four cups."

Magnan lifted the lid of the handsome Yalcan teapot and peeked inside. He sniffed. "Hot water," he said sadly. "Just as his Excellency specified."

"Would I louse up an order, pal?" George said cheerfully, and went away.

"Cheeky fellow," D'ong said. George paused to jot quickly.

"Excellent cook, though, of course," the Grotian added in a stage whisper.

"So. Hot water to top off a lunch of live shrimp and dead issues," Smallfrog remarked with the joviality of a hangman inquiring as to the most comfortable adjustment of the knot.

"Ah, sir, as to the rather unusual events—" Magnan started, only to be cut off by a peremptory Ambassadorial gesture.

"Never explain, Magnan. Unless I order you to, of course. With your friends it isn't necessary, and with your superiors it doesn't work. An interesting entry in your form 163-9, Ben: 'This officer has an unusual sense of humor.' Perhaps it won't sound *too* bad when the Promotion Board is mulling it over. Shall I pour?" He lifted the pot.

"Hot water, Mr. Minister?" he inquired tonelessly of D'ong who eagerly offered his cup for filling.

"I'm sure Your Excellency appreciates Magnan's little jest," Smallfrog said heartily.

"But, sir, I—" Magnan's voice trailed off. Smallfrog whipped out a pen and made a note on the tablecloth. "Decided to ignore my instruction never to explain, eh?" he muttered.

"I wasn't going to explain. It's all George's fault, obviously. I was just going to tell you—"

"What, *you* tell *me?*" the great man inquired in a

tone of Stunned Incredulity (702-c). "Never pass the buck to an inferior, Ben," he added sternly.

"Sir, if you knew the half of it, you'd doubtless have occasion to use your 709-x." (Total Astonishment)

"Try my b," Smallfrog said, registering Near-Total Astonishment. "Magnan, you amaze me. I always thought you a highly career-motivated chap, but now, suddenly, you pile the Pela of insolence atop the Ossion of incompetence. To say nothing of the live shrimp."

"No matter, Freddy," D'ong said soothingly, as he groped in a side pocket with a seven-fingered hand and brought out a small filter-paper packet, limp and stained, with a short length of string attached. Calmly he dipped it into his cup, the contents of which immediately turned a rich amber. He withdrew the bag and with a courteous nod, dunked it into Smallfrog's cup, then, in turn, into Magnan's and Retief's, dyeing each the same deep color.

Smallfrog hesitated, then lifted his cup and sipped carefully. A smile contorted his meaty features. "Gad, sir," he said. "Orange Pekoe, my favorite. Ann Page, too, if my palate serves me aright."

Magnan tried his. It was tea, no doubt of it.

"A delightful affair," D'ong said, rising. "I really must hurry off now. I have a pressing appointment at three." He bustled away, employing approximately five short legs in a gait more rapid than graceful, Retief escorting him.

"Charming fellow," Magnan mused, still sipping his tea.

"Harrumph," Smallfrog said by way of prologue. "Gentlemen, I don't need to tell you . . . this is a critical moment for Terry-Grote relations. Lying as it does squarely athwart the lanes of expansion of Terran Manifest Destiny, Grote, though a trivial world in itself, can pose an awkward problem should Groaci influence become dominant here. But I must ask you, Ben. Did you see what I saw? Or am I hallucinating?"

"Hallucinating, sir? Oh, hardly that, sir. After all,

all you've had is some ketchup and a cup of hot water."

"Skip all that, Ben. But did you see what that fellow *did?* Brewed four cups of hearty tea from a single tea bag. By gad, sir, there's a trick that will cinch that Deputy Under-Secretary slot for me if I can report how it's done. That is to say, an apparent suspension of natural law such as this must surely be looked into!"

"To be sure," Magnan agreed suavely. "And I imagine it would be a feather in the cap of the officer who is able to bring the information to you." He rose. "I'd best hurry off at once and tell Retief."

"Sit down, Magnan. I fear you don't fully appreciate the gravity of the matter I've entrusted to you. Never mind about whatsizname: see to it you don't let the secret of the tea slip from our grasp. Start by following D'ong. See what you can discover about his habits, way of life, all that. If you succeed in this mission, tea bag-wise, there may be laurels in the offing for you yet. That's all. I'm counting on you, Ben."

"At ease, Jim," Magnan said testily as the big Marine sergeant at the Embassy gate snapped to Present Arms. "Did anyone go out just now?"

"Yessir. Went thataway." Jim rolled his eyes to the right, indicating the broad avenue curving away under the shady boughs of the imported heo trees.

"Funny thing." Jim grounded his power gun, abandoning the attempt to maintain the Position of a Soldier. "For a second I didn't get it: saw him come ankling down the steps and along the walk—D'ong, it was, nice guy, usually stops to chat a minute, you know—but this time he did some kind of a tricky side-step and jumped right out of sight. Back of the bushes, I guess. Figured he hadda take a leak or whatever these guys do after a few beers—but I checked and nope—nobody there except Mr. Prutty from the Econ Section smooching that neat little secretary of his, Miss Rumpwell. That's some duty, Mr. Magnan: while I got to stand out here four on, eight off, this clown gets ten times my pay for keeping the help harmoniously adjusted to life at a hardship post—leastways that's what he told me while she was getting her buttons done up. Some guys have all the luck: I invited her out three times and got a chill-off that'd give a Eskimo frostbite, and then she goes for that crummy civilian—no offense, Mr. Magnan."

"None taken, Jimmy, but to return to Foreign Minister D'ong: what explanation did he offer when he emerged?"

"That's the screwy part, Mr. Magnan, he didn't, I mean he didn't emerge-like. Next I seen of him he was back outside the gate moving right along. But I swear he never passed me."

"Hmmmm . . . that seems rather odd, Jimmy: he came down the steps and along the walk, you say, and then down the street—without passing through the gate. Perhaps you dozed for a moment."

"Not me, Mr. Magnan. What I figure, there's a secret passage or like that, he ducked into."

"But why, Jimmy?"

"Beats me, Mr. Magnan. But come to think of it, I seen that little Groaci nose-picker, Fishfilth, or whatever, hanging around acrost the street. Had a little pink parasol, made him look like a five-eyed Madame Butterfly. Maybe he had something to do with it, huh?"

"I suggest you forget the matter, Sergeant," Magnan said stiffly. "Perhaps you blinked at just the moment he slipped past. No point in blowing it up into an interplanetary issue."

"OK, but I'm gonna keep a sharp eye on the next local comes in here."

"Quite right, my boy. Now I must be off. By the way, if Foreign Minister D'ong or Mr. Retief should pass by in the next few minutes, just detain them in a casual way until I get back."

"I'll see what I can do. You don't want me to arrest anybody, I guess."

"Gracious, no, Jimmy. Arrest? Whatever for?" Magnan passed through the great wrought-iron gate and hurried away along Embassy Row. He passed the high board fence which concealed the deep mud-pit which was the Yalcan Consulate General, the placid pond under which lay the Rockamorran Legation, and the haughty classic façade of the Sulinoran Mission to Grote. Next there was a broad vacant lot with a "For Loan" sign almost invisible among the pizzle-weeds, then the low, unprepossessing structure housing the Jaque Chancery. Beyond it, impregnable behind a high stone wall, the Groaci Embassy resembled an Assyrian maximum-security prison as visualized by Cecil B. De Mille. Magnan slowed to a casual saunter, veering close to the plate-steel gate to dart a quick glance through the four-inch keyhole.

"Hi, Ben," a breathy voice called from beyond the gate. "Anything I can do for you?" Magnan executed a two-step, registering astonishment.

"That 709 of yours needs work, Ben," the same faint voice commented. "What brings a Terry First Secretary, on foot already, to the gates of the Groacian Mission on such a warm afternoon?"

"Just passing by, Fith," Magnan replied in a tone of Casual Indifference.

"Don't waste a 301 on me, Ben," Fith suggested. "If you expect to get a glimpse of some nefarious do-ings right out in the driveway, forget it. Ambassador Shiss is too old a campaigner for that. He's got a special nefarious-stuff room for that kind of caper. When you see a news release that cites 'a confidential Groacian source' that means the dope is hot from there. Not that us peace-loving Groaci go in for skulduggery, you understand."

"Of course, of course, Fith—but what in the world are you, a company grade officer, doing pulling two on and four off, while lesser personnel are keeping the help harmoniously adjusted to life at a hardship post?"

"Oh, I see somebody's been slipping you dope on life in the Groaci Foreign Service, Ben. I didn't realize your system was so good. As for the guard detail: well, Ben, frankly, His Excellency has had it soft for me ever since he caught me climbing into a tub of hot sand with the Lady Trish last Wednesday, when the old goof was supposed to be safely off watching a game of flat-ball over at the Inertian Consulate. All perfectly innocent, of course; her ladyship just asked me to check the temperature of her bath for her, to be sure she wouldn't get any damage to the ziff-nodes from that high infra-red radiation, you know."

"But of course, Fith—we're both beings-of-the-world. By the, way, I don't suppose you've seen anything of my colleague, Mr. Retief?"

"Nope, I'm just keeping four or five eyes out for that character D'ong, the local Minister of Foreign Affairs, supposed to be here any time now. You don't happen to see an official limousine coming with the poor boob in it, do you?"

"No—but here's the poor boob himself."

Magnan whirled at the soft voice behind him. D'ong stood at his elbow, a serene expression on his rather lumpy features.

"Why, Ben, fancy meeting you here," he said. "I hardly expected the pleasure again so soon."

"Well, that's diplomacy, Your Excellency. One keeps running into the same people—like Fith, here—just beyond the gate, that is. He was Consular Officer at Slunch when I was a mere Third Secretary. And then later, at Furtheron, we both served on the Chumship Team, arbitrating the Civil War. That's where I got this gash on the arm." Magnan turned his cuff to expose a crescent-shaped scar.

"Nasty," D'ong commented. "Got that in the war, did you?"

"No, at the conference table. Between us, Mr. Minister," he continued in a whisper, "While Fith, like all Groaci, can be a charming fellow, he has a tendency to bite when crossed."

"Well, enough of nostalgia for the moment, Ben," D'ong said. "I musn't keep Ambassador Shiss waiting. Until tomorrow at the jelly flower judging, then?"

"Ah, Mr. Minister—"

"Just call me D'ong," the Grotian said affably. "All that formality gives me a swift pain in the zop-slot."

"Sure, er, D'ong," Magnan agreed. "I was just saying, why don't you and I just sneak off for a couple quick saucers of tea, and let old Shiss stew in his own juice for a while. After all, protocol requires that *he* ought to be calling on you, instead of vice versa."

"I couldn't think of it, Ben. One doesn't stand up a fellow being, no matter how tiresome he may be."

"Frankly, D'ong, I have a feeling Shiss is up to no good. I don't like the idea of him enticing you in there all alone. Suppose I just go along as an escort, sort of, you know."

"I hardly think—" D'ong started, and paused at a sudden outburst of breathy Groaci shouting from beyond the wall. There was a rasp of a bolt being withdrawn, and the massive gate swung back. A platoon of Groaci peace-keepers in flaring helmets and chrome-plated greaves with red and green jellybeans emerged in a ragged column of twos.

"To surround the soft ones instanter!" a non-com whispered in harsh Groaci. The troops at once formed a ragged circle around Magnan and D'ong, power-guns at the ready.

"Here, here, I protest!" Magnan cried. "Captain Fith!" He fixed the officer with an Indignant Stare (491–a). "You're making a serious blunder! Call off your boys at once!"

"You know how it is, Ben," Fith said in his accentless Terran. "Orders are orders and all that jazz. Instructions were to pick up this clown here—" he indicated D'ong with a twitch of a stalked ocular—"and you just got caught in the works. No hard feelings."

"*Au contraire,* I shall have very hard feelings indeed unless I receive an immediate apology—and Minister D'ong too, of course."

"To desist from fraternizing with inferiors," a hoarse Groaci voice called from beyond the wall. "To do your duty at once, Captain—ah, Major, that is, as soon as you have him bound hand, foot, and incidental members and deposited in my office."

"You see how it is, Ben." Fith said sadly. "His Excellency is taking a personal interest in this caper." He turned to address the corporal of the guard.

"You heard His Excellency. Tie him up! Be quick about it, nest-fouling litter-mate of drones!"

The corporal paused to jot a note on his cuff, then laid hands on Magnan, who huddled close to D'ong.

"Not the Terry—*him!*" Brevet-Major Fith snapped.

"Steady, Ben," D'ong murmured. "I'm sure there'll eventually be a nice note of apology from the Groaci Foreign Office. But—" he broke off, grasping Magnan's wrist as the Terran groped in the Grotian's jacket pocket.

"What in the world do you want with that, Ben?" he inquired mildly. "It's only an old tea bag."

"As to that," Magnan hastened to explain, "I merely intended to save it from the clutches of the Groaci."

"Whatever for? It's just a souvenir of my Great-aunt R'oot's visit to Terra a few centuries ago. I keep it for sentimental reasons. Poor auntie passed away last week, leaving me a few hundred million in gold squiggs and green stamps. Decent old girl. I remember when she used to dandle me on a knee she extruded just for the purpose. Alas, poor, kindly Aunt R'oot. I won't be seeing her again, unless she decides to furfle—and I don't see why she should."

"To . . . to furfle? Goodness, D'ong, how does one furfle?"

"First, one has to be dead. Quite dead, you understand, Ben. Indisputably beyond the quaffling stage."

"Mmm . . . 'beyond quaffling stage'," Magnan repeated, nodding wisely. "Dead, you say?" he inquired abruptly.

"No gossiping among the prisoners," the penetrating voice of Ambassador Shiss called from beyond the wall. "Let's get this show on the road, Lieutenant," he added sharply.

Fith leaped as if prodded by an electrospur. "There

goes the old promotion," he mourned. "Hustle 'em inside, boys," he added to his troops.

A moment later the silent street was empty.

At the Terran Embassy gate, Retief paused as the
Marine guard snapped to attention, then cleared his
throat.

"Uh, excuse me, Mr. Retief," the boy said. "But
Mr. Magnan was asking for you. Did he get you OK,
sir?"

"Not yet, Jimmy. Which way did he go?"

"He was headed for the Groaci Embassy, looking
for D'ong. Funny thing about old D'ong: he slipped
right past me. I hope I didn't goof letting him get
away with it."

"Not at all, Jim. I'm going to stroll down that way
and see what there is to be seen."

"Watch yourself, Mr. Retief. I don't trust them
Groaci no farther'n I can throw one."

Retief ambled along the shaded walk, enjoying the
cedar-scented evening air. Grote's large pale-blue sun
was near the horizon, and the shadows were dense beneath the heo trees. Nearing the Groaci Embassy, he
studied the high grayish-ochre walls, topped with corroded spikes. Before the gate he paused, stooped to
pick up a flattened tea bag from among the trampled
leaves. He studied it thoughtfully, dropped it into his
pocket, and approached the peep-hole in the massive
metal gate. He rapped on it twice, and it slid back
to reveal a cluster of eye-stalks in plain G.I. eye-shields.

"Evening, Captain," Retief said. "Where's Magnan?"

"To imply that I, a peace-loving Groacian national,
doing his simple duty, am aware of the comings and
goings of Terry First Secretaries?" a breathy voice
replied, then added in accent-free Terran: "Shucks, Retief, I just came on duty. You had an idea Ben was
here?"

"Never mind, Fith. I just thought maybe we could
skip the formalities and get right to the point: if you
boys are holding Mr. Magnan in your compound

against his will, we'll have to call out a squadron of
Peace Enforcers to make it clear, one more time, that
you can't get away with it."

"Curious fancy on your part, Retief. Why would we
Groaci be interested in detaining a mere Terry?"

"Skip it. Where's D'ong?"

"You refer to the feckless local Foreign Minister?
He is, I believe, closeted at this moment with His
Excellency, Ambassador Shiss, discussing means of
enhancing Grote-Groaci relations—not that it's any of
your business."

"Better check your manual, Fith. This is too early in
the negotiation to start using your 931-yup (Tentative
Insolence). Better stick to a 21-boo (Cautious Imper-
tinence) for the present, or old Shiss will have you on
the carpet for impairing Terry-Groaci relations."

"Mmm. To withdraw now, Retief, to see to my
routine duties, such as inspecting my sluggards all
unaware, gold-bricking in the therapeutic sand-pit, instead of cleaning their pieces as instructed. Ciao." He
slammed the peep-hole cover.

Retief went along to the corner and glanced down
the narrow avenue that ran along the north side of the
Groaci Embassy compound. The leaf-strewn sidewalks
were deserted. A lone Yllian delivery van was slumped
at the curb near the rear gate to the compound. Retief
noted that it bore a legend painted in Yllian characters
that resembled the word 'egg-nog', indicating that it
was the Yllian Consul-General's formal garbage truck.
He noted as he passed it that it listed heavily to star-
board. A sour odor of fermenting refuse hung over the
grubby vehicle. Retief snorted and tried the gate. It
was solidly locked. He stepped back and kicked it at
lock height. There was a metallic tinkle and the gate
swung ajar. At once, the snout of a Groaci power-gun
poled through the opening, then withdrew. There was a
creak of unoiled hinges behind Retief and he turned to
see a heavy gray-skinned Yill ponderously emerging
from the side door of the garbage truck.

"You Terries got a eye on this dump, too, huh?"

the Yill said in a glutinous voice. "Some funny stuff going on around here. One of our boys came over to deliver a birthday stew to His Groacian Ex, the AE and MP, and never came out again. Swell glimp-egg stew it was, too, aged six months, just ripe enough, but not *too* ripe, you know?"

"How long ago was that, F'Lin-lin?" Retief inquired.

"About two weeks, come sundown; hey, I just noticed—they goofed and left the gate open."

"Careful," Retief cautioned as the Yill approached the gate, "There's a power-gun just inside."

"Sure, I know all that stuff," F'Lin-lin said carelessly. Reaching the gate, he thrust it open, and instantly stepped back and flattened himself against the fence beside it. When the gun muzzle poked out F'Lin-lin grabbed it, and held on.

"Watch it," Retief advised. "If he's on the ball he'll set it at low beam and maximum choke and it'll be red-hot in a few seconds."

F'Lin-lin grunted and released the gun, which at once withdrew, while the Yill blew on his palm and muttered. Retief took up a position against the fence on the hinge side of the gate. After a few seconds, a finger-like member poked out hesitantly. Retief caught the six-inch stalk, tipped by a bulbous blue ocular, and held it gently but firmly as it twitched frantically.

"Nice going, Retief," F'Lin-lin said. "I always wanted to pull one of their wiggly eyeballs out by the roots. Interesting to see how much stress it'll take to do it."

"To see anything, Quilf?" a breathy Groaci called from beyond the gate.

"Not precisely to *see* anything, Whiff, but there's something rather curious going on. It got completely dark all of a sudden, and—well, better give me a hand. No! Not to try to drag me back. I have my eye fixed on something interesting."

At once a second Groaci thrust out his head, all five eyes erect and alert. Retief grabbed him by the neck and assisted him out. The Groaci made a vengeful swipe with a heavy knout, missing Retief's head by an inch. Retief caught the weapon and wrenched it from the other's grasp. He snapped it in two and returned the handle end to his assailant.

"Be nice, Whiff, and I won't tell anybody what happened. You can explain that you broke it over my skull."

"To be sure, Terry; a consummation devoutly to be desired. Why are you skulking here?"

"Where's D'ong?" Retief inquired.

"Closeted with His Excellency, vile miscreant! Leave go of me before I get you had up before one of them do-gooder committees that are always trying to uplift us emergent types."

"Keep your ears clean, fellows," Retief said and released the pair, who at once scuttled away.

"Shall we?" Retief inquired of the Yill and indicated the abandoned gate, now swinging wide to reveal a cobbled court lined with stalls occupied by poorly maintained Groaci ground-cars. A lone Groaci in a ribbed hip-cloak leaned casually against the wall by a dark, doorless archway, fingering a six-foot pike. He came to a slack-twisted position of attention as Retief approached, covering the agitated twitching of his eye-stalks by pretending to adjust his top-three-grader eye-shields.

"What's up, Retief?" he inquired in his breathy voice. "I guess it was you that spooked Private Quilf. What did you say to that 'apporth o' cor 'elp me?"

"Nothing much, Sergeant. I just caught his eye and gave him the nod. Obliging fellow."

"Left the gate open, too," the sergeant said. "Quilf is overdue for a few hours on pots and pans, I guess. By the way, what are you like violating the sacred precincts of the Groacian Mission and all for?"

"Just dropped by to remind Mr. Magnan of Staff Meeting. Which way?"

"I got to hang around here, I guess. I see that Yill no-good, F'Lin-lin, hanging around out there. He's their Embassy driver, but I don't trust the bugger. That's how come I made him park on the street."

"What's your name, Sergeant?" Retief asked.

"Yish," the Groaci replied.

"It seems to me I remember you from somewhere," Retief said. "Squeem, perhaps?"

"I was there when the dam let go," Yish conceded. "I lost my stamp collection in the flood—and I've never been convinced you weren't behind the collapse of our lovely new dam."

"Several hundred yards," Retief agreed.

"So I have a personal score to settle—as well as my job to do, wise guy." The Groaci jabbed suddenly at Retief with his broad-headed pike. Retief moved aside sufficiently to let the sharp point slide past him and nick the door frame behind him. Yish withdrew it, jabbed again. "To stand still, vile miscreant!" he hissed half-heartedly as he missed again. This time the point lodged firmly in the hard wood, forcing Yish to change grips and heave backward in an effort to retrieve his weapon. Retief grasped the shaft with his left hand and jerked it free, allowing Yish to stagger back. The off-balance Groaci relinquished his grasp on the pike and sat down suddenly. Retief reversed the weapon and prodded the fallen sergeant medium-gently.

"On your feet, Yish, before you lose any more face than you have to," he said quietly. Yish got up, dusting his crumpled hip-cloak, several of the umbrella-like ribs of which were now hopelessly buckled. Retief went past him through the entry. Behind him Yish yelled frantically.

"To go after the cheeky rascal! Don't you see he's about to violate the sacrosanct precincts of the chancery itself!"

Retief stepped behind the shelter of the archway and thrust the shaft of the pike out across the opening a foot above ground level. The first Groaci through tripped over it and fell sprawling. A moment later two more landed heavily on him. Another five seconds, and half a dozen Groaci were disentangling themselves from the heap. Yish advanced more cautiously, paused to look with disapproval at his disordered command.

"I think you'd better schedule your boys for another thirteen weeks of basic," Retief suggested, "with the emphasis on obstacle-course work."

"You jape, vile Terry, but you'll rue the day you violated the Groacian Embassy."

"Don't spoil your best move of the day, Yish. Your orders were to get me inside, remember?"

"To be sure." Yish moved off, reshaping his chap-fallen recruits into a column of ducks.

Retief looked across the court at the adjacent façade, blank but for an immense iron-bound door, flanked by a polished brass plate lettered "Embassy of the Groacian state" in long-tailed Groaci characters. Yish had succeeded in lining up his troop in an irregular double column before the massive entrance.

"You're doing fine, Yish, considering what you have to work with," Retief called. "Now all you have to figure out is how to coax me inside."

"Coax, indeed, rash alien!" the sergeant responded. "To be sure, my chaps carry traditional pikes, but doubtless you noticed they also carry blast-guns of the latest Bogan design. To doubt even so crude a Soft One as yourself can fail to recognize who wields the whip here—and who cringes on command. You'll be herded inside at a word from me."

Retief strolled across to the great entry. "Doors locked?" he inquired in a casual tone, and poked at the vast portal with a finger. It swung easily back, revealing a gloomy and cavernous interior hall, dim-lit by tapers on tall wrought-iron standards. Retief stepped inside, followed by a sudden yell from Yish, who came hurrying after him. A narrow spiral stair led upward at the far side of the great hall. Aside from a number of impervious-looking doors set in deep recesses, the surrounding walls were featureless stone.

"To stop there, snooping alien!" Yish croaked, winded by his dash. "To place you under arrest on the spot!"

"For what?"

"Trespassing, resisting arrest, invasion, violation of Groaci sovereignty—"

"Hold it—you make me sound like an enemy planet."

"To rue the day you intruded here, Terry evil-doer!"

"You planned to herd me in here at gunpoint, or possibly pike-point," Retief said. "And now you're all upset because I saved you the trouble?"

"To have a point there, Retief. Nonetheless, to hurry along now with—"

"Where's Mr. Magnan?"

"That, Terry, is a secret of the Groacian state. No more questions. This way."

Yish stepped off smartly toward one of the doors; Retief followed. The Groaci used a large electrokey of archaic design, pushed back the door, revealing a narrow flight of steps leading down into darkness. He flipped a wall switch and a baleful red glare sprang up. "You're the host," Retief said. "You lead the way."

"The way is quite obvious, nor is there any alternative, my Retief," Yish said. He made an odd motion of several eyes, and a black-clad Groaci stepped from the shadows behind the door, delicately fingering a foot-long stiletto.

"Hired muscle," Yish said. "My apologies, Retief, but that's the way it has to be." The hit-man edged toward Retief, who stepped forward to meet him. As the Groaci went into a menacing crouch, Retief caught him firmly by the neck, upended him, producing a rain of coins and other small objects, shook him once, and tossed him over the railing. It seemed a long time before a heavy *crump!* announced his arrival below. Retief picked up the knife his would-be assassin had dropped. "Cheap goods," he commented. "If that's hired muscle, I wonder what the free stuff is like."

"Well, you know how it is, Retief. You can't hardly get no good help these days."

"I heard that," a resentful voice wheezed from below. "Some loyalty. And after I got a sprung gusset in the service of the state, and all."

"Still, he's tough," Retief conceded.

"Well, yes, Hiff knows how to take a fall. And now, if you'll just follow me, Retief . . ." Yish started down the stone steps. Retief followed.

"But I demand to see the Ambassador at once!" Magnan repeated for the fifth time, and for the fifth time Fith signaled to an underling to tighten the straps securing the prisoner to the conversation rack.

"No use being a sorehead about it, Ben," Fith reminded the Terran. "Actually you surprise me; I expected you, as one who has survived staking-out in the sulpher pits of Yush, to stand up to a routine interview in more spartan fashion."

"It's merely the indignity of the thing," Magnan explained in a rather sulky tone. "After all, this wickerwork strait-jacket hardly allows a person to breathe."

"Just spill a few official secrets, Ben, and you'll be breathing like sixty in a trice. By the way, what's a trice?"

"It's what you'll be in jail in, as soon as my chief learns of my situation."

"Your chief? You mean old Froggie? Forget it, Ben. Now, how about starting with whatever it was you and Retief figured you'd accomplish snooping around here today?"

"We were hardly 'snooping,' as you so insolently put it, my dear Fith. Actually we were innocently waiting for Foreign Minister D'ong, whom we understood was last seen headed this way."

"Ah, yes, the insidious D'ong. I've had my eye on that fellow for some time. Something not quite kosher about that chap."

"Nonsense: it's just that he whiffles easily."

"You've remained adamant under the torments of the toe-tickler and the Tantalizing Tasties," Fith said, finishing off a package of smoked gribble grubs. "And even endured half an hour of tape-recorded staff meeting—in an alien tongue, yet. But you'll not so easily shrug off the up-coming technique: I have three or four well-trained fellows here who'll take great pleasure in screening a program of old Nelson Eddy movies. Thereafter, a broken man, you'll only be too happy to sob out your trivial secrets. Why not save all that and speak up like a good fellow?" He waved back a Groaci in G.I. eye-shields and a plain O.D. hip-cloak, who had appeared at the entry wheeling a bulky old-fashioned movie projector. "Don't think we'll be needing that, Flish," he muttered.

"Nelson Eddy?" Magnan said in a voice that was almost a whimper. "Couldn't we just start off with the Andrews Sisters to kind of warm up?"

"No use pleading for mercy, Ben. Though an affable fellow by nature, I'm as implacable as a burb-lizard in performance of duty. But just now I must step out a moment and see how your fellow-rascal, D'ong, is enjoying his visit." Fith followed the drab technician from the chamber. Magnan sighed.

"Come back!" he cried abruptly just as Fith was about to pass from view. "I understand your implied threat to poor, harmless D'ong. Rather than permit him to be subjected to the torment, I'll—I'll tell you what you want to know."

Fith re-entered the chamber promptly. "Now don't let your imagination run amok, Ben," he said soothingly. "I merely intended to divert him with a couple of early Roy Rogers films." He shuddered involuntarily.

"You'll find the magic tea bag near the gate, jostled from my grasp by your ruffians." Magnan blurted.

Fith waved all five eye-stalks in a vertiginous pattern. "Are you kidding, vile Terry?" he inquired conversationally. "Magic tea bags, already." He stepped outside for a word with his helper, then returned, rubbing his anterior hands together.

"Well, Roy it is," he said with relish. "And Gene Autry's next. I might even trot out Vera Hruba Ralston, if you prove troublesome."

Magnan moaned faintly, his eyes following every

move as Fith and his aide set up the projector and screen.

At the foot of the steps, Retief waited while Sergeant Yish assisted the injured hit-man to his feet, netting a sharp rebuke as he tried to dust of his employee's hopelessly sprung hip-cloak.

"We've been goofing around long enough, Yish," Retief said. "You know why I'm here. Where is he?"

"You are here, my dear Retief, because, in spite of your crude animal physique, I finessed you here as delicately as King Kroog enticed the fip-maiden into the sauna."

"Oh. I thought the Ambassador's orders were to keep me out of the building on pain of beheading."

"I suppose something of the sort was said, but this is different."

"Just take me to Mr. Magnan and I'll forget to mention the matter to His Excellency."

"I'm taking you as fast as I can, ain't I?" Yish said sullenly. Retief followed him along the low-ceilinged passage past barred cell doors, where what looked like large fish bones lay heaped on the stone-slab floors, among rusted chains. Ahead a dim light burned. By its glow Retief saw Fith emerge from a doorway and stride jauntily away. He brushed past Yish and hurried to the door Fith had used. It stood ajar; he stepped through as Magnan, tight-trussed in a form-fitting wicker cage, muttered;

"This is a matter for publication in the Galactic Review of Interplanetary Excesses. 'Gentlemen, it is with regret that I forward the enclosed MS detailing my abuse by a power whose name begins with Groaci, in gross violation of diplomatic immunity. Now, if you yourselves were out in the great arena of Galactic diplomacy, instead of sitting behind a desk in the GRIPE editorial suite, you'd not be so critical of my having let slip a few trivial GUTS classified items.' So there!

"Oh, it's you, Retief; I was just dreaming of giving

a piece of my mind to those ivory-tower critics of mine."

"Don't worry, I won't tell anybody."

"You mean about the GUTS security violation?"

"No, I mean about talking to yourself. By the way, just what Galactic Utter Top Secret info did you divulge?"

"I . . . I told him where to find the magic tea bag—but it was just to save poor D'ong from being put to torment."

"Commendable, Mr. Magnan." Retief picked up a reel of film from beside the projector. "Are you a fan of Roy's?" he asked.

"I've never considered myself such, but candidly, I was on the verge of participating in an impromptu Rogers festival."

"Curious. Where's D'ong?"

"Closeted with His Excellency, Ambassador Shiss, I shouldn't wonder. He did have an appointment, you know."

Retief examined the harness restraining Magnan, then jerked the straps loose. The wickerwork fell away. Magnan stepped down from the conversation frame with a sigh of relief.

"Vera Hruba Ralston," he muttered. "Nelson Eddy, Eugene Autry."

"Planning a show?" Retief inquired. "Sounds like rather unlikely casting."

"By no means. They're all on the same bill, Fith assures me. Free admission, too, though the seats seem rather confining. And no popcorn, just gribble grubs; and you know how it is once you've had too much of a good thing."

"Or even of a bad thing. Speaking of which, I'll excuse myself from the Rogers revival. Ta."

"Retief! Wait! Where are you going? That nasty little five-eyed sneak, Fith, may come back at any moment."

"I'm going to drop in on His Excellency, the Groacian AE and MP."

"Now, Retief," Magnan said severely. "As your immediate supervisor, I must caution you to do nothing rash."

"Actually, Mr. Magnan, I haven't yet thought up anything rash to do."

"Excellent. Perhaps you're learning restraint at last."

"I guess it had to happen. But why should we be any more restrained than we have to? After an hour in a Groaci conversation frame, I should think you'd like being unrestrained."

"Ah, yes. To be sure, Retief. General Fith stepped a bit over the line restraint-wise in trussing a Terry First Secretary and Consul in that fashion. Still, he merely hinted at the other torments he had planned—he stopped short of actually screening them."

"So—inasmuch as you have the general well in hand, it seems logical for me to tackle his boss."

"Ummm. I trust you employ the term 'tackle' figuratively."

"I don't expect to have too much trouble with the old boy. After all, he's a career bureaucrat, too."

"Retief, need I caution you not to rely on any fellow-feeling from that sneaky, five-eyed little devil? Though of course he knows the rules."

"Nope."

"I thought not. Just employ standard diplomatic techniques; Shiss is enough of an old campaigner to yield gracefully to a proper approach."

"I assume from that you'd be against my braiding his eyes together, or pinching his air bladder shut."

"Correct. Go in there like a true bureaucrat, Retief: let him know we've got the dirt on him, though of course we wouldn't dream of being so uncouth as to give it to the media—as long as he confides in us just what his object in kidnapping D'ong might be."

"Where is poor old D'ong?"

"I haven't seen him. Fith adamantly refused to confide in me."

"I'll snoop around and find him."

Retief left the cell, encountering Sergeant Yish waiting rather furtively, just outside.

"This is hardly equitable treatment, Retief," the Groaci hissed. "General Fith may be along at any moment, asking embarrassing questions—especially if he sees a Terry loose in the off-limits area."

"Just tell him we're on our way to call on the Ambassador," Retief said. "Which way?"

"Just down this way," Yish replied sullenly, pointing to a lightless entry.

"His Excellency maintains an office in the dungeon wing?" Retief asked.

"Naw. This is just the short-cut to the elevators."

Retief entered the dark and narrow passage behind the Groaci non-com. "Just in case anybody gets in our way," he told Yish, "Keep in mind that I'm holding a blast pistol."

"Oh, sure, Retief. Shucks, you don't think I'd try to pull a swifty, do you?" Yish scurried ahead, stopped before a bank of unlighted gray-painted elevator doors. In the adjacent wall was another, elaborately decorated in scarlet and gold.

"Let's take that one," Retief suggested.

"Perish forbid!" Yish exclaimed. "That one's for the exclusive use of His Excellency!"

"He won't mind if we go up in it, as long as we don't meet him coming down."

"True. But one never knows—on the other hand, he never comes down here, and that's an express car, Chancery Tower to sub-dungeon, non-stop. So I suppose we're safe."

They rode up uneventfully. Mirrors on two walls reflected the tall, powerfully built Terran dressed in a late mid-afternoon sub-informal coverall with the CDT crest on the pocket, and beside him the spindle-legged Groaci NCO in the drab hip-cloak and dun eye-shields. The third wall was occupied by an array of control buttons of many colors and shapes beneath a placard reading (in translation): Peril! Only one control switch is not booby-trapped. The Officer of the Day has the code. The safe button will open the doors at the

Chancery level. All others will detonate an explosive charge. Authorized personnel only. S/the Ambassador.

The car stopped. A faint humming sound was audible.

"Seen the O.D. lately?" Retief inquired.

"To have trapped you neatly, impetuous Soft One!" Yish hissed. "To be no way out for you now. As for myself, I expire with enthusiasm. My only regret is that I can only experience hara-kiri once in line of duty, so to get on with it."

"Very dramatic." Retief said. "But pretty silly. Just get busy and open up, Yish. No one will ever know you skipped your big chance to do your number."

"Wild Goroonian Glump-beasts could not wring the secret from me, vile Terry!"

"Probably they wouldn't even try," Retief agreed. "But I'll bet a valuable collector's item against a plain set of Hong Kong-made eye-shields you'll be eating lunch in half an hour with your appetite intact."

"Never, crass violator of hallowed Groacian tradition!" Yish shifted position, folded his arms, and leaned back against the wall. At once colored lights flashed, buzzers buzzed, beepers beeped, and a faint odor of Celestial Queen incense was wafted on the air. Also, the doors slid smoothly open.

"Drat! I blew it!" Yish said casually, moving away from the treacherous control panel.

"Sure you did. It was the thought of lunch that confused you," Retief said soothingly. "Anybody could have made the same mistake. You can go play in the sand now, Yish. If I need you I'll call."

"You're a regular guy, Retief," Yish said in his badly accented Terran, and wedged himself into a corner of the car in an attempt to disappear.

The room on which the doors had opened was a spacious chamber with wide windows overlooking the Embassy fungus gardens. The walls were paneled in pale yellow blinwood, and hung with richly brocaded tapestries that Retief recognized as of Fufian manufacture. Behind a wide desk upholstered in violet-dyed tump leather at the far side of the room, sat Ambassa-

dor Shiss, an individual unusually scrawny even by
Groacian standards, but richly arrayed in a pink velvet
tunic of Terran cut adorned with scarlet aiguillettes,
purple shoulder-boards with major generals' insigniae
and gold Austrian knots. His platinum eye-shields were
jewel-encrusted.

"What's this?" he barked in perfect Terran. "Yish,
I see you skulking there in my personal VIP lift. What's
the meaning of conducting this interloper into the
Presence—and unannounced at that?"

"Why, hi there, sir." Yish chirped. "I hope you
don't mind our popping in this way, but under the
circumstances one had no time to phone ahead for an
appointment."

"Skip all that jazz, Private Yish. You'd better hang
up your jock when you report in for confinement to
quarters. Your career is at an end." The irate diplomat
turned a pair of eyes on Retief, keeping three on Yish.
"Now, as for you, Retief," he began. "Wait a minute,"
he interrupted himself. "Where's Magnan? My alert
troops spotted the pair of you as you were scaling the
wall. I do hope you're not so naïve as to be trying
to pull some kind of swifty on me, splitting up like
this."

"By no means, Mr. Ambassador. My colleague was
detained on a cultural exchange matter with General
Fith."

"Is that damn fool playing with his Roy Rogers films
again? I've told him once if I've told him a thousand
times—Roy's not a spot on Gene. But no matter—I
didn't summon you here to natter of these trivia."

"That's right, Your Excellency."

"Eh? What's right? Never expected to hear you
agree so easily."

"You didn't summon me here," Retief said.

"And you'll have a heck of a time leaving without
an invitation. To you this gracious structure may
appear no more than an ordinary masterpiece of Groacian institutional architecture, but beneath its homey
exterior lies the framework of a Groaci Number Nine

fortress, of the type we normally use on these crude outpost worlds. You've intruded here, Terry—and you'll rue the day you thought to violate my Embassy and live to tell the tale!"

"Consider me deeply impressed," Retief said. "Where's Foreign Minister D'ong?"

"Your insolence is exceeded only by your naïveté," Shiss said chillingly. "Yish! Get Fith up here at once. But be polite; after all he's a brevet general and you're only a private last class, so be *very* polite about it, or he'll have you court-martialed. Retief, you may be seated, there." He pointed to a padded bench by the elevator. Retief pulled out the deep easy chair beside the desk and seated himself, then lit up a dope-stick and puffed smoke at the Groaci, causing the latter to snap his nostrils shut after a single snort of irritation.

"Now, just what's *your* interest in matters of state passing between His Excellency the Foreign Minister? And you know I hate those stinky dope-sticks, which doubtless is why you lit it. But I'm determined not to permit you to distract me by these petty tactics."

"Let's get back to D'ong," Retief suggested. "And this is a top quality Groaci Hoob-flavored stick I'm smoking."

"Um. Let us place our fingering pieces on the table. Naturally I recognize that Terra, like Groac, must interest itself in Grote, the latter lying as it does directly athwart the trade lanes to the Inner Arm. But Groac, I assure you, does not intend to be out-maneuvered and left in the cold favorable-treatmentwise. Thus my appointment today with the Minister. Not that its any of your business—or Freddy's either."

"But where is he?"

"Alas, he failed to turn up, the upstart! I, the Ambassador Extraordinary and Minister Plenipotentiary of the Groacian state, stood up by this petty functionary of a petty world. Intolerable!"

"Doesn't sound like Minister D'ong," Retief said. "He's very sensitive to the feelings of others, and punctual to a fault."

"Bale! Like all inferior life-forms, a category which includes all non-Groaci, and between us, quite a number of the latter, he's not to be relied on in matters of great import. And now that we've established such a delightful rapport, I really must be off for a few moments to attend to a number of trivial administrative details of the kind that plague even the great." He entered the elevator, chair and all, and the doors closed on him.

Retief sipped his Pepsi and studied the room. To the left of the bar he saw a panel apparently identical with that in the elevator. He put his glass on the desk and went across to it. The buttons were of various sizes and colors. Retief turned his back to the panel and carefully leaned against it, depressing all the buttons simultaneously. Bells rang, a siren wailed, lights flashed, and the sprinkler system went into operation. In addition, the bar slowly slid aside, including the mirrored back-bar, revealing a softly-lit room, garishly paneled in gilt panels of deeply carved wood, carpeted with an oriental rug in puce and magenta, with mauve curlicues. At the far side, D'ong sat in an over-stuffed chair, eating popcorn from a greasy paper bag, his eyes fixed on a small screen on which Roy Rogers' face grimaced while the sound track moaned of love on the range.

"Come in, Retief," D'ong called rather absently. "Join our group. You know General Fith."

The latter emerged shyly from an alcove, averting his eyes from the screen.

"Gosh, Retief, how'd you get old scooter-butt to tell you how to open up the secret chamber and all?" he said. "You must have something on the old boy. As a part of his Exequatur ceremony, he had to swear a great oath in Urg's blood he'd never tell."

"We reached an accommodation." Retief said. "He left the room and I risked blowing up the building."

"Figures," Fith said, picking at his earplugs. "Shucks, Retief, I'm kind of glad you dropped in, in spite of various old injuries. You know, Yish had the complete Columbian Exposition issue, as used in the early Terry-

Luna mail service. Genuine top-notch Groaci forgeries, with Luna surcharges and the works."

"Too bad about the collection," Retief said. "Maybe you fellows should have considered that before you set out to starve, flood, and burn out the South Squeemans."

"I had nothing to do with that. I was just a civilian at the time, doing my job and keeping my buccal orifice shut."

"Like me," Retief said, and turned his attention to D'ong. "Mr. Minister, the US cavalry has arrived. Are you ready to go?"

"Heck, no, Retief, we're just getting to the good part, where Roy mounts his wench and rides off into the wasteland."

"I think maybe you've got Trigger and Dale confused, D'ong."

"I confess I pay little attention to names. But how I admire the *savoir faire* of the cowbeomen, who, in times of strife, think first of love. Always they and their faithful mates couple joyously as they dash off across the plains, hero and villain alike! Silly of me to be so sentimental, I know, but nostalgia is such sweet sadness—how it reminds me of my honeymoon with C'lunt, so long ago."

"That's understandable, of course. Sort of."

"One would have to truly know dear C'lunt to empathize fully. He's *such* a darling."

"He?"

"Didn't I explain? C'lunt is my first husband."

"Then you're a female. I owe you an apology, or something. I assumed you were a male."

"Me, a male? That's ridiculous, Retief. After all, our Grotesque males are only seven inches in height."

"Ah, that makes things clearer. But I don't think I've ever met a male Grotesque socially."

"Oh, no. They don't mingle with civilized folk. All they do is jump up and down and screech—and now and then go for a nice ride in the desert, of course."

"Why do they jump up and down and scream?"

"They say it pisses them off to be only seven inches tall."

"I still think you're mininterpreting something."

"What matter, Retief? The message of art transcends all barriers, eh?"

"Very probably. Nice cell you have here."

"You like it? Frankly, Retief, when I was first escorted here so enthusiastically by my welcoming committee (Ambassador Shiss is *so* thoughtful) it was rather plain."

"Too bad Ambassador Smallfrog didn't think of having you assaulted and dragged inside the Terry Embassy. I see he missed making a few points thereby."

"I take no offense, Retief. No doubt it was merely an oversight on his part."

"You say the room was plain when you arrived." Retief studied the golden cherubs and nymphs gamboling across the walls. "They redecorated in a hurry to your specs?"

"Not they, I," D'ong said with shy pride. "General Fith explained that there'd be a slight delay before His Excellency the Groacian Ambassador could see me—about ten years or so. Accordingly, I set about brightening things up a bit. Bare stone is rather austere for a ten-year wait, don't you think?"

"Agreed." As Retief and D'ong chatted, Fith had edged silently toward the open door. He slipped silently through and the heavy panel swung shut and sealed with a complex *click!* like the door to a bank vault.

"Oh-oh," D'ong said. "I guess you're stuck in here with me, now, Retief."

"Looks that way," Retief said calmly.

"Curious," Ambassador Smallfrog said mildly, lolling back in his hip-o-matic. "If we weren't on the twenty-eighth floor, Magnan, I'd swear I saw that chap F'Linlin—you know the one I mean, Ambassador K'Yip-yip's driver—sullen sort of fellow—peering in at the

window just now. You don't suppose the Yill are somehow involved in this matter, do you, Ben?"

"Gracious, I shouldn't wonder, Mr. Ambassador.
After my harrowing experience, my head's still awhirl."

"Um. Mustn't brood, Magnan. Pity we can't send a
squad of Marines over there to search the Groaci compound from ridge-pole to refuse pits and catch the
scamps red-handed—but of course, to violate a friendly Embassy would be unthinkable."

"Let's think about it anyway," Magnan suggested.
"It seems Retief didn't find the place too hard to
burgle."

"Surely you jest," Smallfrog said icily. "As conven-
tion-abiding bureaucrats, we have no choice but to
chalk one up for Shiss and his boys, after which we
can rest on our oars until morning when Shiss arrives
to express regrets to the Grotian Foreign Office. A pity
poor D'ong must meanwhile be submitted to durance
vile. And all just because he's such a dear, lovable
chap, too. I suppose he naïvely revealed the magic tea
bag to Shiss just as casually as he did to us. Magnan,
do you believe in magic?"

"No, of course not, but it happened all the same."

"Good. I thought maybe I was hallucinating. Did
D'ong do a little levitating and possible resuscitate a
few dozen frozen and boiled shrimp?"

"Gosh, sir, that's impossible!"

"Of course. I didn't suggest it's possible. I merely
point out it happened. But these trivia are quite outside
our interest cluster. I assigned you the task of ferreting
out the secret of the four-cup tea bag. Nothing was said
about parlor tricks."

"But where's Retief?" Magnan queried his chief im-
petuously. "We can't just forget the whole matter and
abandon him to his fate in a Groaci dungeon."

"I suppose you're right, Ben. In spite of the fact that
the fellow clearly exceeded instructions in going so far
as to attempt something actually constructive, certain
small-minded critics of the corps might indeed adopt
a negative, or even antagonistic attitude were it known

he disappeared forever under such unconventional circumstances."

"Quite. And all for naught. We still don't have the secret of the magic tea bag," Magnan mourned.

"Harrumph. You must avoid use of the word 'magic,' Ben. Once again, you risk laying this Mission—and even myself—or *your*self, that is—open to criticism. I think miraculous tea bag communicates the essentials without the undignified connotations of the other term."

"Gosh, yes, Your Excellency. I was just thinking how you go right to the heart of a matter, side-stepping the pitfalls that trap lesser bureaucrats."

"To be sure, Ben. Still, one can't help wondering what Shiss is doing with the fellow."

Magnan yelped and grabbed for suddenly flying papers as the French windows swung suddenly open. Retief stepped into the room and handed Magnan a sheet he had caught. Magnan yelped and retreated behind a chair.

"Retief! Goodness knows you've had His Excellency and myself on tenterhooks wondering what happened to you. And here you are, safe and sound. Heavens! You could at least give a person warning before, uh, just appearing out of nowhere like that!"

"Not out of nowhere; precisely, Ben." Ambassador Smallfrog corrected gently. "He came in through the window, quite obviously. Take a chair, Retief. You realize, of course, there'll be an entry in your file regarding your rather excessive zeal in invading a friendly Embassy. Ambassador Shiss has just been on to me about it. Seemed quite agitated."

"I was held up a few minutes getting D'ong back to her office," Retief explained.

"Thank goodness she's—you did say 'she,' Retief?— Safe!" Magnan gushed. "Oh, for a cup of tea right now," he sighed. "Having tasted that delicious brew this morning has quite revived my old addiction."

"See what I can do," Smallfrog said grumpily. "Wouldn't mind a dish myself." He poked the phone control.

"George, three cups of strong tea in my office at once," he commanded.

"Just make that hot water," Retief suggested and placed a puckered tea bag on the Ambassadorial blotter.

"Retief, you've got it!" Magnan cried. "I mean you see what comes of following my instructions precisely. After he was once inside, of course," he added confidingly to Smallfrog.

"These details hardly matter now, my boy," His Excellency said jubilantly, phoning in the new order. "Good to know poor old D'ong is back safely in the Foreign Office," he continued. "See here, Magnan: D'ong will surely feel grateful to the Terran Embassy for release, if the beggar has any human feelings at all. Now's the time to scoot over with a most-favored-nation treaty all ready for signature."

"Certainly, sir! Retief and I can have it back, taped and sealed, in a trice!" Magnan glanced around, looking puzzled. "Goodness, where *is* he?" he inquired vaguely, as he shifted to look behind him at the empty room.

Smallfrog waved a casual hand at the curtains blowing at the open windows. "Oh he just stepped out," he said. "That fellow F'Lin-lin was hanging about out there, you'll recall. Forget these trivia. Ah, here's our hot water now."